To Cathy

Thanks for riding along

Frank.

MW00667374

THE APPRENTICESHIP
OF
NIGEL BLACKTHORN

PART I

ACROSS THE PRAIRIE

To Cathy

Thanks for
Riding Along

Frank.

THE APPRENTICESHIP
OF
NIGEL BLACKTHORN

PART I

ACROSS THE PRAIRIE

Frank Kelso

Beachfront Press

A Beachfront Press Book

Copyright 2017 by Frank Kelso
All rights reserved

ISBN: 978-0-9906025-9-0

Cover photograph by Caroline Gardner, Mountain Center, CA, taken on supply run by Lee Livingston Outfitters into the Absaroka Mountains near Cody, WY

Cover design by Charlene Raddon

Second edition: 2019
V4

All rights reserved. No part of this book may be reproduced in any form or by any electronic, mechanical, or other means now known or hereafter invented, including photocopying or recording, or stored in any information storage or retrieval systems without the express written permission of the publisher, except for newspaper, magazine, or other reviewers who wish to quote brief passages in connection with a review.

Please respect Author's Rights.

The Apprenticeship of Nigel Blackthorn is a work of historical fiction. The names, characters, places, and incidents are either the product of the author's imagination, or, if real, used fictitiously.

Visit the website: TheApprenticeBook.com
Join Frank's Blog, Traveling the West at - http://frankkelsoauthor.com

Beachfront Press, LLC
25778 John M Snook Dr, Suite 2402
Orange Beach, AL 36561

Dedication

Thanks to those fans who follow my Facebook, Twitter, Instagram, Pinterest, and LinkedIn pages. Special thanks go to my mentor, and writing partner who kicks me in the butt to keep me focused on better writing, my friend, John O. Woods.

A tip o' my hat to Bruce and Barbara Blasch for introducing me to Owyhee Wilderness area in Utah and white water rafting on the Payette.

A special thanks to Ed Haefliger and Caroline Gardner for their wonderful pictures of pack mules at work, just as they did in 1853.

No dedication, or even my books, would be complete without the support and encouragement of my lovely island bride. Thank you for all you do for me, but mostly for tolerating my grumpy behavior. I have the T-shirt to prove it.

Frank Kelso

Other Books by Frank Kelso

The Posse – an anthology of 8 western stories

California Bound (Co-Author – John O'Melveney Woods)

Zach's Gold (Book 2 in Jeb & Zach series)

Juan's Revenge (Co-Author – John O'Melveney Woods)

Short Stories

Flop-eared Mule
The Windmill
True to the Union

Links to Frank Kelso Social Media

Please visit Frank Kelso's web page: frankkelsoauthor.com

visit Facebook: www.facebook.com/AuthorFrankKelso

visit on Twitter: @authorfrankelso

linkedin.com/in/frank-kelso-89b077100

authorfrankkelso.blogspot.com

TheApprenticeBook.com

facebook.com/thepossebook.1

facebook.com/CABoundBook/

facebook.com/TheApprenticeBook

Chapter One

June 19, 1853

Nigel Blackthorn's father, John Blackthorn, a Methodist minister, gave his family no choice but to leave Wales in 1852. God had called him to bring Christ to the wild heathens on the untamed prairies in the American West. The promise of land and a stipend mattered little to him.

Eight months later, while loafing in the shade, Nigel surveyed the West Texas prairie through the tent's flap. He welcomed a day's rest after his father parked their wagons beside a stream last night. The thirteen-year-old considered splashing in the stream below his tent. Like many youngsters, he'd grown weary of traveling every day. *There's nothing to do.*

His missionary family established their wagon camp among the cottonwoods straddling Nebo Creek, which meandered into the nearby Canadian River. The clear water from the two streams nourished a lush green meadow at their junction. The family's oxen grazed untended in the meadow, recovering from several dry camps on the parched trail south to Fort Adobe.

"Nigel should be helping," his oldest sister, Georgiana, said from the cook fire.

He laughed aloud while he lazed in the tent, listening to his sisters carp.

His sisters groused he *never* did his share, griping that mother coddled him.

Nigel refused to consider their complaint—*cooking is a woman's work.*

After stretching on his bedroll, he placed his hands behind his head. The noon sun heated the tent, eliminating any thought of helping his sisters—*it's too hot.*

In his usual booming pulpit voice, Papa said, "You are spoiling him, Elsbet. He has to learn." He'd overheard Papa say this to his mother before, and it often carried a sharp edge.

"I'm not," Mother replied, "he's too young yet. He can't work as much."

That's the way Nigel liked it. With that pleasant thought, he grew drowsy. The stream's gurgling water lulled him, letting him fall asleep, oblivious to the world around him.

Nigel awoke, startled by a thunderous noise. His heart thumped.

"What was that? That a gunshot?" he called aloud.

As if in response, his sisters shrieked.

Girls. They screeched about everything. *Harold, our wagon driver, must have shot at another skunk.* Nigel sat up, listening. *Wait a minute. Horses? Those are pounding hoofs—why are they running? Who's coming?* He rose from his bedroll.

Mother swept the tent flap aside, rushing inside, wide-eyed, and gasping.

"It's the heathens. Grab your shoes." She pointed behind him. "Go beneath the tent. Slither into the bushes. Sneak across the stream. Hide on the other side." Out of breath, she gasped, "Hide! Don't let the heathens catch you. Don't listen to our screams. Don't listen to us. Pray for us. Pray for us all."

Tears flowed when she pushed Nigel under the tent's back edge. Her golden locket glinted in the sunlight leaking through the flap. She called after him, "Hide until they are gone. Don't look back on this. Don't look back. Ever!"

He ducked under the tent's flap before sliding into the stream like his mother instructed.

~~~~~~

After rushing from the tent, Elsbet remembered the prairie lark she once watched, squawking to draw a predator away from her hidden ground nest. Mimicking the bird, she screamed for attention. She must distract the savages long enough for little Nigel to hide. *Please Lord, please let my little baby survive all this.*

Her prayers shifted once a bare-chested warrior grabbed her by the hair.

She didn't want young Nigel to gaze upon her attack. What happened next to Elsbet and his two sisters, Georgiana, seventeen, and Eugenia, fifteen, passed beyond brutal into savage.

~~~~~~

Nigel crossed the babbling stream, too frightened to enjoy wading in the water.

Papa shouted, "Forgive them Lord, for they know not what they do."

Nigel climbed into the hollow bole of an ancient, lightning-struck cottonwood tree. Inside, their screaming faded, but not enough to diminish the shrieks of terror piercing the air—pleading and pitiful.

He tried not to listen, recalling Mother's guiding words, "Don't listen to our screams."

How do you *not* listen to their screams? How do you *not* listen? He sobbed, placing a fist in his mouth to stifle his noise while he prayed, as his Papa taught him. He prayed for them all.

Smoke rose from the camp while the heathens whooped and hollered in triumph. They warbled high-pitched war cries. They created such uproar, even the oxen bellowed in fear. He covered his ears, attempting to block the sounds. After an hour, the noise faded but for the crackling fires. Time flowed and the evening grew darker as smoke obscured the campsite.

He prayed for his family. He prayed for them all.

The gurgling stream beckoned him, but fear held him fast. His parched throat ached. Nigel wanted his mother. At this point, he'd welcome his sisters, but he dare not raise his head to search for them. Tears streamed on his chubby cheeks. He held his hands to cover his mouth, afraid to make a sound. Only thirteen, he didn't know what to do, or how to survive alone. He never bothered learning to cook. No one knew where he hid, or even to search for him.

On June 9, his birthday, his family departed from Fort Atkinson, Kansas, near the Cimarron Crossing on the Santa Fe Trail. Their two wagons rolled south into the West Texas prairie led by a hired scout. The family expected to find the peaceful Cherokee in the Indian Nations, north of the Canadian River. The scout became lost, and rode out alone to find Fort Adobe, letting the heathens kill his family. He prayed for his family because it was all he knew to do without them. He prayed as his earthly father taught him to pray to his Heavenly Father.

He must have fallen asleep. Darkness surrounded him. *Had a horse whickered?*

Had the heathens returned? Renewed terror stabbed at his heart.

Are they searching for me, again?

No thumps of hoof-beats had sounded, or rustling movement in the brush. Night masked their movement, if they searched for him. Frightened and alone, he had no idea what to do. His mouth grew so dry, it hurt to swallow. In a baby's crawl, he reached the stream, sipping the cool water one handful at a time. After each handful, he glanced about but failed to see past his nose. He trembled at each sound. He slithered up the bank across from the smoking ruins, hiding next to a fallen tree. Mumbling more prayers, he cried himself to sleep, praying for his lost family.

His Mother's last words came to him unbidden.

Don't look back on this.

Don't look back.

Ever!

Chapter 2

June 20, 1853

Nigel jerked awake. In his dream, Mother shouted, "Run, the wild heathens will catch you!" Hunger pulled at him, but he feared moving. Thirst tugged at him, but he feared moving. He scanned the woods, shifting only his gaze before recognizing the eerie light of false dawn. Smoke clung to the burned campsite. It drifted into the trees across the stream, carrying a strong, sour smell he failed to identify. He knew he must wade across the stream, *and soon*. He crawled to the water to drink a few handfuls when an urge caused a new shiver. He realized he needed to "make water." Right away, once he thought about it.

"I must be sure my sisters aren't nearby if I make water," he whispered aloud, but jerked upright once realizing he didn't know what happened to his sisters, or if they still lived. The idea of such frightened him anew. He stayed hidden beside the stream until full daylight, listening for the noise of anything moving. He failed to glimpse any movement. He shook with fright, alone and uncertain, not knowing what to do. He prayed—for that was all he knew how to do alone.

Hunger forced him to cross the stream. He hadn't eaten in twenty hours. For a lad his age, it seemed a lifetime. On hands and knees, he crept into the camp to find his tent knocked down, his blankets gone. One glimpse of the smoldering ruins of their wagons froze him in place. His father lay beaten and bloody beside the charred cover of his Bible. They had tied him to a large wheel, which now lay on the ground next to the smoking wagon ruins. Arrows stuck from his chest.

Nigel grew so frightened he struggled to breathe, just gasping. His stomach heaved as if he needed to throw up, but with nothing to expel, he dry-heaved. The wagon bed, frame, and axles had burned, collapsing to the ground. Charred lengths of wood remained, smoldering in several places—the rest, in ashes. The sour, burned-fat stench grew stronger near the wagon.

He crept behind the smoldering wagon bed, where his father lay tied, thinking he'd seen Mother's shoes on two sticks in the wagon ruins, wondering, *why did her shoes hang on sticks?*

Nigel missed two heartbeats comprehending the horror of what made the "sticks" holding his mother's scorched shoes. He shrieked, collapsing into the ashes of his mother's body among the wagon's ashes. Lying in the ashes, he sobbed in shuddering convulsions. He lay there for hours, without food or water, nearing delirium. Lying in the ashes, beyond hope, he prayed.

Nigel pleaded with God to return his family, promising he'd work hard every day, and never whine about work, *ever*. He promised God he'd work so hard, his family would never complain about him again. He sobbed until no more tears came, only pain. He lay unmoving until sunset, buried in the dark ashes of the burned wagon, next to his beloved mother.

~~~~~~

In the scant light of late evening, a solitary figure entered the campsite in silent caution, rifle at the ready. After the stranger surveyed the carnage, he sighed, before praying aloud in *Français*.

"*Mon Dieu. Mon Dieu*. Must they be so savage? Is killing them not enough?"

Pascal LeBrun crossed himself several times. Like many frontiersmen, he often spoke aloud to himself. He shifted to signal his hidden companion when a movement caught his eye.

A black apparition rose unsteadily from the funeral pyre—a wavering shadow in the fading light. Ashes scattered as the ghost-like wraith rose, becoming a smoky, wavering illusion.

Pascal stood transfixed, mouth gasping for breath, as cold sweat drenched his face.

"*La misericorde de Dieu*—God's mercy. *Misericorde*! W-W-What are you?"

"I am Nigel," replied a hoarse, dry voice in a faint whisper.

Pascal crossed himself, and again, saying prayers he thought he'd long since forgotten.

"*Non, non*. You are *Noir ... L'ange noir de la mort,*

the Black Angel of Death. *Merci, mon Dieu!* It is not my time." He shuddered, gasping for air.

Pascal edged closer, pointing his rifle at the vaporous mirage wavering above the ashes. He leaned forward, poking the mirage with his rifle's muzzle. After his iron muzzle touched it, ashes fluttered from the object he thumped. Easing a step away, he heaved a sigh of relief.

"*Misericorde.* I thought you '*le Noir,*' the black spirit of death, rising to avenge these poor pilgrims." He crossed himself several times, mumbling prayers with each.

"I am Nigel," whispered the dark wraith a little louder.

"Well, you might not be '*l'espiri noir de la mort,*' but you are *Noir,* a dark one."

"No, I am Nigel."

"*Oui, oui.* Nigel is a fine name for an English gentleman at foxhunt, but here on God's wild and unforgiving prairie, that name will be a fight-starter. The question before us is, are you *porcelet noir,* a dark little piglet? Or *louveteau noir,* a dark little wolf cub? God's will be done."

Unbidden, Nigel said, "Amen." His empty stomach gurgled, its noise carried in the camp.

Pascal harrumphed. "You growl like a little wolf cub."

The tall man shifted to wave at his companion, waiting with a rifle at the camp's edge.

"LaFleur, take this *Noir* to the Canadian. Dunk him several times until he comes up clean— clothes and all. Then drag him to our camp. Feed him a bowl of stew. I'll soon follow."

Nigel wiped his mouth, slobbering at the thought of food.

After LaFleur and *Noir* departed, Pascal gathered a tent's remnants for a burial shroud. After breaking the arrow shafts, he placed the man's body alongside the woman's remains from the burned wagon. He scavenged through the camp, seeking clothes for the boy but found none.

Upon finding girls clothes, he crossed himself, saying prayers for a quick and merciful death, but feared it that wouldn't happen if captured by the Comanche. He used a torn canvas wagon cover to wrap a young man he found at the far edge of the burned wagon camp. He laid the bodies together.

"We shall bury you in the morrow," he said aloud before wading across the stream toward his small camp west along the Canadian River, away from these evil spirits.

In their camp, Nigel devoured the hot bean stew LaFleur offered for supper.

"Manners, manners," Pascal barked. "Will you eat it all, leaving us none? Don't eat too fast. You'll vomit—then it's wasted. There is too little food to waste any. Learn that, *vite.*"

"I'm hungry. There are more beans in the pot. May I have more?" Nigel asked.

"*Non.* That is tomorrow's dinner. We build one cook-fire each day. Pace yourself."

When Nigel surrendered the empty wooden bowl, he had licked it clean.

The tall man tossed Nigel a ripped man's shirt

from his family's camp.

"Hang your wet clothes to dry on a bush. Wear this shirt. Grab a blanket from the pack to sleep on the ground. We'll bury your family on the morrow before we flee this evil place."

"Did you find my sisters?"

"*Non.* Do not dwell upon them. It's best to think of them as in heaven already—pray God shows them His mercy. Sleep now, first light will come early."

Nigel asked, nodding at the silent man, "Does he talk?"

"*Non,*" Pascal said before he turned to his work in the camp. "He is LaFleur. His father wanted him to become a poet, calling his first born *LaFleur deA'Lune*, Flower of the Moon."

The tall man stood before asking, "Was the young man one of your sister's husband?"

"Oh, no. My sisters never married. You must mean Harold McDougal, one of the men from Scotland, who came to work at my father's mission. The scout, Mr. Jimmy Greenlee, taught him to drive the wagon when we started along the Santa Fe Trail from Westport Landing. On the trail, Mr. Greenlee taught Harold how to shoot to help protect us from the heathens. My sisters thought Harold cute, but that's revolting." He wrinkled his nose as if someone farted.

Pascal glanced to the heavens before muttering, "*Mon Dieu.* Why did these ignorant pilgrims come to the prairie so unprepared?"

Nigel observed the men performing their evening

chores, working without a word between them. He lay near the fire to study their activities, but he fell asleep after three eye-blinks, his mumbled prayers lost to an exhausted sleep.

Light came early, as predicted. Nigel struggled to sit, more than a little dazed, before he rose to stand. The men pushed him from their path, no matter which way he turned, or where he moved. The tall man shouted at him, but he failed to comprehend a word the man bellowed.

Confused, Nigel squeaked once before he cleared his throat to speak louder.

"Are you speaking in tongues? I don't understand a word you are saying."

"Ha-Haw," Pascal cried, laughing. "Have I rescued a wandering Protestant preacher who quotes scriptures?"

Nigel took the tall man's comment as a serious challenge, drawing himself up with pride.

"No, sir. My father is Reverend John Blackthorn, a Methodist Minister. The American Board of Missions requested my father come from Wales to convert the heathens to Christ."

"*Mon Dieu*! If the Jesuits hadn't thrown me out before, this would do it—rescuing a Methodist minister." Pascal laughed aloud. "I must remember *Anglais* for you in the morning, but in the evening, for LaFleur and me, it will be *le Français*—which you shall learn. I thought you an idiot who understood nothing," he said over his shoulder, while packing the camp.

"So now, in *Anglais*, collect water to wash the cooking pots and gear. The tin plate by the fire is your breakfast. Eat while you work, *ti-Noir*."

"You said first light. I can barely see," Nigel whined, like he did with his mother.

"*Oui*, we let you sleep. You shall not be so lucky after today. You will rise with us. We have buried your parents and the young man. Carry water in the pots to douse the fire, stirring the embers to quench all embers. After washing the pots, put them in the pack on top. When you are done, wade across the stream to your parents' grave. Say your prayers at their grave to tell them goodbye while we load the train. We must move, leaving this evil place behind."

At the stream, Nigel washed a fire-blackened iron pot in the river, but grew alarmed at the approach of clopping hoofs. Hidden in bushes alongside the Canadian River, he glimpsed LaFleur lead a string of small horses with big ears toward the camp's clearing.

When Nigel returned to camp, the noise of Pascal shouting and cursing at the animals overwhelmed him. He recognized the curse words, such as, "Damn it to Hell," which Pascal shouted in a constant stream of profanity—in English.

"Stop! Stop! You must *not* take the Lord's name in vain. Papa says only coarse, low-born people, like muleskinners, shout curses as a way of working."

Pascal whipped about, staring at him. His comment stunned the tall man into silence.

"Haw-EE-Haw-EE-Haw-EE-Haw-Haw," Pascal brayed, sounding like the mules he loaded. He laughed so hard, tears came into his eyes. "*Oui,* little preacher's son. What do you think we are?" He gasped for breath as he laughed even harder.

Nigel jerked away in shock. In his turn, he gaped slack-jawed at the older man.

"Y-Y-You mean? Y-Y-You mean you're going to skin these poor animals alive?"

He shifted to glance back and forth between Pascal and the mules.

"Haw-EE-Haw-EE-Haw-Haw," Pascal brayed, again.

With a twist, Nigel glanced at LaFleur, farther along the line of mules, with arms across his stomach in laughter. The mute barked like a dog, laughing so hard he too shed tears.

Nigel didn't get it. Thinking they made sport of him, he scowled at the laughing men.

"Oh, *petite Noir*," Pascal gasped. "If you can make me laugh like this, I think I'll keep you around for my jester. It's good, and healthy, to laugh unbridled now and then."

"You mean you aren't going to skin them?"

"*Non, non, ti-Noir.* A muleteer is a man who works mules to carry trade, as do I, Pascal LeBrun, or to pull wagons. The *ignorant* muleskinner uses a whip on these stubborn animals cutting their skin with his harsh whip. A '*coarse muleskinner*' curses them while his whip breaks their skin, and often breaks their spirit. It's a derogatory term, because it says the muleteer can't handle his animals without beating them.

"I, however," Pascal said, while pulling himself taller and lifting his chin, "*I* am a muleteer *par excellence*. I never beat my mules, as you will learn. Your father was correct, however. You should not curse or take the Lord's name in vain. I shall not allow you to curse."

"But what about you?"

Pascal laughed while he waved his hands, palm up, palm down, several times.

"After the Jesuits exiled me, I'm damned forever. A few curses aren't big sins anymore."

Confused, Nigel asked, "What are these Jesuits you keep mentioning?"

"It's the Society of Jesus. We are Catholic priests," Pascal said, shaking his jacket lapels.

Nigel stared at Pascal, his popped eyes wide in fear, as if the man sprouted horns. He struggled to breathe as he leaned away, gasping, "Papist? *You're Papists?*"

"Haw-EE-Haw-EE-Haw-Haw," Pascal brayed, falling on the ground from laughing so hard. "*Papists?* Papists, he asks?" Pascal muttered between trying to take in gulps of air. He struggled to rise while still laughing his braying laughter.

"*Non, non, ti-Noir.* The Jesuits aren't Papists, but we let the pope think we are."

In the background, LaFleur's barking laughter continued unabated.

Pascal shook dirt from his clothes, doing his best to restore civility.

"Now you know the worst, *petite Noir*. You've

fallen in with the lowest of the low. Not only are we coarse muleskinners, who blaspheme God's holy name, but we are Papists, to boot. Poor *Noir*, what will you do? Go with us? Or wait for another wagon train?"

A little taken back, he asked in a soft voice, "B-B-But, you wouldn't leave me here?"

"*Non, non.* I wouldn't do that, not alone on the prairie." Pascal's head shook as he spoke.

"I don't want you casting any of your Papist spells on me with your foreign tongues, or using your secret hand-signs, or Catholic tricks to convert me." Nigel surprised himself with the boldness of his reply.

"*Non, non, ti-Noir.* You're too clever for any of that, now that you know what we are," Pascal said, smiling at LaFleur, who shook his head at the boy's comments.

"Enough frivolity. Wade the stream—say prayers for your parents. *Tout de suite!* Give them your blessings before you pray for God's blessing and mercy upon them. Pray for your sisters, that they too are in heaven, finding comfort in God's mercy. Follow when we move on."

"How will I know?"

"Oh, you'll know, but you'll be far away, so my curses won't burn your tender ears."

Nigel waded the stream to kneel beside the earth mound where Pascal had placed a simple stick cross. He said prayers for his mother and father. He missed his sisters, truly hoping they slept safe. He prayed they reached heaven to enjoy

God's mercy. *Even if he is a Papist, it's right that he suggested I pray for my sisters to receive God's mercy.*

He burst into sobs, his head falling forward onto the grave, staining his face with tears and dirt. A fleeting vision swept past of his mother's kind face smiling at him, with the sunlight glinting from her small golden locket. He remembered her last words. "Pray for us. Pray for us all." And so he prayed for them. He prayed for them all.

Why has God abandoned me? Why has God abandoned our family? Why? Why?

He stood after a while, wiping the tears and dirt from his face with his hands. He took one last swipe at his runny nose with the back of his hand before swiping his hands on his pant leg. He trotted across the stream as the sounds of the mules faded in the distance.

I must hurry.

And his mother's last words came to him unexpected rush.

Don't look back on this.

Don't look back.

Ever!

Chapter 3

June 21, 1853

Nigel ran to catch Pascal at the head of the mule train, counting the mules as he passed them—eighteen in the string Pascal led. LaFleur rode behind and to one side, leading six unburdened mules, four loaded mules, and two unsaddled horses. He recognized the cooking pot he cleaned earlier on one of the loaded mules, realizing those mules carried their food and camp supplies.

While he trotted past the mules, he considered his future. *Mayhap, Pascal will let me ride one of the horses like he and LaFleur do. I've never ridden a horse. This might be fun.*

When he came even with Pascal, he panted for breath. "The mules move faster than I thought they could." He couldn't keep up at a fast walk. At the mule train's head, he glimpsed an unburdened horse with a leather strap around its neck where a brass bell hung. The bell tinkled in rhythm with the horse's motion, while Pascal rode alongside guiding the belled-horse.

Nigel panted while pointing at the horse beside Pascal. "What's that horse for?"

"Millicent is a mare, a female. The mules like the shape of her lovely rump. They are lulled by her bell song. They follow wherever she leads them. She's their *madrina*, the 'bell mare.' Think of her as a grandmother leading the children. And I, clever Pascal," he winked, "have whispered words of love in her ear, so like all females, she follows me wherever I go."

Nigel glanced around at Pascal before he frowned, his eyebrows knitting.

"Where is your whip? If you're a muleskinner, don't you need a whip?"

"*Non, non, ti-Noir.* I said 'an ignorant muleskinner' whipped his animals. Why would mules work for me if I whipped them? They're quite stubborn. I let them gaze upon beautiful Millie's rump while listening to her melodic bell song. I feed them when I let them rest as needed. In that way, they work for me like a free spirit, without the need of a whip."

With his face full of bright-eyed hope, he glanced at Pascal mounted on his horse.

"What do I ride upon?"

"Ah, *Noir*," Pascal sighed. "This is where the lessons begin."

"What lessons?"

Pascal speared Nigel with a hooded eye.

"This prairie is hard and unforgiving. It will kill you, if you're soft and weak. The lessons will teach you to become hard like the prairie, so it doesn't kill you. I'll tell you this now, but you won't remember. You'll come to think LaFleur and me are as hard and unforgiving as this prairie, that we're cruel or mean to you. It's not so. It saddens me to bury good Christians like your parents. They died because they failed to prepare. Your lessons will prepare you so I don't have to bury you after you grew careless, and let the prairie kill you."

Nigel surveyed the great expanse, unbroken to the horizon, while a shiver spiraled along his spine.

"You make the prairie sound like it's alive."

"*Oui*, it is alive with all manner of things that kill." He swept his arm wide. "Gaze across it. It is full of unseen dangers. It's not the soft grass that it appears. The Redman is the most dangerous being living on the prairie. Sometimes, we trade with them in peace. Other times, they try to steal our horses and mules, as though it's a game between us. If the Redman catches you alone, he may kill you for sport, or to test you. You must be wary—don't turn your back on them, ever. The Redman views us the same way. The white man treats them badly, so they are wary of us, too. It's a tragedy that the whites and the reds are destined to kill one another."

Pascal took a deep breath while surveying the prairie around him before he continued.

"Learn right now that you did the correct thing when you hid that day when the Redman raided your camp. You know how I can tell you hid, *petite Noir*?"

"No," Nigel whispered with downcast eyes, ashamed he'd hidden while his family died.

"You survived. That attack became your first

lesson. Look for ways to avoid danger or a fight. Don't be afraid to retreat from danger. It isn't 'brave' to rush into every danger—it's just stupid. The stupid and the greedy don't survive on the unforgiving prairie. If the Redman raids our train today, I will tell you to hide, and survive."

Pascal twisted about in his saddle to scan the prairie around them without breaking the stride of the mules. To a pilgrim, the land appeared flat and featureless. To a plainsman, the land breathed—heaving into rises or ridges or sighing into draws or hollows. The man's gaze studied the ground, taking note if they crossed another's trail. He glanced at Nigel, walking alongside.

"*Petite Noir*, you must learn that little things can kill you just as easy. If you step in a gopher hole, and break your leg, you could die there if you don't have a companion nearby to help you. There are rattlesnakes, scorpions, poison waterholes, dry waterholes, wolves, and, when in the mountains, cougars. You must learn to recognize these dangers before you are at risk. Then, you must learn how to avoid danger whenever you can. That is, if you are to survive."

The former Black Robe took off his hat, wiping his brow with a sleeve.

"For your next lesson, did you say prayers, asking God's blessing for your sweet mother this morning?"

"Yes, sir," Nigel replied, with tears beginning to form.

"Do you miss her?"

"Yes, sir," Nigel half sobbed. Tears streamed from his eyes.

"*Oui.* She will have a place in your heart, but she isn't here on the prairie with you anymore. What did you say she told you at the last?"

"Pray for them. Pray for them all."

"*Oui*, you did. You shall continue to do so. What else did you say she told you?"

"Don't look back on this. Don't look back. Ever," recited Nigel.

"*Oui.*" Pascal waited for a dozen seconds. "Are you a Mama's boy?"

Don't look back. There is nothing left behind to see. Not anymore.

After a longer pause, Nigel said, "Not anymore."

"*Oui.*"

The two continued along the trail in silence for ten minutes.

"Let me explain what these lessons mean. LaFleur and I are tradesmen. We travel this prairie from place to place to sell trade goods, or haul *cargas,* as they say *en español.* We must travel in a swift and quiet manner. While we're in the open like we ride now, we're in danger. We don't speak often. Of course, LaFleur can't talk anyway." He waved a hand gesture, as if batting a fly. "LaFleur and I use hand signs or other signals. You must learn them. Don't shout or raise your voice. Sound carries far across the open prairie. A Redman might pass us unnoticed, but he will seek those making noise, so you must learn to work in silence. A Redman will notice a shout for miles—

only a white man shouts. If they fail to hear or see us, we may pass in safety."

Pascal leaned away to spit bitter pieces of a dried-up trade cigar he chewed.

"It takes cooperation between us to do this every day. If you want to eat our food, you must work, too. This means when we stop to rest or camp for the night, I'll assign you tasks. I expect you to learn them, and do them without my asking, or go without food that night. You must learn to respond to my orders, even if what I say makes no sense at the time. I may not have time to explain in an emergency. I must know you'll do what I say, when I say, *tout de suite*, quick and quiet. I don't want your whining or dawdling to get one of us killed if in danger."

Pascal rode in silence while he glanced at the mules before studying the nearby plains. By summer's middle, the rolling prairie had dried, withering to various shades of brown from light tan to dark-brown wallows. The buffalo dug wallows into the ground with their horns or hoofs to loosen the dry soil. They coated their shaggy hide with the dry dirt to reduce infestation by flying pests like the carnivorous blowfly, which laid its eggs under their hide.

"The danger isn't always out there," Pascal said, sweeping his arm across the horizon. "A mule kick can kill you or make you wish you had died. The mules also bite. At your size, you could lose a hand if you stick it too close to a feisty mule. Always be alert, even in the camp. Be careful around the fire, or with hot food or water. Burns and scalds can kill a man on the prairie. These lessons will end only if you don't survive, little *Noir*—they'll continue after you become a man. My goal is to see that you learn to survive as your mother wished. I know you're saddened at the loss of your father and mother." Pascal coughed to clear his throat.

"It may not seem like much consolation, but think of me as your godfather, your *parrain*. Let's say, I'm your *parrain*-Pascal. Mayhap, you won't think yourself so alone and abandoned."

They moved forward in silence for several minutes. Pascal riding while Nigel walked.

"Is that all of the lessons?" Nigel asked, wiping his nose with the back of a hand.

"*Non, non, petite Noir*. It will be as I said. The lessons will continue until you are grown into a man. I'm not used to talking this much, so I rested."

"I'm getting tired of walking. I hoped I could ride for a while to rest, too."

"*Non, non, Noir*. The mules carry trade goods to make us money. There will be no riding for whiny young English boys who have no money. You're tired because you're soft. *Tu est un enfant gate*—a spoiled child. I can tell you spent too much time riding in your papa's wagon. You grew soft and weak because you didn't do any work—that will never happen with me. It's God's penance. You will walk, and you will work, every day until you get tough as old leather."

They continued in silence for five minutes when Pascal twisted to check on the mules before gazing across the surrounding plain. This time, Nigel gazed where Pascal gazed before the man spoke again.

"Each day you will work with us to keep the mules moving or to help cook. There's plenty of work for us. You may think me a Papist. However, the only reason I rest on Sunday is the mules need a day's rest, or they can't carry their load. In the Sunday camp, we catch up on the things in need of repair—something always needs repairing. Sunday is also a day for bathing and laundry. Don't the Methodists preach 'cleanliness is next to Godliness'?"

Nigel sighed while his shoulders slumped, remembering Papa's sermons.

"Yes, the Most Reverend John Wesley said it. Papa recited it often."

Pascal laughed. "You see, *ti-Noir*, we shall have great fun in our lessons."

"You have said that word before, '*ti-*,' or sometimes, '*petite.*' What do you mean?"

"Good. You have an ear for pronunciation. *Petite* means 'little,' so I called you 'little dark one,' *petite Noir*. '*ti-*' is a contraction of *petite*. It's a term used with a child. It's easier to say *ti-Noir*.'"

Nigel nodded, but didn't think he understood.

Again, they moved on in silence for several minutes. Pascal riding, Nigel walking.

"*Noir*, once the Church assigned me to serve as a school teacher for a small parish in the south of

France. I found great joy in teaching young boys like yourself."

Nigel glanced around at him, his face twisted with questioning.

"*Non, non,*" Pascal scolded, wagging his finger at him. "The little boys never landed me in trouble as it did some priests. The lovely mothers led to my downfall, those ladies for whom I gave a different kind of tutoring once they sent their children for a nap. Alas, my *special* lessons with the sweet, young mothers led the Jesuits to expel me from the Holy Mother Church."

"*A fornicator?*" Nigel gasped. "They expelled you as a fornicator?" His eyes grew wide.

"Haw-EE-Haw-EE-Haw-Haw," Pascal brayed, sounding more like his mules than ever. Wiping a tear, he said, "Poor *Noir*, what a den of iniquity we are. You have fallen in with truly wicked people."

"It's not funny. Papa said fornicators will have a special place in hell."

"Oh, he's correct. We shall have the hottest fires," Pascal wheezed, still laughing with tears streaming on his face, "But I'll have company beside that fire, visiting with many old friends, and mote of my enemies. Tell me, *ti-Noir*, do you know what it means 'to fornicate'?"

"No. Mother said I'd learn soon enough. It became Papa's special topic for sermons. In Sunday sermons, he grew red-faced, pointing at different men in the pews, saying how they'd ruin themselves and their families if they didn't repent to mend their wanton ways."

"I would have loved to listen to his sermons, *ti-Noir*. However," Pascal said, heaving a sigh, "We shall save lessons on fornication for another day."

LaFleur clapped his hands to get their attention. Pointing first to his nose, LaFleur signed *Pascal the man to teach fornicating*, which Pascal translated aloud for Nigel.

Both men laughed while using hand signs with rude and crude gestures. Whatever Pascal responded, passed in *Français,* interrupted by their laughing, and gesturing.

Nigel shook his head, piffling his disgust of their crude gestures and body movements.

Again, they moved in silence for several minutes—Pascal riding and Nigel walking.

"Do you know what time it is?" Pascal asked, while he surveyed the nearby prairie.

"No, sir."

"You must learn to glance at the sun, or your shadow, using the sun or the stars to tell time. It's almost nine o'clock. At nine o'clock, we rest the mules for twenty minutes or more depending on the water available. We allow them to drink or graze, but we don't unload them at the morning or afternoon rest. We unload them for a two-hour *siesta* at noon before unloading again at night. You'll soon learn what we do when I assign your tasks. Do you read?

"Why?"

"*Non, non.* I ask—*you answer.* Remember that lesson. I'll tell you why later. Answer."

"Yes, sir. I can read," Nigel responded,

remembering the threat of no food.

"Can you do sums? Subtraction?"

"Yes sir. I can do double columns in both."

"Good. And multiplication?"

"Not so good, sir."

"Geography? History?"

"England's geography and Church history, sir."

"Geometry? Algebra?"

"I don't know what those are, sir."

"Well, you'll learn in time. After the morning rest, I'll put you on the mare with an English book. I want you to read aloud. Breathe deep, lift your head, and speak with clear, crisp diction. At the end of a page, we'll discuss what you've read."

Nigel whined, wrinkling his face as if he bit a sour apple, "You mean like *school*, sir?"

"Of course, like school. Do you want to grow up to be a dunce?

"What's a dunce?"

"It's an ignoramus who can't think."

"What's an ignoramus?" Nigel asked in a soft voice, hinting at his reluctance.

Pascal laughed before he twisted to peer at LaFleur, who placed a finger on his nose tip, while he barked his own laugh. Glancing at Nigel, he said, "Ha. An ignoramus is someone like me who thinks he can teach a dunce like you."

"When do I rest?" Nigel asked, again with his soft voice tinged with doubt.

"Tonight, when you lie down to sleep," Pascal replied before he dismounted.

Chapter 4

June 21, 1853

At the morning rest, Nigel trod beside Pascal along the line of mules, starting from the front. Pascal checked the girth strap of each packsaddle to assure it hadn't loosened or shifted. He showed Nigel details to check, explaining what each meant. He called the packsaddle, Grimsley. They had bought them at Fort Atkinson from a Santa Fe Trail supplier. Until they learned how to strap one on a mule, and how to load it, they exercised great care to prevent the new packsaddles from galling, or rubbing, the mule's back into a raw sore. Pascal checked bridles and leather train-line connecting the mules into a hitched line, on alternating sides. The heavy, pleated-leather train-line had a three-inch metal ring every fifteen feet, with a one-foot chain on the ring clipped to the mule's bridle. The leather train-line kept the mules in line and moving together.

"We tie the mules to alternate sides so they don't bite or kick each other when they are bored or tired at the end of the day. If not for showing you what to do this morning, I'd have met LaFleur at the middle of the line. Remember, without the mules, we don't make any money—without money—we'd starve. Take care of the mules first."

Pascal gave Nigel a pat on the shoulder, pushing him away.

"Now, go with LaFleur. He'll show you the waterskins. Have a cup or two now. He'll give you a strip of venison jerky. Suck on it, don't chew and swallow. Make it last until siesta. LaFleur will teach you how we fasten the waterskins. It'll be your job to be sure they're full and fastened in place before we ride each morning. You may think it's easier to fill them all at once in the morning. However, you'll learn that mornings are busy. If you fill a skin when you see one empty, it'll save time in the morning. When you are done with LaFleur, return to me with a saddle blanket. It'll be time to move again—I'll begin your lessons. If you have to piss, do so before you return."

"Mother said I mustn't say that word. I ought to say 'make water.'"

"I'm not your mama, and *I* piss." Pascal sighed. "There are no *pissiors* on the prairie. I piss like a stream from a fire hose—I go where I wish, when I wish."

Later, when Nigel returned, Pascal said, "Put the blanket on the mare before jumping on. The blanket protects her back so you don't scratch her or rub her raw with your plump butt."

During the morning lessons, Pascal interrupted Nigel's reading.

"You mentioned the American Board of Missions sent your father West. Do you know who they are, or where they live?"

"I listened when Papa told Mother, while we still lived in Wales. A Methodist minister, Nathaniel Wyeth, visited to preach in our village. He spoke about converting the heathens. Papa said he felt a calling to bring the word of Christ to these heathens. He got excited when he talked about how pretty this country would be, saying we could have our own land. Most of what I learned came from my sisters—Papa didn't talk to me about moving. Mother said The Board accepted Papa for a new mission church in the colonies. She said we'd sail across the Atlantic to join with other ministers to serve on mission land while converting the heathens."

Nigel adjusted his hat, glancing across the prairie as Pascal had done before he continued.

"At first, I found it exciting, taking the boat from Portsmouth, England, to Boston. Mama and my sisters stayed sick the whole time. They said they never wanted to sail again. I roamed all over the ship by myself because Mother grew too sick to notice. The sailors acted weird on the ship. I learned to avoid them below decks. After a few weeks, it grew boring. I cheered when we landed. I liked Boston—it's a really big city. We had fun seeing so many different things, but Mother grew afraid my sisters and I would get lost. She held us as if we were children. My big sister said Boston was not as big as London, but how'd she know, she never visited London."

"Let's get back to the American Board," Pascal said, interrupting Nigel's wandering.

"The Board was in Boston. They housed and fed us, and the other missionaries, until they sent us West. We expected to travel to the Or-e-gon Territory with another ten ministers, their families and workers—men like Harold McDougal. Our train had twenty wagons when we left Westport. I had more fun with all the wagons together. Georgiana, my oldest sister, said the American Board of Missions paid Papa a stipe- ... a stipe-something."

"A stipend? A little money each month?" Pascal suggested.

"That must be it, because Papa never had any money before we came to Boston. Mother said once we built the mission church, the American Board would send another wagon with more goods, seeds, a milk cow, and chickens. Mother really wanted her own animals and a garden. She liked to talk of what she planned to grow in her garden. She spoke of her own land as if a dream. She found this land so beautiful and green, she wanted to stay forever."

"*Oui, oui.* But this is not Oregon. Where are the rest of the wagons? How did your family end up here alone?"

"I don't know all of what happened. My sisters said the bishop asked Papa to take part in a special mission serving English-speaking Indians called Chur-keys."

"You mean Cherokee?" Pascal asked. "The Yankees drove them from their lands when the whites found gold on Cherokee land. The Yankees moved them to the Indian Territory east of here. That happened a dozen or more years ago, before I came this far south."

"Well, anyway, the bishop hired our scout, Mr. Greenlee, to lead us to meet the Cher-o-kee. He claimed he visited Fort Adobe to trade twice before. Told my papa he knew the way."

"Why would the Board send one family here alone? Even if you found a peaceful congregation, living without friends and neighbors is difficult."

"Another minister and family with two more workers had planned to come with us in another two wagons, but the minister's wife grew sick, so they couldn't come. I think she was having a baby—as if I'm not supposed to know what happens when a woman swells that way. Two brothers of the minister's wife came with her, but they wanted to come later with the minister and his family. We expected them to meet us in the Indian Territory in the fall."

"You're sure the American Board of Missions is located in Boston?"

"Oh, yes. They had a big building with their name on it next to the Wesleyan Church. We lived in a building they owned across the street from the church. We didn't need to pay rent or buy the food. They had food all the time. I really liked being there."

Pascal and he continued with the lessons in English until siesta. LaFleur served the siesta meal cold—they built no fire at siesta. Dinner consisted of last night's supper of bean stew served with hardtack biscuits. Cold, the stew had the consistency, and taste, of lard. The mules rested, but Nigel and the men didn't. It seemed to him that they worked more during siesta than they did in evening camp. He looked forward to his lessons, so he could ride and rest.

Pascal ordered him to lie down for a nap. The idea of a nap miffed Nigel. *I'm not a baby that needs a nap,* but he fell asleep as soon as he closed his eyes.

The evening camp came at another stream. He learned the animals needed water to refresh after working all day, so they camped near water. Everything became a lesson to learn.

The mules make the team money—the mules come first. Young boys must work to eat.

Nigel fetched dry wood before scraping a fire pit while LaFleur and Pascal unloaded the mules near the camp. Nigel learned the only places to find wood for the fire came near streams, where the trees grew—no trees grew on the open prairie. LaFleur unloaded the supply mules where he intended to camp. He used a pack shovel to show Nigel how to dig a proper fire pit while Pascal led the unloaded mule-train and unsaddled horses to a grazing area. LaFleur showed him how to start a small fire with flint. The mute man dug the pit more than eighteen inches deep to keep the fire inside the pit. LaFleur used hand signs to say, *No fire on ground.*

If one lit a fire on top of the ground, the unending wind might blow the fire into the grass, setting fire to the camp. There were few rocks on the prairie to build a fire-ring for containing embers. LaFleur's small fire, built at the pit's bottom, didn't create much light to avoid attracting any Redmen who might be nearby. Nigel learned to collect dry, fallen wood, so it didn't create any smoke—Redmen might spot a smoky fire. If spotted, it would lead Redmen to them.

With the heel of a hand-axe, LaFleur drove two, one-inch-square iron bars into the ground on opposite sides of the fire pit before he hung a one-half-inch iron rod between them. The square bars had iron loops at the top to hold the cross-rod. He hung the bean pot over the fire to cook the evening meal. The silent man had many gadgets in his camp-packs—each with a place and a purpose. The second pot would cook after the first finished cooking. He motioned Nigel to follow when he led the unloaded supply mules to the grazing area near the camp.

Pascal picketed the horses before he untangled the hobbles used on the mules. Nigel learned Pascal favored a front-to-back hobble to prevent the animals from wandering away or being "spooked" into a stampede. LaFleur taught him how to tie the hobble, which consisted of a four-foot chain with a U-shaped metal piece on each end. He placed the open U along the narrower pastern between the hoof and fetlock on the front leg before tying the open end with a leather thong he took from a leather pouch he carried at his waist. The iron "U" rested on their hoofs to prevent chafing the tender skin below the fetlock.

LaFleur pulled the front leg rearward to loop the other open U around the alternate rear leg between hoof and fetlock. Again, he tied the open end with a leather thong. The smith had curled the tips on the open U in a tight loop to keep the thongs from sliding off after tied in place.

Pascal strolled near, regarding their work for a moment.

"You must learn how to do this. LaFleur will teach you how to tie the knot. Examine the leather thong before you use it. If it's worn or dried-out, don't use it. It'll break in the night, letting the animal wander away. I don't want to lose a mule because you didn't learn how to tie knots or used a worn thong. LaFleur will show you how while we eat. I'll go prepare our meal while you two finish."

After striding toward the camp, Pascal called over his shoulder, "LaFleur, teach *Noir* how to approach a mule or a horse so he doesn't get kicked or spook them."

Night had fallen by the time Nigel sat on the ground to eat—the same old bean stew with pork belly pieces. Nigel gazed at the pot after he licked his bowl clean.

Pascal barked at him. "Wash the pot in the stream before you go to bed. Fill the skins."

~~~~~~

LaFleur snapped his fingers at Pascal after the lad strolled to the stream to wash the pots with a waterskin slung over each shoulder. The mute wrote on his slate, *He is a louveteau—wolf cub. Engouffrer—wolfs food—like one.*

"*Oui*, I'll have to put more beans in the pot with him around."

~~~~~~

When Nigel returned, Pascal grunted a laugh when he glimpsed him.

"Tonight when you say your prayers for your family, say a little prayer of thanks to Mr. Grimsley, the saddler. He promised to ship those new packsaddles in May. If he had, LaFleur and I might be three hundred miles from here today. It is unusual for us to travel this far east on the prairie. We only came this way because I found a contract in Fort Atkinson to deliver supplies for the army post at Fort Belknap, Texas." Pascal asked as an afterthought, "Do you know who your family expected to meet at Fort Adobe?"

"No, we were to meet a Cherokee guide at the Fort to lead us to the Cherokee lands so Papa could establish a Methodist church with them. The bishop said the Cherokee are peaceful heathens, already converted but without a minister. Mr. Greenlee, called them Agency Indians, but I don't know what that means."

"You're sure your father said Fort Adobe and not Bent's Fort?"

"Yes. Mr. Greenlee said Bent destroyed his Fort. He knew about Fort Adobe, but when we camped the last night, he planned to ride alone to search, to be sure. He never came back."

"He missed it by fifty miles," Pascal grumbled. "The fool led your family to their death. If he led you to Fort Adobe, your men might have fought off the Comanche, but there's little water there if Redman decided to wait. Didn't that idiot scout know Fort Adobe is abandoned?"

"No," Nigel responded, shaking his head with bewilderment. "No. He said we would find fur traders and friendly Indians there."

"Not in four or five years has there been any real activity there. That is why the younger Bent closed it after Pueblos killed Charley Bent in the Pueblo rebellion at Santa Fe, in what, eighteen-forty-eight, during the Mexican-American War. What a colossal blunder the Mexicans made in that war—so close—and then lost it all."

Pascal fiddled for a while with repairing a leather braided-line before he spoke again.

"What I don't understand is why send those missionaries to Oregon? Who asked for them? Who wanted them?"

"When we lived in Boston, I listened to the ministers talking to one another. They said at first, the Methodists from England sent missionaries to a place called 'Oh-wy-hee,' before they sailed to Oregon across the Pacific, a yearlong trip by boat. Later, the American Board sent wagons along the Oregon Trail, following the trail a group of Mormons made while pushing handcarts. The ministers reported the American Fur Company agreed to help the Board because the Hudson Bay Company brought Catholic priests from Canada to convert heathens at their posts. The American Board wanted more ministers converting the heathens than priests."

Nigel peeked under the brim of his hat at Pascal after he made the last remark.

"Bah! A pox on all their houses. I don't know who is worse, the devils at Hudson Bay or that devil, John Jacob Astor, at American Fur. Shame on the Methodist Church for getting into bed with that thief, Astor. He never ran an honest scale."

"The Board told us we'd go to the Owyhee mission at the ford on the Snake River at the Oregon Territory border," Nigel said. "I remembered because I couldn't imagine a river of snakes. Once at the Owyhee mission, they'd assign each minister to a different location. From there, each minister would go his own way. In Boston, they reported the Owyhee land had snow-covered mountains, but I haven't seen any snowy mountains around here."

"*Non, ti-Noir*, you'll not see snowy mountains here in Texas. We'll add geography to your lessons so you learn about all those places. Hawaii is an island in the Pacific Ocean. The mission called Owyhee is near Fort Boise, and it *is* on the Snake River. LaFleur and I went to Fort Boise when we first came to this land. I wondered when I first heard that name, where it came from. I thought it a word from the Redman's language." Pascal grunted aloud, "Now you come from England to explain it. They spelled 'Hawaii' as O-w-y-h-e-e.

Anglais, bah."

After several minutes of silence, Pascal sighed aloud. "To have come all that way with such hopes for serving our Lord, only to be led astray by a fool scout."

Following another long period of silence, Pascal glanced at Nigel with a shrug.

"You are blessed by the Lord, *ti-Noir*. God must have a grand plan for you to have brought us all this way to rescue you." Pascal chuckled aloud.

"Well, God should've sent you a day earlier, so you could've rescued my family, too."

"I'm sorry, *Noir*, but if we rode a day earlier, we would not have come to your family's rescue. I told you, we hide from hostile Redmen. They have too many warriors for the two of us to fight while expecting to survive."

Nigel twisted his face in anger, squeezing his lips in a line. His family died because of a "fool scout" who lost his way. "You say we must survive, when you should have helped."

"*Non, ti-Noir*. If we died attempting to rescue you, you would not survive either."

Nigel burst into tears. "It is God's fault for sending my father here instead of to Oregon with the others."

Pascal pulled Noir into a hug, while attempting to show compassion.

"I know you are hurting, but we poor sinners cannot understand God's plans. We are to do our best each day as God sends us where He will. You must learn to accept His will."

Nigel grimaced—the pain and grief eating at him, causing his chest to ache.

"How can you accept His will so easily, when He threw you out of your Church?"

Pascal shook his head, waving a hand signaling the negative. "*Non, petit Noir.* God didn't dismiss me. Weak men, like myself, did that on their own."

"You aren't weak. You live here on the prairie, where it so dangerous, yet you survive."

"I survive. Yes, that is my penance. As to the other, I'm still weak in the flesh, I don't repent, too often I seek comfort in a woman's bosom, and I revel in my sins."

"I have heard you say that word before. What is a penance?"

"A penance is God's little punishments in life before His final punishment for your sins after death. Enough liturgical philosophy for tonight. Say prayers for your family. Go to sleep."

Nigel spread his blanket before lying down to sleep, but it eluded him. He had made it through a second day without his family, still frightened, and so alone, even with these men.

How can I go on without my family?

Nigel said his prayers, as his father had taught him. He prayed for them all.

Chapter 5

June 22 to July 1, 1853

The next day came as a repeat of his first day. Up before light, eat a meager, warm gruel with a few pieces of jerky for breakfast, clean the gruel and coffee pots, dump water on the fire, put the waste in the pit, and then fill in the fire pit with the dirt removed the night before. Next, fill the waterskins before loading them, the cooking pots, and the supplies on the camp mules.

Pascal's loud curses echoed while he and LaFleur pushed and shoved the mules into place forming the train-line. They lifted each packsaddle by its wooden tree, needing one from each side, all the way along the line, loading eighteen mules. Each mule carried a packsaddle weighing over three hundred pounds. The men broke into a sweat, breathing hard by the end of loading the saddles, which they did twice a day.

The mule team carried as much as one wagon—5,400 pounds. A loaded wagon traveled fifteen miles a day on smooth flat land, but far less on rough, broken ground. The mules traveled twenty miles a day, even on rough, broken ground, as long as the mountains had a goat path.

Nigel paid no attention to Pascal and LaFleur's appearance when they first found him. He'd been overjoyed to have someone. Anyone was better than being alone on the prairie. At first, they resembled tall, husky men with trim chin-beards. Each one wore his long hair tied behind their head with a piece of leather cord woven into a pigtail along his neck.

He studied them, noticing Pascal's brown eyes, hair, and beard with red highlights where the sun lightened it. LaFleur, the bigger of the two, had a thick chest with a flat belly, blue eyes, light brown hair, and an even lighter beard. The sun bleached his hair to near blond in front and on top. Watching them load, he noticed they stood taller than his father, over six feet tall, with big arms, chests and legs. He grasped how strong, after the pair lifted the three-hundred pound packsaddles, moving them with ease. However, he thought them old, like his papa—at least thirty years old.

Nigel's daily routine didn't vary often in those first weeks. Walk until the morning rest, ride the *marina* with the blanket, read the English book, and answer Pascal's questions. At siesta, they off-loaded packsaddles to let the mules graze. Always a cold meal in a cold camp with no fire at siesta. They performed endless chores during siesta, but each took time for a short nap before the men reloaded the mules. Nigel walked, or trotted, until the afternoon rest, then he rode the bell mare during *Françoise* lessons, and anything else that came into Pascal's mind.

Pascal found no water that day until nearly dark, which made setting up camp and getting the animals into hobbles a lot harder, which also took longer. They had little conversation in the evening camp with everyone exhausted—rest became more important. Nigel ate, washed the pots, and filled two waterskins before mumbling his prayers as he fell asleep.

Each new day likened the day preceding. They shook him awake in the dark before dawn. He worked until he dropped exhausted on his blanket each dark night. Breakfast never varied, warm gruel and jerky. The siesta meal always served cold, beans and pork side-meat cooked the night before. The evening meal made fresh each day. They ate jerky and hardtack biscuits during the morning and evening rest.

Nigel learned the men issued water sparingly throughout the day—water came only with meals or rest stops. He drank coffee in the morning because it helped him wake up while allowing him more to drink. He learned to fill a large leather bag with water each morning after placing eight cups of dry beans inside to soak all day, while the train moved. The beans grew plump, ready to cook by evening. One fire-blackened cast-iron pot held four-cups of beans and pork side-meat, for tonight. The remaining beans cooked in a second pot, served the next day, cold at siesta. The menu never changed.

Pascal said, "Beans, beans, the musical fruit, the more you eat, the more you toot."

The men wore wide-brimmed straw hats with a flat crown they called Panama Plantation hats. The Plantation hat provided them better shade than his father's black wool hat that Pascal tossed to him the first night in their camp, sounding apologetic.

"It is a little something to remember him by," Pascal said when he handed him the hat, and said, "don't lose it." *Noir* soon learned why a hat became so important in the relentless sun. Unfortunately, his father's hat had a small brim, letting his neck and ears sunburn. LaFleur taught him to use a spare cloth to make a kerchief around his neck. The kerchief kept the sun off his neck. He found it handy to wipe sweat from his face, or grime from his hands.

Pascal carried a small cask of olive oil they used for everything: cooking, first-aid, leatherwork, and gun oil. LaFleur helped him apply olive oil on his sunburn. Nigel applied it every day until his skin became darker and less sensitive to the sun.

He noticed Pascal and LaFleur dressed in layers. As the day progressed, they shed the heavier leathers they donned when first rolling from their blankets. However, as they traveled farther south, they dressed with fewer and lighter clothes. Pascal told him few things on the prairie grew white naturally. Animals, like the deer, antelope, and rabbits flashed their white tails to alert others of danger. If a Redman glimpsed a flash of white, he knew it belonged to a white man, focusing his attention on tracking it. Pascal told him not to wear any white, not even for underwear or stockings, brown or green the preferred colors, but he accepted black, dark blue and dark reds. Everything related to survival: clothes, work, camp, eating, even drinking water. He watched everything they did, trying to understand how these men lived on the prairie alone.

He learned in a hard lesson that Pascal had no tolerance for the whining and complaining his mother allowed. Pascal denied him a meal at siesta. Pascal gave him instructions only once, and in a soft voice. Nigel learned to pay close attention, doing whatever task Pascal requested.

During one discussion, Nigel asked, "Why does it happen that way?"

Pascal shrugged. "Water runs downhill."

Nigel thought about that answer for a minute. "That answer makes no sense. What does 'water runs downhill' have to do with my question, or anything?"

"It has to do with everything, *ti-Noir*. In nature, things are the way they are, water runs downhill, *always*. Just because you don't like it that way, or you think it shouldn't be that way, doesn't mean you can change the nature of things. You must learn to accept the nature of things. The rattlesnake will strike, if you come too close. The Redman will kill strangers on his land. Water runs downhill. Observe what is natural, learn not to resist the natural way things occur."

He gaped at Pascal, brows wrinkled in confusion. *What on earth is he talking about?*

The only way Nigel knew Sunday arrived is Pascal rested the mules. It seemed he worked harder on repairs and washing clothes than he did while the mule train moved.

"Do I take a break for my lessons before the siesta?"

"There is no siesta in camp on Sunday. The siesta rest is for the mules. Be happy, it is Sunday. You don't have lessons on Sunday." Pascal gave him a wink.

"Oh, thanks a lot."

After they settled to eat their evening meal, Pascal said, "Your shoes look like they are coming apart. Why didn't you say anything? Learn to fix broken equipment as soon as you can. If you can't walk, you're no help. How do you expect to earn your keep?"

"Where am I going to buy new shoes out here?"

"Buy? *Buy?*" Pascal barked, grimacing like someone had farted in church. "Have LaFleur show you how to make hard-soled moccasins. They'll be better for your feet than those store-bought shoes. LaFleur will make your first pair, but watch him, then start working on your next pair, so LaFleur doesn't have to show you twice."

LaFleur snapped his fingers while barking a laugh, then rubbed a rock on his palm.

Nigel asked, "What is he saying?"

"Pay him no mind. He's rubbing flint on his skin to sign 'skin-flint' because he thinks I'm too cheap to buy anything. I tell you both. We're tradesmen. We sell, we don't *buy.*"

Monday morning, he learned the mules were smarter than he thought. When Pascal and LaFleur led them into the camp where the saddles had been unloaded two nights before, the mules sought their own packsaddle. Pascal said each smelled their packsaddle, knowing where to wait. The problem became that they stopped when they found their pack. They didn't want to move to get linked to the train-line. That's when Pascal and LaFleur pushed and shoved them into line. Of course, Pascal cursed a blue streak all the time he wrestled the mules.

He studied as LaFleur led six unburdened mules with a notch cut in their left ear. On each Monday, they arranged the rested mules to stand next to the first six mules in the train. Then LaFleur took the last six to tie them with the pack animals. They loaded the notched-ears with the six packsaddles from the last mules. After those six mules had packsaddles, Pascal lead them to the front of the line before connecting them to the train-line with the fresh ones in front.

Each Monday, they placed the six mules that rested for a week in the front of the train-line, allowing the last six a week carrying no load.

"Over the years, we've found the mules moved at a better pace, acting less troublesome, if they had a regular break from carrying their heavy load. We aren't only being kind to the mules. It makes less work for us in the long run," Pascal said.

Nigel walked alongside Pascal.

He helped close morning camp, and then he

walked. He did his lessons, *Anglais* in the morning, and he walked. He worked on the harnesses or riggings during siesta. And then he walked. He did lessons in *Français* in the afternoon and evening camp. Pascal told him the mules spoke better *Français* than he did, but LaFleur always gave him a smile and signed "good." He learned to enjoy the lessons, and not only because he rode. Pascal made the lessons entertaining.

And he walked. In the ten days after they rescued him, he walked two-hundred-eight miles to Fort Belknap, Texas.

Pascal told him not to blame God for his loss. He prayed for his lost family each night.

He prayed for his family, but he wondered if God listened.

Nigel wouldn't look back on this. He left nothing behind him to see—not anymore.

He wouldn't look back.

Ever!

Chapter 6

July 2 to 5, 1853

The Army Quartermaster Sergeant at Fort Belknap acted particular about tallying Pascal's load of supplies. The sergeant searched for some excuse not to approve Pascal's load, but scratched his head with his pencil, frustrated he found nothing missing. A lieutenant observing nearby asked him to explain the delay before ordering the sergeant to sign for the complete load.

Pascal asked the lieutenant, "Are there any Army supply trains going southwest to serve the Army forts along Marcy's route to the Pecos?"

The lieutenant shook his head. "They wouldn't come from here. You'd have to go east to Ft Worth to ask the quartermaster about deliveries to other Texas forts." He stopped before turning away. "You might go into Weatherford. It's the last civilian junction on the road from Fort Worth. They supply many of the little settlements from there. Also, Charles Barnard built a new trading post south on the Brazos near Comanche Peak. He may need trade goods delivered."

"*Merci*, Lieutenant. I know both George and Charles Barnard. I don't like that braggart Sam Houston, or the Torreys, who are the Barnard's partners. However, if I can make a profit from them, it'd be a good reason to visit Charles again. I don't understand him setting up a trading post in the middle of Comanche territory, for those lands are buffalo grazing grounds, near Comanche Peak. Building there will stir trouble with the Redman."

"I believe Charles bought out his partners a year or so ago, including Senator Houston. Charles moved the new trading post past Techuacana Creek farther west up the Brazos from the old Waco campgrounds. He doesn't want the Comanche or Lipan Apache who trade at his post to come too close to the new village the white settlers established at the old campground."

Nigel waited to ask questions until they tramped toward the waiting mules.

"Why did the sergeant keep checking your delivery? Couldn't he count?"

"He's a common thief," hissed Pascal. "He expected to claim I shorted the *cargas*, hoping I'd bribe him to cover up the shortage. Afterwards, he would steal what he claimed had been shorted, selling it to put more money in his own pocket. I think the lieutenant is suspicious. He's watching the sergeant." With that, Pascal spat on the ground and rubbed his foot over the spot on the ground. He learned when Pascal spat like that, he hexed someone he didn't like.

"Let's get the mules moving this afternoon. There'll be no need for siesta rest since the mules aren't carrying a load. Mayhap, we can get to

Weatherford by dark tomorrow, giving us a late morning the following day while we wait for the town to wake up before our business. We'll need to find water nearby to camp and clean up. I want to talk to the merchants to find us some trade goods we can sell further west or a load of *cargas* for transport."

Pascal called to LaFleur to move out.

Nigel struggled to keep up, walking alongside the mules. They almost trotted forcing him to do the same. *Pascal is right, the mules are moving easier. It is like they sense the change.*

Evening camp flowed at a more relaxed pace without heavy packsaddles to unload. The mules covered a longer distance the next day, with shorter rest stops, and a faster pace.

More trees grew in this part of the plains with more creeks and streams. Trees along the creeks and streams grew taller, not like in England, but still tall for the prairie. Camp settled into a more relaxed rhythm on the second evening, but he sensed Pascal and LaFleur acted worried. They didn't laugh and joke as usual that evening. *Something is wrong, but what?*

The next morning, the men behaved as if it were Sunday, washing themselves and their clothes. Pascal retrieved his "business clothes" from a camp pack. *Maybe it's going into town that has them agitated.* Nigel didn't have any spare clothes, using the spare shirt from his father to cover himself until his clothes dried after washing.

A little unsure, he asked, "I know you don't like to buy, but I could use another shirt, if they have one in town."

"We'll see," Pascal responded while he continued to get ready for the ride into town.

LaFleur, who remained in the camp, gave Nigel a long hug before they departed.

Pascal rode his horse while Nigel walked to Weatherford. In town, Pascal pointed Nigel to the general store in the settlement before handing him two copper pennies.

"Buy yourself a treat while I do business here. Wait for me at the store."

~~~~~~

Pascal heaved a sigh after Nigel trotted toward the store.

"There is no point delaying this. I must get it done with."

Pascal strode into the sheriff's office and, to his surprise, found Sheriff Tom Watson, a man he'd know years earlier, when Tom rode with the old Frontier Rangers. Later, Pascal heard Tom had suffered a severe injury in an Indian fight, limiting his ability to mount a horse.

Pascal cried, "Tom, I don't believe it! When did you become the sheriff here?"

Tom spoke in a high-pitched, Southern drawl to greet his friend.

"Pascal, you ol' rascal. I sees them injun's ain't scalped you yet."

"More sadly, I haven't been chased or shot by a jealous husband either."

"You're pretty much out your territory being east this a way, ain't you?"

"*Oui.* I came across the smoking ruins of a pilgrim wagon train on the Canadian south of old Fort Adobe. Five missionaries expecting to convert the Redman from his heathen ways let themselves be slaughtered by those very heathens."

"Well, you give me a passel of them Yankee Blue boys to ride with me, we'll convert as many of them Comanche as we can get in our sights." Tom hated the Comanche for what they had done to his family. He spent years with the Rangers chasing them to seek his revenge.

Pascal handed Tom a folded sheet made into a letter with a wax seal.

"I'd like you to get this letter sent East reporting Reverend Blackthorn's family died on the prairie. The letter is for the American Board of Missions in Boston, the fools who sent the missionary party onto the prairie."

"Yes sir. I can do that. It'll be in the next mail East. I'll sees it's reported right proper."

"There's a problem. A young boy survived, Nigel Blackthorn. I asked the Mission Board to take him in, but until then, I guess he'll go to an orphanage."

"Oh, golly dang! Poor little lad. How old is he?"

"He just had his thirteenth birthday."

"Oh! Oh, that's not so good."

"What do you mean?"

"I thought him a li'l babe. But a young sprout of thirteen? He'll suffer awful in that infernal orphanage. You know my pappy has slaves back in Mississippi, but I wouldn't even put one of them Nigra children in the orphanage, it's so bad."

"What can I do with him? Where can I send him?"

"Keep him. Work him hard. If'n he's on the prairie with you, he'll grow up straight, becoming a strong, righteous man, not be beaten like a dog in that danged orphanage."

"But he eats more than LaFleur and I together," Pascal sputtered. "He's all hands and feet. He can't seem to walk without stumbling over himself or dropping something."

"I can tell you ain't got no children."

"None the Church will recognize."

"Well, he's a getting a growing spurt. You keep on feeding him, an' he'll just keep on getting bigger. You'll have a big ol' boy doing the work of two men when he's growed."

"But right now, he eats like two men."

"Why sure. Look at it this way—you don't have to pay him."

"It'd be cheaper to pay him than feed him. I can't be raising a pilgrim out on the prairie."

"Oh, pshaw. Kit Carson, Jim Bridger, Jedediah Smith. They 'twas lads when they came West. I thought you a learned man, some kind of churchman. Is *such* what they learned you?"

Pascal drew away at the implication, but persevered in his argument.

"It's no life for a young boy out there with LaFleur and me. He needs boys his own age."

"Nah. He needs somebody to care for him, raising him to know right from wrong. You'll do right fine—so'll that young'un, too, with you to look out for him. He'll get no caring or learning in the orphanage, just beatings."

Pascal glowered at the sheriff for a minute before he strode through the door. Outside, he stood gazing into the distance across the prairie. *I told LaFleur we shouldn't ride to the smoke ... Avoir ce qu'on pouvez.* (You get what you deserve.)

"Ahhh," he sighed before he spoke aloud, "This will change things."

Pascal prowled around the village asking who shipped? Who received? What is in short supply? What did they have in excess? What products are expensive? What products are real cheap? What is the price of wheat? Corn? Cattle? Did anyone buy or sell mules? Horses? Did the Army resupply the forts? He found people willing to gossip.

The clock had passed noon when Pascal ambled to the general store to find Nigel sitting on the porch, his shoulders slumped, and his body sagging while his chin rested on his hand.

"What is wrong, *Noir?* Spent all your money?"

"No, sir. I spent one penny on candy, but I'm saving the other penny."

Pascal smiled with eyes shining in pride. "Ah. A good lesson learned."

"I ... I worried you ate without me."

"Well, I guess I'll have to feed you."

Pascal glanced around, spotting a house behind one of the business buildings. A sign on the house read, "Room & Board – Meals served."

"We'll march to the boarding house to inquire if we're too late for their noon meal."

"All right!" Nigel jumped up, moving at a trot, when Pascal mentioned food.

The meal cost two bits, including a glass of lemonade and a piece of pie. Pascal grumbled, but he paid.

Pascal had to admit he hadn't seen *ti-Noir* happier. He watched *Noir* finish a large china bowl of beef stew filled with potatoes, peas, carrots, and onions in a thick flour gravy and fresh flour biscuits on the side. These weren't trail hardtack you had to soak in liquid before chewing.

The landlady took a shine to Nigel, bringing him a big glass of cool buttermilk.

Nigel said he never had it before, but he drank it all, ending with a big sigh, "Ahhh."

Pascal thought he'd have no room for the pie, but it disappeared in three bites.

The landlady smiled, gazing upon Pascal with favor.

"It's a joy to watch a growing boy eat. It all went in, and ten minutes later he'll be hungry again. If he grows into those big hands and feet, he'll be a big one when he's full grown."

"It's what everyone says."

"If you bring that youngster again, please come a little later, like you did today, so my regulars get plenty to eat. Let them have a head start, so to speak," she said, smiling at Pascal after they stepped onto the porch.

"*Oui*, I understand. You've been a gracious hostess." Pascal took her hand, bowed, kissing the back of her hand, "Mayhap, I could visit later this evening for some dessert?"

"Mayhap," she said, still smiling, while she took her time in withdrawing her fingers from his grasp before sashaying into the house.

Pascal strolled with Nigel to the general store, where they entered to ask the woman at the counter to show them ready-made clothing in Nigel's size.

"One size to fit him now, I think, and then a size larger for when he grows. Nothing fancy. A work shirt and pants in each size and four pairs of dark stockings."

The woman motioned for Nigel to come to her. She placed ready-made twill pants and cotton button-front shirts against his lean body to find out what size might fit him.

The woman set aside the pants and shirts she'd selected for Nigel before asking, "Do you want long underwear for him?"

"Do you have anything lighter weight than those red wool long johns?" Pascal asked.

"Yes, we just received red cotton two-piece sets that are lighter than the wool flannels," she said, pointing to another pile of red garments. "They button at the waist."

"Alright. Two sets of the cotton long johns. He'll outgrow them before winter."

She nodded in agreement, smiling.

"Do you have dried or compressed vegetables?" Pascal asked, "Or anything like it?"

"Yes," the clerk answered. "The trail folks have wanted them ever since Captain Marcy wrote how it expanded his food supply. We've some dried citric acid like Marcy used."

"*Oui*, I'll take the largest container of the dried vegetables and the smallest of the citric. I met Marcy's party at the Horsehead Crossing on the Pecos. It must have been two or three years ago. He's as opinionated as most officers, but better at caring for his men. It surprised me how well he worked his mules. I'd like to review his maps. Were they ever printed?"

"I wouldn't know."

"Too bad about the maps. Do you have dried beans or rice? Mayhap, some corn meal?"

"We've got red beans in fifty-pound sacks. Don't carry rice. We might have a twenty-five-pound bag of corn meal someplace in back."

"*Oui*, I'll take two sacks of beans and one corn meal. I'll pay for it now, but send a pack mule for them later this afternoon."

"We close at six o'clock today, opening again at seven tomorrow morning. It's Saturday, folks will be getting supplies all day. There'll be a lot of folks in town. We'll be busy."

"*Oui*, we'll be back before six o'clock today. How about a slab of pork side-meat?"

"Don't carry it. The blacksmith at the livery barn makes smoked bacon, if he has any. He keeps it in a sawdust pit underground on the shady side of the harness shed in the rear."

"*Oui. Merci.*"

"If you're going toward Austin, you ought to ask the blacksmith about taking his horses. He sells wild ponies to the ranches farther south. I think he's got a passel in his pasture now."

"Ah, that's good to know. *Merci beaucoup.*"

~~~~~~

Pascal and Nigel tramped to the blacksmith to ask about buying smoked bacon.

The blacksmith said he had a few left. After a glance at Nigel, he asked if Pascal could send the lad into the sawdust pit, fishing around until he found two slabs for them.

"They is wrapped in burlap on the outside with plain cotton on the inside," he said. "Smoked 'em myself. It'll keep a good while on the trail. I had me some hams, but they's all gone. They don't keep too good on the trail, but they's powerful good while they last and the hock sure does flavor the beans."

"*Oui*, but you don't have any." Pascal raised his eyebrows. "I hear you sell horses to folks farther south. Would you be interested in having us string your horses south to save you the time of riding there and returning?"

The blacksmith, Jake Salter, glanced at Pascal, his eyebrows furrowed.

"How much you charge?"

"It depends. Are the stallions fixed? Are they a wild mix of mares and stallions? Have they been shod? Are they raw or broke?"

"Only got four mares. The regular buyer wanted mares, if I had them. The rest are geldings. I fixed them 'bout two weeks ago and I shoed them, too. I been waiting for 'em to settle down before I move 'em on south."

"Are they bit-trained to bridles? Are they saddle broke? Or are they still wild?"

"Well, they're a might bit raw yet. They might could use some work, but you ought to do that while you drive them."

"*Oui*, if they were trained to a bit and saddle broke, I'd charge three-dollars a head to deliver, but raw, un-broke and needing work, it'll have to be ten-dollars a head."

"Ten dollars! Why, I can't pay no ten dollars. I wouldn't make no money." The blacksmith hollered, waving his arms. "Why you might as well stick a gun to my head to rob me. Ten-dollars! That's outrageous."

Pascal smiled, recognizing the ploy as a negotiation tactic to lower the price.

"*Non, non.* The usual price for breaking new ponies is seven dollars. You know that as well as I. The other three dollars is the cost of stringing them all the way south. It's a fair price."

"No, I can't pay no more than seven dollars for both breaking and driving down there."

"*Non, non.* I couldn't do it for less than nine dollars and fifty cents a head. You'd have to throw in that small saddle over there, so the lad can ride them every day to gentle them down."

"Well, if you're going to gentle them like that, I might could pay eight dollars."

"I might go to nine dollars a head, but if I do, I'll need bridles for one-half of them so they get used to the bit in their mouth and learn to respond."

"Well, I don't know about bridles for half of them, but I might could give you a half-dozen. Now, you're sure you'd break them, ride them every day, wiping down afterwards?"

"*Oui*, that's why the lad is along. He's here to work."

"Alright, nine dollars. It'll save me some time if you string them along south, breaking them along the way."

"Let's call that a bargain. Who are the ranchers paying for the horses?"

"I'm selling a dozen to James Tracer at the Bar-J ranch, southwest of the old Waco village, upstream from the old Torrey Trading Post Number-Two, but up the west bank of the Bosque River, south of the Brazos. I've dealt with him before, giving him my best price of twenty five dollars a head.

"I'm selling six geldings to Alvin Richter in Austin for thirty dollars a head. I ain't never dealt with him before, so you watch him."

"Now, let's be clear here." Pascal glared at him, a hard face, as only Pascal could do. "I ride there to learn they have already paid you, or paid you in part, and have paper to prove it, I'll come here to saddle you like one of my mules. I'll work you until you drop, then whip you when you do. I've done it before, and if you don't believe me, ask your sheriff, he saw me do it when he rode with the Frontier Rangers."

"My God. That story's true? I'd never thunk it," he said, shaking his head. "Well, I'm safe. I told you true."

"*C'est magnifique.* I enjoy doing business with you, my good fellow." With that, Pascal shook the blacksmith's hand to seal the bargain.

"I'll give you one hundred ninety two dollars for the dozen and one hundred thirty six dollars for the six. You sign a bill of sale for three hundred dollars in *gold*. I'll collect my fee out of their payment. This way, you're paid and done when I take the herd. Understand that if either buyer gets pissy or doesn't want to pay, the horses are mine to sell where I can."

"I'll settle for that price if you're paying in gold, but you won't have no trouble with that Bar-J outfit. Can't say about Mr. Richter. He came through three weeks ago, gave me his address, said he wanted a half-dozen good riding horses next time I'm down there, and said Indian ponies is fine. If he don't want them, you can get thirty dollars a head anywhere in Austin or San Antonio. For sure, if they is settled down and ride gentle."

"I'll try to find a load of freight for delivery on south that way or some trade goods I can sell. When I have a load for the mules in a few days, I'll return for the horses, paying you then."

"Looking forward to it," said the blacksmith as they shook hands again.

"We'll go back to LaFleur now," Pascal said, as he gathered his horse from the hitch-rail. "You two bring a pack mule to town to collect our supplies. We'll let you guard the camp this evening while LaFleur and I visit the town for a dinner, a drink, and a good cigar."

"I thought you told the lady at the boarding house you'd come by for dessert tonight."

"Ah, Yes. She'll be a tasty dessert." Pascal smiled at Nigel, with a wink.

"You mean her pie will be tasty?" Nigel asked, scratching his cheek.

"Yes, I'm sure her pie will taste sweet, too."

~~~~~~

While Nigel plodded alongside Pascal, he thought about the bargaining for the horses.

"I don't understand. You said you're a tradesman. You don't buy, you sell. Why did you *buy* the blacksmith's horses?" He rubbed the back of his neck.

"If the blacksmith trusted me, which wouldn't be smart on his part, I'd have to ride all the way to Austin to collect his money before returning here to pay the blacksmith his due. I'd be doing all the work of breaking the horses plus riding back and forth while allowing him to make all the profit. This way, the blacksmith doesn't have to trust me not to steal his horses, or trust me with his money. He accepted less than the price he wanted for the convenience of having his money, in *gold*, now. This way, he doesn't risk being robbed along the way or risk getting hurt breaking the horses." Pascal spread his hands wide as if revealing all.

"I still don't understand. Isn't that cheating him?" Nigel rubbed his chin.

"*Hors de mu vue*! (Away with you), you impudent pup," Pascal barked, scowling at him. "I cheat no one. I offered the blacksmith a service. My service was money, gold in-hand today, instead of money three to four weeks from now. He paid for my service. It is what a tradesman does, offers something you need, a service or goods, in return for money or other goods. You'll learn there'll be times when I trade one type of goods for another type of goods, where no money changes hands, and if I'm clever, and *I'm* always clever, I make a profit on both ends."

Nigel turned to look at him, his face screwed sideways.

"Don't look at me like that. The Bible says, 'a laborer is worthy of his reward.' First Timothy, verse nineteen. This is my labor. I provided him a service and, for that, I'm paid a fee. If he thought I cheated him, he'd have sent me down the road. This will be your service, too. You'll work those horses to earn your keep."

"How does the blacksmith make a profit if you charged him so much?"

"That's not our worry. However, I'll tell you he gets those horses from ranch hands or drifters trying to make extra money. They find the wild ponies, driving them here to sell to the blacksmith. I doubt he paid five dollars a head for a wild pony, which is half a month's pay for a ranch hand. The smithy made fifteen dollars a head depending on what he paid, just for shoeing and fixing. No one got cheated, we each made about the same."

"But you still have to break the horses?" Nigel ran his hands through his hair.

"Yes, but that won't be as hard as it sounds, and you'll help."

Nigel jumped in the air, getting excited about the prospect of riding.

"Does that mean I get to ride every day?"

"Well, I don't know if I'd go that far, but we'll talk. Let this be a guide in your future lessons. You must be able to add sums and multiply in your head with speed, or you'll be the loser in trades like this. If you need a paper and pen to figure sums and numbers you'll starve as a tradesman. Pay attention and learn your lessons. There is a reason for each of them."

Nigel ambled a little farther, still thinking. "There's another thing I don't understand."

Pascal snorted. "That's a surprise."

"You asked if he 'fixed' the horses. The blacksmith said they're geldings, he did it himself. What does that mean?"

Pascal snorted before laughing aloud.

"You didn't grow up around a farm, did you?"

"No, sir."

Pascal waved for him to come closer, put a hand on his shoulder to whisper to him. "You have a man's parts in your pants. You know, those two little marbles in the sack?"

Nigel nodded.

"They *'fix'* a male horse by cutting off the 'hang-y down' part. Afterwards, *he* is no longer a male horse, *it* is a gelding."

Nigel stood still with his mouth open in a perfect "O." "N-N-No. They cut them off? Doesn't it hurt?"

"Haw-EE-Haw-EE-Haw-Haw," bellowed Pascal. "*Oui*, it hurts!"

Pascal snorted when Nigel walked differently, as if he wanted to cross his legs.

Nigel wondered aloud. "Why? Why would you do such a thing?"

"We need to add animal husbandry to your lessons. You'll learn, as you get older, and your juices flow, that man isn't all that different from a stallion. To answer your question, a stallion is too feisty and territorial. He'll bite and kick if another stallion comes close to one of his mares. They'll fight to the death to keep another stallion from being nearby when a mare's in her season. When the stallion is that way, he can be dangerous to ride. After you remove the 'hang-y down' parts, the feisty stallion is no more. *It* is a gelding, a reliable working animal."

The puzzled squint on his face betrayed his confusion. "Did you fix your mules?"

"*Non, non, ti-Noir.* Mother Nature did that for me. Understand the mule isn't a natural animal, it's half horse-half donkey, nature can't tell which, so she won't let a mule reproduce. I've heard of a mollie, every now and then, that produced a spud, but from a stallion, not from a jack donkey. You see the stallion, like man, will take any port in a storm."

Pascal laughed after a wink at Nigel.

Nigel shook his head, squishing his eyebrows together. "All of this is quite confusing."

Pascal laughed at his quandary.

"*Oui*. And one day soon, it will become clear, as you snort and prance like a stallion every time a little filly comes by."

Nigel gave Pascal his "preacher's son" sour face of disgust.

Pascal laughed with gusto.

When they returned to camp, LaFleur jumped into the air, clapping before pointing at Nigel. LaFleur pointed to his nose, pulled down the corners of his mouth in an exaggerated frown, slumped his shoulders, stomped his feet before pointing at Pascal, and then to Nigel.

Nigel grew confused, failing to understand. "What's he doing? What's he saying?"

"Don't pay any attention to that clown. He's making sport of me," Pascal said.

LaFleur grabbed Nigel, pulling him to where Pascal stood after he stepped from his horse. He, Pascal and Nigel danced in a bear hug.

"What's he saying?" Nigel asked again. "What's he saying?"

Pascal tugged himself away from LaFleur, shouting, "Stop. Stop."

Then Pascal turned to Nigel with a solemn face as he shook his head, as if in sorrow.

"LaFleur signed we're a team now. I'm making you my apprentice. You'll learn to be a tradesman like LaFleur and me. Without a doubt, I'll be damned for leading you into this life."

LaFleur continued his barking laugh, dancing in circles while holding on to Nigel.

"What do you mean, I'll be your apprentice?"

"Do you know what it means to serve as an apprentice?"

"I think you learn a Master's trade like a cooper or a blacksmith."

"It means you'll learn *this* trade. You'll work harder, for longer hours, receive even less thanks than before and, if we ever profit from this wandering, you'll have a share."

"You mean I'm staying with you and LaFleur?" Nigel shouted. "Forever?"

"*Oui*, if you wish."

By that time, Nigel whooped like a wild Redman while he and LaFleur danced in a circle.

"Enough of this frivolity," Pascal shouted. "This changes how we do things. *Noir*, it'll change your lessons and your training. You'll have to learn everything we do, and more, you are no longer just a helper. I'll have to think about this some more. LaFleur and I'll discuss it tonight when we go into town. In the meantime," pointing at LaFleur, "You quit dancing the jig. Put a packsaddle on one of the mules to fetch the rest of the supplies in town.

"*Noir*, bring us a mule. Don't dawdle. LaFleur, if you need anything from the store, take money with you. Look at what I bought while you load the mule. Buy any supplies I missed from the store. We'll leave *Noir* to guard the camp when we visit town tonight. Now get moving, before I reconsider this foolishness," he said to their backs as they hurried away.

~~~~~~

Pascal turned to survey the camp, muttering aloud to himself.

"I knew I made a mistake when I traveled east into the settlements. We can't go back to Fort Atkinson. I'll not re-cross the heart of Comanche territory to go north again. It's too hot and dry on the prairie to go there now. Even worse, there's no profit in competing with the wagons on the Santa Fe Trail. There aren't other trading posts between Atkinson and Bent's new Fort, so I'd lose money dragging empty mules that far. It's going to be even hotter riding south."

He worked on a harness needing repairs before he muttered aloud.

"LaFleur must check all the chains and metal works tomorrow, while we have a blacksmith to make repairs or forge new pieces. He'll have to show *Noir* how to make some wood and leather hobbles for the horses. I don't want to spend good money on metal hobbles only to use them a few weeks." He worked for a while in silence, but soon muttered again.

"The roads are better here in middle Texas than farther west in the open prairie, which means too many wagons here for me to make any profit in cartage, and too many stores to sell my trade goods. Townsfolk claimed a stage service runs from Fort Worth to Waco, on to Austin, and south to San Antonio. Others reported stage service from settlements on the Gulf of Mexico to San Antonio. Too many people are coming to Texas. It's getting crowded.

"The Redman is already upset because there are too many whites. It'll only cause more bloodshed. It is God's Mercy that the Comanche, Kiowa, Cheyenne and Lakota haven't made peace among themselves. If they ever joined, they'd drive the white man across the Mississippi. It's good that the Redmen distrust each other as much as they distrust the white man."

He roamed around the camp, checking on the pot hung over a low fire before stirring it.

"LaFleur only made beans for the two of us. Well, that'll be about enough for *Noir* when we go to town. I'll have to be more careful when talking to the ladies, if *petit Noir* is nearby. He watches everything. And he asked questions, *ce'l questions*! (What questions!) *Son questions vous rendre fou.* (His questions drive you mad.) Why this? And why that? It's why I like silent LaFleur as a partner."

Time passed while he considered plans for their future.

"We'll go south to Comanche Peak to visit Charles Barnard's trading post to see if he has any ideas on what would be profitable trade goods between here and Austin, or maybe San Antonio. In earlier times, I'd take him a cask or two of gunpowder, but I don't want to encourage selling weapons to the Redman. Ah well, we shall learn about his trade goods when we see him."

Thinking of weapons, he continued to ramble aloud.

"We'll have to get *Noir* some kind of rifle for teaching him to shoot. I don't think he can handle a man-sized weapon yet. I don't want to waste the ammunition for him to learn. I'll have to find him a target rifle in a .22- or .25-caliber. I don't remember seeing any signs for a gunsmith in Weatherford. I'll wait until Austin to find those things. Too many changes, too quick. We'll get careless, letting someone get hurt, or worse."

Chapter 7

July 6 to 11, 1853

The next few days frustrated Pascal. He failed to find a full load of freight to haul south to Austin or even to San Antonio. It forced him to carry less than a full mule-train load, while they worked the horses south to Austin for their only profit.

Pascal and LaFleur loaded the mules early the morning they planned to leave. The men started them along the trail with Nigel on the *madrina* in the lead. Pascal told Nigel the plan.

"LaFleur and I will get the horses, catching up with you before the morning rest. By the siesta rest, we'll corral the horses, unloading the mules."

"Why? I don't understand?" Nigel said, placing his hand on his left check.

"You don't have to now. It'll become clear later. Don't stop to talk to anyone. Don't dawdle on the trail, the mules will get restless, becoming troublesome. I showed you Comanche Peak yesterday. You'll see it when you ride from the trees, south of the Brazos, after you cross the ford on the Clear Fork. Stay on the *madrina*, taking her across the ford at a trot. Don't slow down until the last mule is on the other side."

"I know. You showed me all this yesterday. I can do this."

"We shall see. We shall see," Pascal muttered aloud when he rode away.

Pascal and LaFleur caught up with him at the time for morning break, as planned. Nigel reported he didn't have any problems, and he never noticed anyone on the trail.

"*Oui*, you did well. I'll ride farther downstream to find a place to corral the horses. Keep the train on the trail until you see me come back, guiding the bell mare to me when I signal. I'll use the mules to form the backside of the corral. Let LaFleur drive the horses past you first, then you come behind with the mules."

Nigel fidgeted in his saddle, growing excited at the prospect.

"Are you going to break the horses now?"

"In a manner of speaking. You'll see when we begin."

Pascal returned within an hour, signaling LaFleur to bring the horses. Nigel followed them toward the riverbank. Pascal selected a "horseshoe bend" in the Clear Fork of the Brazos River with an eight to ten foot drop-off down to the river. The horses wouldn't jump from a steep drop-off into the river. Pascal guided Nigel and the *madrina* to close the open land-end of the horseshoe with the mule-train, closing "the corral" on the horses.

Once stopped, LaFleur and Pascal unloaded the packsaddles from the mules.

Nigel failed to understand the change in routine, calling, "Why are you unloading? It's only the morning rest."

"Breaking horses can be done several ways, *ti-Noir*. If you do it like the horse wrangler or cowhand, it's hard on the horse and the rider can be thrown and injured. I use an easier way. These horses aren't used to carrying anything on their back. In fact, panthers will leap down upon them from a tree, to kill them, rather than chasing a horse from the ground. So the horse has an in-bred fear of something leaping on its back. When a wrangler saddles it, and then jumps on the horse, the poor horse reacts as if attacked. It becomes frightened, trying to buck the rider from its back, and sometimes it does, but the horse remembers being frightened.

"I, clever Pascal, train in a different manner with less work for us and less stress on the horse," Pascal said while he worked across from LaFleur to unsaddle the mules.

While Pascal spoke to Nigel, LaFleur tramped to the riverbank, returning with an arm full of eight-foot tall saplings cut by an axe. Pascal instructed Nigel to observe and learn.

"Pay attention to LaFleur. Study how he strips the small branches to create a fork with a five-foot stalk below. While he's trimming the forks, remove the bridles from ten mules."

Pascal roped a horse, bringing it outside of the "corral" to stand next to LaFleur.

LaFleur placed a cloth blindfold on the horse's

eyes. Below the blindfold, he laced a soft leather cuff on the horse's long nose. The cuff wore additional thongs hanging from each side. He slipped a bridle over its nose and cuff, fastening the bridles buckles. The horse shifted its hooves, stamping in nervous agitation, but it didn't buck or rear. The animal shoved its tongue against the metal bit as if it didn't like the taste of the metal bit in its mouth.

LaFleur lifted the sapling fork he'd prepared. He measured to where he wanted the height of the stalk under the horses chin before removing the bottom part with a hand-axe. By spreading the two fork branches, he placed one fork tine on each side of the horse's muzzle. He passed the tines up inside the bridle, so the fork's stalk hung beneath the horse's chin.

He tied the fork tines to the leather nose cuff, holding the sapling in place under the nose. From his pouch of leather thongs, he tied the upper branches of the tines to the bridle on each side. This arrangement let the four-foot solid stalk hang below the horse's chin like a beard.

"*Noir*, the horse must drop its head to kick or buck," Pascal said. The fork under his chin hits the ground, preventing the horse from dropping its head. This doesn't hurt the horse. It confuses them, but it doesn't frighten them, which makes saddling much easier for us and the horse."

LaFleur stepped close to the horse with a saddle blanket. He rubbed it along the horse's nose and cheeks, letting the horse sniff it—it smelled of mule—a scent the horse knew. He rubbed the horse's neck, and then its shoulders, never lifting the blanket until he came to its back, where he stopped, leaving the blanket in place. The horse shifted its weight, but didn't react or buck.

Pascal held the horse's head, stroking his nose, and speaking soft words, while LaFleur placed an empty packsaddle on the gelding. The saddle startled the horse, but Pascal held him steady, stroking, and talking. The horse tried dropping its head to buck a few times, but the forked stalk kept its head up. The fork confused the horse, causing it to whicker, and shake its head while shuffling its hoofs, but it didn't buck.

LaFleur tightened the cinch, connecting a breast collar, and a head-stop, which is a line between breast collar and the bridle, to prevent the horse from lifting its head up. He attached rawhide lines from the bottom of the fork stalk to the breast collar rings on each side, limiting the horse's ability to shake the stalk back and forth. On the trail, the front breast collar and the rump breech strap keep the saddle centered, fore and aft, preventing it from sliding when going up or down hills. These straps also prevented chafing the animal's back caused by the pack sliding.

In between tasks, Pascal pointed at the horse's rump strap. "I've seen muleteers use a crupper under the tail instead of a rump strap. I don't use a crupper because it galls the tail, forcing the mule out of service. LaFleur tried different versions of a rump strap. This one works best at keeping the pack from sliding forward when descending steep hills."

After the packsaddle remained in place for several minutes, the animal settled its hoofs again. LaFleur loaded the packsaddle with forty pounds of trade goods. The horse reacted to the weight, shuffling to buck and rear, but the fork stalk and head-stop prevented it. LaFleur led the horse for a trot in a twenty-foot circle. When he completed three circles, he removed the blindfold before leading the horse to trot around three more times. The horse fidgeted, shaking its head and snorting, but learned to accept the weight of the light load in the packsaddle.

While LaFleur walked the first horse around in a circle, Pascal led the next horse from the corral. LaFleur returned the horse wearing a packsaddle to the corral. They repeated the process again. Pascal sent Nigel to the riverbank with a hand-axe with instructions to cut more saplings with the fork high enough to use as LaFleur had shown him.

The men rested at noon to eat their usual cold meal before they continued loading the horses with packsaddles. They finished about the usual afternoon rest time once they fitted eighteen horses with packsaddles. The horses continued moving in the corral, unaccustomed to saddles, but rigged with the forked stalk and head-stop, they couldn't buck or rear. However, they could neither graze nor drink. While the horses grew accustomed to carrying a packsaddle on their back, they also learned to have the bridle's iron bit in their mouth.

"We'll leave the packsaddles on until sunset, but wear their bridles overnight," Pascal said. "Before dark, we'll unload the packsaddles. We'll take groups of six to the river, letting them drink, before grazing inside the corral area. They shouldn't need to drink again until morning, when we do this over again. It'll go quicker the second time. We'll add more weight tomorrow. By the day after tomorrow, we should be able to ride south again."

The evening camps proceeded at a more relaxed pace than usual while they "broke" the horses to saddles. Nigel observed more than he worked that day, but found his curiosity piqued.

"Why is it when you curse, you only curse in *Anglais*?" Nigel asked in *Françoise*.

"My papa agreed with your papa. Only coarse men of low breeding curse while working, like the *Anglais*. He said if I must curse, I had to curse in *Anglais*. Besides, the *Anglais* have all the good curse words." After his last comment, Pascal leaned close, slapping the bottom of Nigel's foot while he winked.

"Ha-Ha. Very funny. I'll remind you I'm Welsh, so such a joke doesn't apply to me."

Pascal laughed aloud. "Who's joking?"

Within two days, Pascal and LaFleur trained the eighteen horses to accept a saddle and bridle. While a few still acted unsettled when ridden by

Pascal or LaFleur, they didn't buck or rear-up. They accomplished the "work" part of "breaking" the horses with relative ease, and in a few days, without injuring either men or horses.

Pascal continued using the horses to carry packsaddles so they'd not forget they are work animals, expected to carry a saddle every day with a man's weight on their back.

During this time, the mules grew more vocal, braying often at the packed horses.

"Mules are smarter than horses. They're laughing at the horses," Pascal said.

The mules seemed to enjoy just trailing along without being loaded, while watching the horses carry the mules' packsaddles.

The morning Pascal readied to move south, he called, "Now we shall see if *ti-Noir* is a horseman."

"I get to ride? Hooray! No more walking." He waved his arms above his head.

"*Oui, Noir.* Riding horses is part of your work, as is wiping them dry after you ride. Don't run them to a lather. I don't want to wear them out or spend unnecessary time cooling them down. As to 'no more walking,' I think you're right. I think you need to run now."

"Run?" Nigel shouted. "To where? And why? Why run when we have horses to ride?"

"Someday, *Noir*, the Redman will attack, killing your horse. Or you'll not see a gopher hole, letting your horse step in it, breaking its leg. Understand you can do nothing for a horse with a broken leg but end its pain. Such things have happened to

LaFleur and me. You must be able to *run* away, or you won't survive."

"Is this another lesson?"

"Of course. Why do you ask?"

Pascal adjusted his saddle, getting ready to mount. He directed Nigel to take the first horse from the string, saddling it with the small saddle, as they taught him.

"Come back to me when you are mounted."

When Nigel came alongside, Pascal leaned forward with hooded eyes and grim mouth.

"Let us speak to your apprenticeship, *ti-Noir*. I said earlier, the lessons will continue until you are grown. I tell you again, but you don't believe me, yet. The prairie is unforgiving and hard. If you're to survive on the prairie, you must be as hard as the prairie. Your father was forgiving—he wasn't hard. He wasn't prepared for this prairie, and he didn't survive. Even worse, his family didn't survive. He may as well have shot your mother and sisters back in Westport Landing. It'd have been kinder than to allow what the Redman did.

"I know it hurts to hear such, but you must learn to be strong in mind and body to survive this prairie. If I make life easy for you, like your mama did, you won't survive. You will suffer like your mother and sisters did on that terrible day."

Nigel sobbed with tears streaming across his cheeks. "Why are you saying all these mean things about my family?" He sobbed in great gulps. "I thought you liked me. I thought you wanted me to come with you?"

"Listen to me, *ti-Noir.* Do you remember the day I found you in those ashes, all black with soot? I asked then, 'Are you a dark little piglet? Or are you a dark wolf cub?'"

Pascal paused to glance behind, making sure the horses stayed in line.

"If you're a piglet, others will feast on your bones, and on your labor. They'll trample you in the mud. If you're a wolf cub, you'll do the feasting as you grow. When you're grown, men will be wary, walking or talking in soft tones around you, lest you strike.

"I'll teach you all that I know, but the strength to survive must come from within you. I can show you what to do, but you must learn to make the strength your own. Learn that your mind must be stronger than your body. Without a strong mind, a strong body doesn't know what to do, becoming another man's tool. You'll still be a piglet, just a *strong* piglet.

"Your honor, your discipline, your pride will come from your strong mind. I can teach only so much. What you learn and apply will make you the man you will become. The pride, or the honor, of a man is not his strength or how smart he is.

"*Une homme de honour c'est une homme de parole* (A man of honor is a man of his word). *Une homme donner sa parole, respecteer sa parole* (A man that gives his word, must keep his word.) *Meme en depit de la mort, honour.* (Even in the face of death, honor.)

"It is how you will be measured as a man."

Nigel wiped his nose before he gazed at Pascal with his eyebrows furrowed.

"Does this mean more lessons?"

"Haw-EE-Haw-EE-Haw-Haw," Pascal brayed. "Of course it means more lessons, *ti-Noir*. And it means you run, morning and evening, every day."

Pascal laughed his great braying laugh, slapping his thighs while reveling in the humor.

Through his tears, Nigel glanced at LaFleur, who laughed his barking dog laugh. He pumped his legs up and down, running in place, and pointed at Nigel—*Run*.

And so Nigel ran in the morning after the train started moving. He exercised the horses when he finished running. He rode four different horses before his lessons and rode four different horses during his lessons, a half-hour for each horse. They spoke the morning lessons in English. He rode six horses after siesta before riding four different horses during his lessons, a half-hour for each horse. They spoke *Français* in the afternoon lessons and in the evening camp.

Nigel liked to run before he ate his evening meal. He found he slept better and learned he had fewer sore muscles if, after his evening meal, he bathed in the stream to get the sweat and the grime off his body before bedtime. In the heat of summer, he found it refreshing.

He prayed for his family each night before sleep came, but sleep often won.

Pascal and LaFleur encouraged his prayers,

saying God's purpose is hidden from man.

LaFleur wrote on his slate, *Not dwell on their loss. It will make you bitter. Remember their love for you. Our Lord called them home. Accept His wisdom. Cast no blame.*

He heard their words but struggled to accept their meaning.

One day was like another.

And so he ran.

He didn't look back.

There was nothing back there for him.

Chapter 8

July 12 to 13, 1853

After they finished an arithmetic lesson one morning, Pascal told Nigel the story of Charles Barnard's wife. They planned to visit Barnard tomorrow. No one knew all the details of Juana Cavasos Barnard, but he knew a few things.

"In the late summer of 1844, the Plains Comanche raided Matamoros, along the Rio Grande near the Gulf, capturing several Mexican women for slaves or trade. One of those taken was eighteen-year-old Juana, the daughter of Maria Josafina Cavasos, and granddaughter of Narciso Cavasos, the holder of one of the largest Spanish land grants in Texas. It isn't clear how long the Comanche held her captive because there are different versions of that story.

"However, in late 1846, while the Comanche traded at the old Torrey Trading Post Number-Two on Techuacana Creek near the Waco Indian Village, George Barnard purchased Juana from the Comanche for three hundred dollars in horses and trade goods, a handsome sum.

"In 1847, Juana married George's younger brother, Charles Barnard. Juana is well respected by the people who trade at Barnard's. Her reputation as a mid-wife is widespread because she's well-versed in folk and herbal medicine learned from the Comanche."

"She is a remarkable woman. You could learn from her because she has learned to survive here in the worst of circumstances—captive of the Comanche," Pascal said.

The next day, before the morning rest, they came to Barnard's Trading Post at the foot of Comanche Peak. Nigel didn't consider it much of a peak, only a rounded hill overlooking the Brazos valley. The highest point around, it gave an unobstructed view of the area. A short, sweet grama grass covered the prairie here, not the coarse short grass he'd noticed around Fort Adobe and north of Fort Belknap. Here, trees grew tall beside the streams feeding into the Brazos.

"The Comanche considered the rolling plains between the Concho and Brazos Rivers their buffalo hunting ground and winter camp," Pascal said. "I came here to trade in earlier years, but I don't ride this way anymore." Pascal heaved a sigh. "The Comanche wanted rifles and liquor. I won't sell those things—and they didn't like it. My refusal made trading difficult, so I don't trade with them now, unless they cross our trail on the upper prairie."

Pascal gazed across the prairie, seeming lost in thought before he spoke again.

"In the early days, when we came west into Canada in 1846, the fur trade thrived, and some men made small fortunes in the beaver trade, but those days are gone forever. The only hides left with a market are the buffalo, and their hides are too heavy and hard to transport without wagons or carts like the Comancheros use. The fur trade is over, which is why young Bent closed and burned the original 'old Fort'—most of the other trading posts are gone, too.

"In the spring of 1847, we traded with the Redman from St. Vrain's Fort on the South Platte, the last good year of the fur trade," he said, motioning at LaFleur. "The Redman traded for flour, coffee, iron points, and foofaraw for the women in exchange for beaver and other furs. We went to Rendezvous on the Snake near the Grand Tetons that year. The "river of snakes" you mentioned. Ah, what magnificent mountains are there, rivaling any of the Alps in Europe.

"In the autumn of '47, we came south to Bent's old Fort for the first time, then on south to Taos and Santa Fe, before going into old Mexico that winter. We deciding we liked Mexico better than those great mountains in the winter with all their snow." Pascal glanced at his friend, laughing while they exchanged hand signs.

"Now that you've reminded me of those mountains, mayhap, we'll head north next spring to travel among them again. We shall have to see what trade we can carry to those north regions. Maybe Barnard will know."

When they approached the Barnard Trading Post, Nigel studied its strange design that left it half-buried. The trading post appeared as a long, low-roofed log cabin built into the hillside. It had no windows and a sod-covered roof. Pascal explained the vertical slits on either side of the only door formed gun-ports needed to drive raiders from breaking in the door. The thick-planked door had iron straps near the top and bottom with iron lugs forming a hinge.

"There are tales Charles built another Trading Post in a cabin almost five miles farther west, near a Shawnee-Delaware village," Pascal said." Rumor has it the Shawnees and Delaware will be moved to the Indian Nations, which is where your family should have gone." He sighed heavily. "It's too late for 'what should have been,' we must work with what we have."

The Trading Post at Comanche Peak had two wood-fenced corrals down-slope from the bunkered Post building, nearer to the Brazos River at the hill's base. Pascal led the animals toward them because he planned to use one corral for the horses and the other for the mules.

While they led the animals to their respective pens, a man and woman walked from the Post building toward the corrals. Pascal waved, calling a greeting to Charles Barnard. Barnard introduced his wife, Juana Cavasos Barnard.

Pascal acted his usual gracious self around the woman.

"I'm pleased to meet you. Your adventures with the Comanche are legendary," he said.

Pascal introduced LaFleur and Nigel.

Juana shrugged away Charles's protective arm

to step forward, taking Nigel by the hand.

"I will take this wolf cub with me while you old men tell lies and drink whiskey," she said before she strode away, leading Nigel to the bunker.

The three men gaped at her in wide-eyed surprise but then shrugged.

"Women," one said aloud, and they chuckled.

Once inside the candle lit Trading Post, Juana pointed Nigel to a rough-hewn table.

"Sit. I've fresh venison on the spit. A wolf cub like you needs meat. Later, I will teach you how to find food out there. You can't survive on beans and jerky like those old fools."

She turned to the fireplace, carving the meat on a tin plate.

"Why did you call me a wolf cub?" Nigel asked, licking his lips at the sight of roast meat.

"I observed you two hours ago when you loped over the rise a mile north of here. You ran from sight, going to the stream to drink, before running to them. When you came trotting alongside the horses, moving easily. At first, I thought you might be a *los Indio*, guiding them."

"How did you know I got a drink?"

Juana chuckled, ruffling his hair as he ate.

"You remind me of *los Lobos* in my country, Mexico. Gray wolves roam these prairies farther west toward the mountains or south to the *Rio Bravo*. Texas calls it the *Grande*. They are always at a trot, or on the run when after game. They are always hungry, hunting, and killing, when they find game, but sometimes—they just kill—as if they need the practice. Now that you are up close, I notice you have the wolf's eyes, that look of hunger, like everything is a possible meal. In this room, I can tell you are not the gray wolf of my home. I think you will be the black wolf, your hair and skin are so dark."

She continued talking to him while she gathered items around her kitchen.

"Men won't like you. They'll fear you like they fear your little brother, the gray wolf. Women will look in your eyes to find you exciting, but they won't understand you're dangerous, and try taming you by bringing you to their bed. Enjoy them as you will, they won't change you. You'll be the black wolf, always."

His face flushed with heat at her frank speech about taking women to bed, forcing him to glance away like a preacher's son.

"Pascal says I am a black wolf cub, too."

Juana grunted when she set a second tin plate of roasted meat before him.

"He's not as much of a fool as I thought if he sees the wolf. When you finish, we'll walk. I can't lope like you young wolves do, but this is a time for walking. You have much to learn."

"Why does everyone want to give me lessons?" Nigel said in a nasal whine.

"You have a lean, hungry look. If you want to satisfy your hunger, you must learn to gather food from every source out there on the prairie. Do you know what berries and roots are good to eat? Do you know how to catch fish with your hands? Can you fashion snares to catch rabbits or other ground animals? Can you live off of the prairie if you're alone?"

He shuddered at the thought of what would have become of him if Pascal hadn't come.

She lifted his head, eying him as if she read his thoughts.

"If you want more to eat than that old man's beans, then I can show you how to harvest the bounty of the plains. If you're satisfied with his beans, go listen to those old men's lies."

"How do you know we eat beans?"

"You've a lot to learn. This is a trading post. I know what white men take on the trail. Now, will you walk with me?"

"Yes, Ma'am." As he rose, he snatched the last piece of venison.

Juana led him across a lush green meadow toward a small stream emptying into the Brazos, asking questions as she walked. "Where did you grow up?"

"Llewellyn. It is in Wales, a part of England."

"I know England. Did your family have a farm?"

"No, Ma'am. My father is a Methodist minister."

"Did your mother have a garden or raise animals to eat?"

"No, Ma'am, not really. We didn't have any land. My mother and my sisters tended a kitchen garden. They kept a few hens."

"Did your papa have a horse or cows, pigs, sheep, any animals?"

"No, Ma'am. We didn't have money for animals."

"You need more than I can teach in a day or two. It is a wonder you and your family survived."

"They didn't. I'm all who remain. If my *parrain,* my godfather Pascal, hadn't found me, I'd have starved to death."

The woman studied him for a long moment, "Comanche?"

"What else? I hate them. When I am a man, I'll kill them—I'll kill them all."

"You can try." Juana stood still for several minutes, gazing into the distance. She sighed aloud, still gazing outside at the prairie before she spoke without turning.

"I had a hard time with the Comanche. I learned their slavery is no different from Mexico's slavery of their native *indios,* or the white man's slavery of the *Negras.* It's all slavery. Do you understand what they do to captive women?"

Nigel's tears formed in his eyes as he shook 'no'.

"They burned Mother. We didn't find my sisters' bodies. I don't know where they are."

Juana pulled him close, hugging him for a moment before they resumed their walk.

"I don't talk about my time. Not even with my husband. He knows the Comanche ways. He understands with kindness. It's been hard for me to forgive what they did, but my husband has helped me understand. It is their way. They treat captives from other tribes the same way. Their enemies treat the Comanche women that way if captured. It is their nature. It is what they expect.

I don't ask you to forgive them, for I haven't. I ask you to understand they don't know better. It is their nature. If you learn the natural way of things, you'd be no more angry with them than angry at a rattlesnake that strikes at you in surprise. It is the way of nature."

"Pascal said something like that. He said 'water runs downhill.' He said you can't change nature and you can't resist it. I must learn to accept the nature of things."

"I forgot the old fool once was a priest. He still carries a bit of their wisdom. Think about what is said. Don't let your hate for them rule your life.

"So that you know, *en español*, we call the godfather *padrino*. It is an honorable thing to care for a godchild." She sighed again, brushing a tear. "Enough of memories.

"Now, to your lessons. You must learn to find food. The land will show you where it is, if you learn to recognize the signs. Examine the ground at your feet. Study it as if it were a book, notice patterns. Scan for a break in the patterns. Observe no farther than the length of your arm."

She turned him around two or three times as if playing a game.

"Now turn to face north. What direction is east? What direction is west?"

After he pointed the correct directions, she smiled and patted his back.

"Good, at least you are learning how to find your way. Now tell me what you observe on the ground beneath your nose to the North and the East."

Nigel surveyed the ground for several minutes. It appeared like grass and dirt to him.

"I don't see any patterns."

"Do you see a dividing line in the grass, like a small path? Focus on the ground starting in front of your right foot."

Nigel responded aloud after studying the ground. "Yes, now I see it. The grass is kind of pushed to one side along there."

"So what pushed the grass aside? Bend lower, search for tracks."

"There are large and small prints in the dust. They kind of resemble each other, but one is bigger."

"Close enough. Now stand, gaze around, and tell me where that little path goes in each direction from here."

Nigel stood, pointing in each direction. "One goes to those bushes near where we came from the Post and the other goes toward the bank leading to the stream."

"Step to one side. Don't walk on their path. Follow to the bushes. Report what you see."

Nigel eased ahead in steps toward the bushes before stopping. He twisted to glance at Juana.

"I don't see the path under the bushes. There is no grass under there."

"Examine the bush. Tell what you see."

"It has green, red, and black berries on it. Ouch—it has thorns."

"There is a saying *en español* that is funny, but I don't know how well it translates. The saying is, 'blackberries are green when they are red.' Do you know what it means?"

"No. It doesn't make sense. How can they be black and green and red at once?"

"Pluck a couple of the 'black' berries from the bush, and then eat them."

"They are sweet but tart. They have grit in them like sand."

"Those are seeds, not sand. Yes, sweet and tart might describe them. Now, pick a red to taste it."

"Ugh! It's hard and bitter, but there's no grit."

"So which would you pick to eat?"

"The black ones," Nigel answered as he picked a few more berries.

"The red berries are not yet ripe. In a few days, the red berries will begin to darken, and then you can eat them. The little green berries are far from ripe. They may need another week of the sun to be ready to eat. If a bush or a tree produces edible fruit, but the fruit isn't ripe to eat, it is called 'green.' The red berries are not ripe, so they are 'green.' Do you understand now?"

"I think so, but it is a silly saying."

"Yes, men think so," she said, smiling.

"Now back to your lessons. What else is there? Closely examine the bottom of the bush."

"I don't see anything. No, wait, there are little bits of hair on some of the thorns."

Nigel got on his hands and knees, reached into the bush, gathering little clumps of fur.

"Sniff it. Can you smell anything? Do you recognize the color?"

"It smells like ... when a man 'makes water.'"

"Yes, some people think that is the smell. The important question is what is it?"

"I don't know."

"Then slowly turn to peer toward the bank where the path leads."

Still on hands and knees, Nigel shifted his gaze right, spotting a rabbit on its rear haunches watching him. "That's a rabbit. This is his fur."

He rose to point at the rabbit. At his movement, the rabbit vanished.

"Yes, a rabbit. But how will you catch him?"

"Our neighbor in Wales used a shotgun."

"Do you have a shotgun?"

"No."

"Then to catch the rabbit, you must trick him. You know the rabbit comes this way to eat the berries. How will you catch him? Do you have a bag of rawhide thongs?"

"Yes. How did you know?"

"It is what you do to survive out here. Be prepared by carrying your needs close at hand. The old fool is training you well, if he has taught you such already."

Juana taught him to make a simple snare for a rabbit, showing him how to build it, how to set it up, and how to use different materials, depending on whether in the woods or in rocky country, where there were no sticks or green tree limbs.

Juana led him around the area, asking him to point out different animal tracks, and asking when he thought the animal made them. She asked him to smell the different animal droppings to learn what each animal scat smelled like, how fresh it was, and what the animal ate. She gave him so much to remember, his mind whirled.

They ambled toward the cabin for siesta when Juana asked if he checked his rabbit snare.

"If you leave your snare unattended, another animal will steal your lunch."

"There's a rabbit in the snare," Nigel exclaimed, as they approached the snare.

"It's your lunch. You must learn how to kill it, skin it, and roast it on the fire."

"Will the lessons never end?" Nigel asked, with an exaggerated sigh.

Juana showed him how to grasp the rabbit by its hind legs before breaking its neck.

"The lessons will end when you are too old to sit a horse any longer, or sooner, if you forget something you've already learned."

"You sound like *parrain*-Pascal."

The skinning and cooking lessons continued until the siesta.

After the siesta ended, Juana asked, "Do you know what do with the rabbit hide? Do you know how to preserve, and how to treat a hide to make it usable?"

"No. LaFleur works all the hides."

"And what will you do if he is not with you?"

"What would I do with such a small skin?"

"You have so much to learn, little wolf," Juana sighed. "A rabbit's fur is very soft. It makes a good lining for your moccasin in the winter. A pair of them will make a mitten for your hands in the winter cold. A pair around the collar of your winter robe will keep the wind from your neck or keep the robe from scratching on your neck. You will learn to take an old wool blanket, cutting it into sections to sew inside your leather leggings or inside your winter robe, lap one piece over the other so there is no piece of hide showing from the inside. The animal hide on the outside will protect you from the wind and wet. The wool pieces sewn on the inside will protect you from the cold. Some leave the fur on the outside of the hide—I do not. It makes the robe heavy when it is wet and it stinks awful when wet. You have yet to spend a winter out here, but this prairie can be so cold that animals will freeze in place if they stop moving. You will be thankful for every piece of clothing that protects you, come winter."

And the lessons continued.

Juana discussed the basics of preparing hides, from rabbits and small game to larger animals, like deer or elk. She looked at his moccasins, rubbing the hides in her fingers.

"Ask the silent one to show you all he knows, he is good with hides. You'll do well if you learn what he knows. When you visit an Indian camp, ask questions of any old woman you notice working hides. Trade her some trinkets or give her a deer with the hide on it. Those old women know more about curing hides than we will ever know."

And the lessons continued.

After the evening meal, Juana took Nigel aside

into a small room in the back. She showed him plants and leaves she had drying in this room. She asked if he could write, and when he said yes, told him to fetch several pieces of paper, writing what she showed him.

"Later, you'll need it to study until you do it so often that you won't need to look at the paper." She showed him yarrow. "Collect it, letting it dry. Rub the dried leaves in your hand until it becomes a fine powder—use it for fever. Add it to coffee to hide the taste. It is bitter." Juana gave him one leaf from every plant she had, telling him to write its name and its use.

"Just as I told you to find an old woman in the Indian encampment, find the Medicine Man, or an old birthing nana. Give them some tobacco or some sugar, or both. Ask them about what they use for different sicknesses. Some of their treatments are very good. Of course, some are useless, but do not say it to them. Learn what you can and try them carefully. Use what works for you. Be respectful, share what you have."

"Why would I want to visit their camps?"

"Lessons. Learn from others. You must learn to observe. Observe the animals, learn what they eat, what they avoid. Let the natural world guide your spirit. Let it be your brother. Now, go run. You've been following me all day, you need to exercise."

"You sound like Pascal," he muttered, stopping in the camp to tell them he was running.

And so he ran.

And he prayed for his lost family when he lay

down to sleep.

They readied for the trail the next morning, up before first light. First, they loaded the packsaddles on the horses. Next, they aligned the horses in a train, followed by the mules in a string behind the train.

Nigel strode to Juana, thanking her for all she had taught him.

He told her he wanted visit again.

Juana smiled at him. "It would be nice to have you visit again." Then she gazed into the distance. "I won't see you again. You'll ride the frontier and the mountains. This land will be too tame for you. Don't blame the Comanche. One day you must forgive them."

Nigel gazed at Juana, his face sagging into a deep frown.

"Is there any chance my sisters are alive? Can we pay to get them back, as your husband did for you? Please ask those who trade here if they have seen my sisters?"

"You must understand each Comanche band is different. The Comanche that trade here are Penateka, the Honeyeaters. The band that rides along the Canadian is the Kotsoteka, the Buffalo-eaters. There are also the Kwahadi, the Antelopes, up on the Llano and by the Cimarron They are busy hunting food for the winter now—the Kotsoteka won't come this far south." With tears flowing freely, she said, "It's too late. Follow the old priest's advice. Pray that God grants His mercy and they find peace in His arms." In tears, she spun away, running to the Post.

Charles Barnard glared at Nigel as his lips curled in a snarl.

Pascal shoved Nigel forward. "Go. Start your run. *Tout de suite.*"

~~~~~~

Pascal apologized that Nigel had upset his wife, but LaFleur interrupted, barking twice before pointing to several riders coming around the slope of Comanche Peak.

"These are my customers," Barnard said. "Curb your pup's mouth. Treat them with respect and pray they have plans for tonight other than following your mules."

"Do you want us to leave?" Pascal asked.

"No. They will think you're trying to hide what you carry, which is bad. Or they'll think you're afraid of them, which is worse. You know trade language. Greet and speak with them."

Five Comanche warriors trotted close waiting until Barnard raised an open hand in greeting. One man guided a horse carrying several buffalo hides and other pelts, but no beaver.

Barnard strode forward to speak with them while Pascal and LaFleur lumbered along.

One Comanche slid from his horse, giving Barnard a traditional greeting among friends. He glanced at Pascal before he spoke in Spanish. "You are the black robe. Have you been reduced to trading pelts like the rest of us heathens?"

"I would starve if I had the Penateka as my competitor. That's why I work the mules to carry trade from post to post," Pascal said, offering five trade cigars to the Comanche riders.

"Good. Did you bring us whiskey and guns?"

"Standing Elk knows I don't trade in whiskey and guns," Pascal said.

"I thought you might not remember me. It's been a few years."

"We met at Bent's before the Army came to ruin it. It is good to visit with old friends."

While the men focused on the interplay, Juana slipped next to Barnard.

She spoke in deference to Standing Elk in his native tongue. After several exchanges between them, she switched to Spanish. "I told this one you carried word of a search for two lost sisters. He said the Penateka have not hunted north or west of the Wichita this season. They have not heard about any captives."

"Thank you for asking," Pascal said to Juana before facing Standing Elk. "I'm a messenger. The soldiers at Fort Belknap asked me to spread the word. I have no idea who the women are."

"If I learn about captive white women, I will tell Barnard because he doesn't cheat in his trade with us. Have you goods to trade?" Standing Elk asked, glancing at Barnard.

"Wait now," Barnard interrupted, "This my trading post. Pascal, take your mules, get moving." He laughed, "I won't have you taking my customers away. Go on, move out."

Pascal made exaggerated gestures, as if miffed at Barnard for sending him away, but he welcomed the excuse to depart.

~~~~~~

Nigel grew concerned when he backtracked to find the train still at Barnard's post, but he noticed the mounted Comanche. He recognized Juana leaving the discussion. Pascal told him to leave, so he waited hidden until he figured what to do. Whatever happened at the post ended while he observed from a distance because Pascal and LaFleur rushed to get the train underway.

When Pascal rode close to where Nigel hid, he shouted, "Saddle one of the horses. We need to move as fast as we can until dark. We'll ride east toward the Waco campgrounds settlement. Let's discover if the Comanche want us bad enough to ride into an area with more whites nearby."

"What's going on? What happened?" Nigel asked while he saddled his horse.

"You'll have to wait until we rest after dark tonight. The Redman leading the Comanche isn't a bad enemy, but he doesn't like whites. If we ride hard, we should make Waco about sunset."

They reached the Waco campgrounds without any sign the Comanche had followed. They set up a cold, dark camp, keeping the animals close.

In the dark, Pascal said, "Standing Elk said they had not hunted north of Wichita this season. He would have bragged if the Comanche held white women captives. I doubt the Penateka have them, but another band may. There is no way to know."

"He's lying," Nigel shouted. "He knows they would get into trouble if they have my sisters. They don't have the courage to tell the truth. They're just lying, murdering savages."

"If you had said that to their face, you would have met your sisters in heaven tonight," Pascal said. "We have no proof who has them. All you know is the Penateka denied holding captives. They have no reason to lie about it. It's not a crime in their eyes to capture women."

"Are you taking their side—believing their lies?" Nigel screamed.

"There are no *sides*. What happened is tragic. We can do nothing to change that. You must learn to control your emotions. If you had thrown this pissy tantrum at Barnard's, we'd have been lucky to survive against five seasoned warriors. Think about Juana becoming their prisoner again. She risked a lot for you. Is that what you want? Your misbehavior could put us at risk. Barnard is right, if you are to continue with us, you must curb your tongue. Is that clear?"

Nigel wiped the snot from his nose, nodding.

"I want to hear you," Pascal barked.

"I'll keep my mouth shut," Nigel said.

"That's not the point, which is why I wanted it out loud. You must share responsibility for our lives as we share responsibility for yours. Don't do stupid things to get us killed."

"I didn't … I don't want you or LaFleur killed. I never thought about Juana. I don't want her captive again," Nigel swallowed an audible gulp.

"She never goes outside when the Comanche trade. It took exceptional courage for her to come to them, asking for a favor on your behalf. Include her in your prayers tonight. Go to bed. I doubt she sleeps tonight."

Nigel didn't find sleep either. He thought about how bad he'd feel if he caused Juana harm. It shamed him that his stupid behavior put women close to him at risk. Never again, he vowed. *I'll protect the women around me. I'll never let another woman be captured.*

One day became like another, no way to tell them apart, just days and days.

Work from dark dawn to dark dusk before falling into an exhausted sleep.

He rode the horses when he returned from running. He rode four different horses before his lessons, and then rode four other horses during his lessons in English. He rode six horses after siesta, and then rode four horses during the afternoon *Français* lessons. He struggled with correct pronunciations. He ran every evening before he ate his meal.

He prayed for his family each night before sleep won—sleep won more often than not.

He thought there couldn't be forgiveness without punishment, but who to punish?

Pascal reminded him he trod on dangerous ground. God meted punishment—not man.

One day became like another. And so he ran.

He didn't look back.

There was nothing back there to see.

Chapter 9

July 14 to 23, 1853

The afternoon after they left Barnard's post, Pascal told him to ride a horse to the top of a rise to describe the other side. He rode to the top expecting some "trick" lesson by Pascal. What he witnessed stunned him—he found an awesome sight, truly awesome! A herd of buffalo ambled along, stretching for miles to the north. His mouth gaped wide as he observed them for ten minutes before LaFleur interrupted his reverie, snapping his fingers to get Nigel's attention.

LaFleur wrote on his slate. *This small herd. On high plains west where we found you, a huge herd surrounded us. They kept coming over rise. Ambled around us, like rocks in a stream. Two days to ride past, herd so big. Mules angry at night. Herd crowded all sides. Bad time for us. No sleep. If mules go crazy-they stampede buffalo. All be trampled. He wanted you see herd. Not see this big again. He afraid buffalo gone. Make war between Red and White.*

After a long while, Nigel glanced at LaFleur, who smiled nodding. They rode to catch up. Nigel babbled in excitement when he came alongside Pascal. After winding down with nothing more to say, he studied Pascal for a moment. "Thank you for sending me to view that herd."

Pascal nodded. "*De rien* (You are welcome— literally, it was nothing), *ti-Noir.*"

They settled into an easy routine of work over the following days.

One afternoon during French lessons, he struggled to ask a question in *Français.*

"Why do you call the Indians 'the Redman' and not Indians, like everyone else?"

Pascal gave him that haughty, superior gaze only a Frenchman can do with aplomb.

"*Voila!* I'm not like everyone else." Then he said nothing more for a few minutes. "I will tell you the stupid Italian had no idea where he was—he was lost! What an idiot!"

"What Italian? Who are you talking about?" asked a bewildered Nigel, in *Anglais.*

"That idiot, Christopher Columbus. He thought he 'discovered' India. He missed the continent of India by half a world. He is heralded as *the great explorer*. Bah! He discovered nothing. He was lost. What an imbecile! The Jesuits in Canada have evidence Norsemen camped in Canada two hundred years before Columbus was born, but the Pope is Italian. He called it heresy for the Jesuits to show Columbus as a fool."

Nigel screwed up his face, more confused than ever.

"What does this have to do with the Redman?"

"Is this India?" Pascal asked exasperated.

"No." Nigel's eyebrows wriggled like wooly worms.

"Of course not," Pascal shouted. "LaFleur and I have been to India. The real Indians are little brown men. *Voila!* This land is not India! Thus, the native people here are not 'Indians!' They are Redmen. Can it be more simple? These people are Redmen, and I'll thank you not to mention that Italian idiot again."

Nigel's eyelids flew wide, as his mouth dropped open, even more confused than before.

"But I didn't ask about the Italian. I asked about the Redman."

Pascal snorted aloud, following it with a harrumph.

"And what about those imbeciles, the *Anglais*? They have their East India Company, as if there is a 'West India.' They've been trading with those little brown men in true India for three hundred years. After all that time, they can't tell the difference between those little brown men and these Redmen in the Americas. If one would be so arrogant as to give the Redman a name other than what they call themselves, it would be Americans.

"The *Anglais* and the Hudson Bay Company have traded with the Redman for more than two centuries, but *they* still think these people are 'Indians'? Two centuries passed, and they failed to notice the two peoples are different colors. Two centuries passed and they've failed to recognize their geography error. The English are bigger imbeciles than the idiotic Italians. The *Anglais* don't know East from West, or Red from Brown."

His face slack-jawed, Nigel glanced at LaFleur who sat laughing so hard he had tears in his eyes. He raised his finger to his lips for silence. Nigel understood he shouldn't ask any more questions just now. It seemed LaFleur had listened to Pascal rant on this subject before.

They traveled southwest the next three days to the Bar-J, selling a dozen horses without incident. What passed unnoticed was Pascal kept the four mares, giving the ranch the geldings, LaFleur and he had been riding. Pascal promised to explain later why he wanted the mares.

The distance from Fort Belknap to Weatherford to Austin is over one hundred ninety miles. The team consumed sixteen days to make the trip. The first three days to break the horses, two days to Comanche Peak with Barnard's Trading Post, a day at the Bar-J, and a Sunday rest on the trail. The remaining days on the trail became boring repeats of one another.

A distance of one hundred ninety miles, and Nigel ached as if he had run the whole way. He wore out the moccasins LaFleur first made for him. He discovered the moccasins he made failed to wear as well as the ones LaFleur made. He asked LaFleur to examine them. LaFleur showed him where he went wrong before helping him make another pair that fit much better.

Pascal made him rework the first pair he had

made, saying, "Don't waste the leather."

The man in Austin, Mr. Alvin Richter, acted surprised when Pascal came to his door to deliver the horses. He strolled from his house, staring at the horses before he straightened to smile.

"They appear in good condition. You've treated them well. Are they saddle broke?"

Pascal waved Nigel to ride a horse on the street.

After Nigel rode about bareback, Mr. Richter jumped on another horse, riding bareback along the dusty street before returning.

Mr. Richter smiled, reaching to pat Nigel's shoulder.

"He's easy riding. I haven't ridden bareback since I was this lad's age." After jumping down, he examined the mouth of three horses. "How long ago did you geld them?"

"A month, maybe five weeks," Pascal replied.

"And they are this well behaved? You have a great hand with horses, Mr. LeBrun. What do I owe you?"

"You owe Mr. Salter, the blacksmith, one hundred eighty dollars for six prime horses."

"Yes, that is what we agreed. Let me step inside to get it." When he returned, he gave Pascal one hundred eighty dollars in twenty-dollar gold pieces, adding an extra gold piece.

"I expected them to need work, but these horses are in good condition and ready to ride. I'm impressed, Mr. LeBrun. Let me know when you have more horses like this."

Pascal smiled. *"Merci beaucoup.* It is a pleasure doing business with a gentleman," but muttered under his breath, "particularly one who pays in gold." He distrusted paper currency.

Pascal appeared in a much better mood after the sale, visibly relaxed, when he called to them.

"We'll find a corral out of town for the mules, if we can. We'll enjoy the 'city' for a few days until I can find trade goods or cartage heading west."

After finding no corrals available, Pascal decided to camp a mile west of town in a meadow with water and grazing land. LaFleur and he visited the town each night. During the day, they stayed busy with work, while waiting to reload with new trade. They repaired or made new leather ropes and harnesses. A master at working rawhide, LaFleur transformed it into usable harnesses and braided ropes. Nigel helped him weave a new train-line with several new metal rings and chains LaFleur ordered from Jake Salter, the blacksmith.

Nigel didn't like visiting towns. Townsfolk gave him weird stares. The town children made sport of the way he dressed. He got into fights with the local boys when they razzed him. Usually, they visited a town to trade or if they needed supplies. Otherwise, they rode around. Pascal scolded him for fighting with town boys because he wanted good relations with their parents, as buyers.

Another reason Nigel didn't like towns resulted from Pascal and LaFleur's behavior. They bathed, donning their "city clothes" to visit the sporting houses. He failed to understand the role of sporting houses, but the preacher's son in him thought they ought not drink whiskey and smoke cigars half the night. While he didn't understand the reasons, he had grown observant enough to notice the men became less critical and more relaxed after a trip to town. He'd seen drunks staggering in town, but never noticed them drunk.

From Nigel's point of view, food was the only good thing about a town. Pascal would treat Nigel to one meal in town if they conducted trade there. Nigel preferred breakfast with eggs, potatoes, meat, and biscuits because he didn't get such food on the trail. Either he ate breakfast or dinner in Austin while there, which he thought better than any penny-candy treat.

If Pascal or LaFleur gave him a penny or two, he saved them. One day in Austin, LaFleur gave him a penny, and then noticed Nigel put it in a small leather pouch he'd made himself. LaFleur snapped his fingers to get Pascal's attention, pointing to the pouch with pennies, before rubbing a piece of fire-starter flint on his palm before he pointed from Pascal to Nigel.

"*Non, non.* He's learning to be a tradesman, not a wastrel," Pascal said, smiling.

One evening, near dark, LaFleur motioned for Nigel to follow him, hand-signing "quiet." LaFleur carried his rifle. LaFleur signed, "Do as I do." He stalked through the woods in slow cat-like movements. Soon he pointed to tracks in the dirt—deer. Moving even slower in the underbrush, he raised his rifle, easing the barrel through an opening, and fired. He shot a doe. LaFleur signed "A buck has a tough hide for harness and ropes while a doe has a softer hide for moccasin tops or carrying pouches." He taught Nigel how to gut the animal before burying the remains so offal didn't attract varmints into camp. LaFleur showed him how to skin the deer, and how to preserve the hide with its mashed brain. He hung the cleaned and dressed deer overnight.

While he cleaned it, LaFleur showed him the new breechloader rifle they'd purchased in Kansas, while waiting for the packsaddles. Pascal had explained people referred to the rifles as Beecher's Bibles after Reverend Beecher who with John Brown, incited a slave rebellion.

Nigel failed to understand all of what Pascal told him, but he thought slavery a bad thing, approving their attempt to stop it. He'd noticed black slaves on their journey from Boston to Westport. He observed that folks treated them poorly. He failed to understand the way people spoke to them, as if animals. He couldn't fathom why they called slave men "boys."

He witnessed so much that he failed to grasp the meaning. He couldn't grasp why they called the rifle a "Bible." He didn't know what "statehood" was, or why people fought over it. But he understood these weapons were Sharps rifles, renowned for accuracy and for faster loading, which became important if the Redman raided.

The breech-loading Sharps used a paper-wrapped cartridge and a soft copper percussion "cap" fit atop the firing nipple. The percussion cap would fire in wet weather, where the old flintlocks wouldn't. He wanted to learn to shoot to avenge his family by killing Comanche.

Between them, Pascal and LaFleur carried four "Beecher Bible" rifles.

Nigel hoped they'd show him how to shoot the big rifle so he could exact his revenge.

The next day, LaFleur showed Nigel how to quarter the deer. LaFleur sold half of the dressed deer to the cafe where they often ate meals. In camp, LaFleur prepared dozens of jerky strips, cooking the rest. Nigel relished roasted venison.

In the evenings, before Pascal and he rode into town, LaFleur worked with a piece of deer hide he kept rolled in the supply packsaddle. After several days, Nigel realized LaFleur had hand-stitched a buckskin shirt for him. During these times, he didn't sit and watch. LaFleur taught him how to work the fresh hides to make useful and needed leather items, starting with long leather thongs, so useful in tying everything, and a leather pouch to carry them. He learned the value of LaFleur's bag of thongs, always carrying one he'd made himself.

When settling on the ground after the evening meal on Saturday, Nigel said, "I spied a Methodist Church in Austin. May I go to church services tomorrow morning?"

"*Certainment* (certainly). You have but to ask when we visit a town with a church. Just because LaFleur and I have been cast out is no reason for you not to visit your church. If you play your cards right, one of those fine Christians will take you home for a nice Sunday dinner."

"It's not why I'm going." He spun to tramp away.

While Nigel stomped away, Pascal laughed before saying, "Take one of the mules tomorrow. You will be too stuffed with food to hike this far."

Nigel had never attended church alone. He always sat with his mother and sisters, while his father conducted the services. He found it hard to sit alone among all these strangers. He noticed people gawking at him when he strolled into the church wearing his new buckskin shirt before sitting in a pew. The minister spotted him sitting alone, asking him to rise and identify himself. The congregation gasped in open-mouthed horror when he told of the Comanche massacred his family. He steadied himself not to cry or let his voice waver in giving a brief report of his family's death. He decided he'd never reveal this story again, if he could avoid it.

The congregation joined hands, offering a special prayer for God's loving care of his slain family. They may have been Methodists, but their service was far different from his father's in England. As Pascal predicted, they held a church supper after services. It appeared as if more people attended the supper than the service. He admitted he hadn't expected this much attention. Nearly every family asked him to join their table, offering to pray for him and his family. He hadn't seen this much food in one place since Boston.

He considered it neighborly to eat a bite of everything, just to show his gratitude for sharing the Lord's bounty. Did he mention pies? Pies—he had forgotten how wonderful his mother's pies had been. And fresh baked-bread—Pascal had camp biscuits, but no baked bread. Hardtack biscuits aren't bread, they're rocks that must be soaked in coffee to eat. He gobbled berry-jam on fresh bread. Nigel realized how you craved such simple things as baked goods and berry jam. By late afternoon, he became grateful for the mollie (female mule) to ride to camp.

Even though they camped near the town, the routine didn't change—up before dawn to tend the mules. They needed to find a new grazing area after two days because the mules grazed the grass low in the first area. The team had no end of work—from dark dawn to dark night.

Pascal instructed him to run each morning and evening, even while waiting in camp.

So he ran.

Late each evening, after washing in the stream, he spread his bedroll, preparing to sleep. He recited his litany of prayers, trying to complete them, before sleep won.

He prayed for his slain family, seeking the Lord's blessing for his mother and sisters.

He prayed for them, as his earthly father had taught him.

Forgiveness never entered his heart—he hardened it to hate the Comanche.

He didn't look back.

Chapter 10

July 26 to August 26, 1853

Monday morning returned to the usual camp routine in preparation for moving out the next day. Pascal signed a contract to haul a full-weight load of dry goods to El Paso. He purchased four more mules to carry it all. *Oh, did he complain about the price!* The new mules used Mexican saddles, which had no "tree" like the Grimsley packsaddles. A Mexican saddles formed a simple cube, three-foot per side, made into stitched leather bags. One cube hung from each side of the mule. A pair of three-inch wide leather belts looped under the cubes before being cinched tight.

LaFleur wrote on his slate. *Long hot trip. Few towns or settlements. Nothing until El Paso. At the Grande. Stay close.*

After they left Austin, heading west, Pascal grumbled aloud to LaFleur about all the wagons. Soon people would stop using mule trains to carry supplies and other trade goods on the plains. The Federal government established U.S. Mail service between San Antonio and San Diego by way of El Paso, called the San-San Mail.

"The fools can't build roads on the prairie—it's not theirs." Pascal said.

Pascal continued his rant, waving his hands, jabbing a finger in the air.

"They talked of the State paying to build a graded road from San Antonio to El Paso to allow wagons and stagecoaches to travel with ease, making the trip in three days. The newspaper reported Senator Sam Houston plans to ask the governor to create a 'Reservation' between the Concho and Brazos Rivers. It'd be Indian Territory, prohibited to white men. George Barnard said Sam Houston convinced him there'd be a Reservation agreement. He said that is why they built their trading post out on the Brazos River. The fools think the Comanche will settle down, living in one place. The Redmen have followed the buffalo for too many years to change now."

Pascal didn't think much of Sam Houston, going on another rant about the man.

"Old Sam got lucky. He caught Santa Ana in a quadroon's bed before they captured him. Sam forced Santa Ana to surrender all Mexican land in Texas. In a bold move, he formed an independent Republic. The first time Santa Ana threatened to take it back, Sam got scared, running to the Yanquis, begging to become a state. Sam Houston surrendered Texas' sovereignty without a shot— what an imbecile!"

Nigel failed to understand what Sam Houston represented, or why it upset Pascal.

Pascal gritted his teeth when the most popular discussions in Austin centered on railroad right-of-ways and construction, followed by plans to cross the Great Plains from east to west.

"Railroads will ruin the prairie. They'll cause the Redman to go to war, without a doubt. Worse yet, those rail barons will drive out the mule trains, even the wagons. Why stink up this beautiful country with smoke and ash? It'll cause wildfires. Bah! What fools! Complete idiots!"

After he tired of ranting, Pascal told them they'd head west but not climb the rugged hills to the southwest. Instead, they'd follow the Colorado River upstream to the Concho, leading to its Middle Fork. From the Head of Concho, they'd ride west to the Gap at Castle Mountain. That route meant forty miles from the last water on the Concho to the Gap followed by another thirty miles to the Pecos River. They expected dry camps along the trail on either side of Castle Gap.

Pascal planned to follow Marcy's southern route to Dead Horse Crossing on the Pecos. He decided to head west on Marcy's route to El Paso del Norte. Once in El Paso, he'd find *cargas* going north on the Rio Grande to Santa Fe, or find trade going farther west past the Gila River. He planned to take the first contract on trade goods going north or west from El Paso.

"In fact," he mused, "if we can find *cargas* going from El Paso west to Tucson, I think I'd take that instead of going north. It'll be winter before we return. I don't go north in winter."

In camp, the evening after they left Austin, Pascal unpacked two new 1851-Model Colt Navy revolvers he had purchased in Austin for LaFleur and himself.

"The new 36-caliber Colts are more reliable and sturdier than the original Colts. The new model has a trigger guard unlike the older Patterson Colt each one used. The new Navy model holds six shots, rather than Patterson's five shots. I stayed with the lighter 36-caliber to save by using the 36-caliber reloading gear we already own.

"If we are forced into a gun battle with the Redman requiring us to use the new Colt Navy and the old Patterson, we've made a terrible mistake. Before we go onto the prairie, we'll take a day for target practice with the new Colts, so we won't be shooting along the trail where we're riding." Then he chuckled, "I want to know how to shoot these new revolvers before my life depends on it, in case the Redmen aren't friendly."

Pascal handed Nigel a long package, instructing him to unwrap it.

To Nigel's amazement, the package contained a German target rifle, called an Anschutz, German for "shoots straight." The Anschutz had an octagonal barrel similar to the Sharps.

Pascal said, "It is just a little 'peashooter' 25-caliber percussion cap muzzle loader, but it's the right size for you to learn to shoot. You'll practice shooting your rifle for ten shots each morning before you run. You'll practice until you can hit where you aim every time. I'll show you how to shoot, but like your other lessons, you must learn the feel of the rifle, understanding how it works.

We can start tomorrow, after LaFleur and I have practiced with our pistols."

Nigel's eyes shone with excitement about the rifle—he wanted to shoot now.

Instead, LaFleur showed how to take it apart to clean it.

He complained, "It isn't even dirty."

LaFleur wrote on his slate. *No. Never get dirty. Always clean. Ready to shoot.*

Target practice the next morning became the first change in the routine for weeks. Nigel enjoyed it. Pascal and LaFleur shot their new pistols first, then cleaned and reloaded them. Pascal called them "cap and ball" pistols, loading black-powder and a lead "ball" into each chamber of a revolving cylinder. Next, he placed a percussion "cap" over each "firing nipple" on the outside of the cylinder. This revolver wasn't easy to load, let alone reload quickly, or on horseback.

In practice, he observed the men failed to hit the wood target every time. However, their misses kicked up dirt on either side of the wood, so they didn't miss by much. Each man wore a covered flap holster across his stomach. Pascal called them "belly guns." Nigel had not seen the pistols out of their holster before this.

Pascal said, "That's a good sign, because it means we have not met any trouble."

When he thought about it, the two men kept the holster hung from the saddle pommel, within easy reach, but not in their way when riding or working the mules. Nigel realized he'd grown so accustomed to seeing the men with weapons, it seemed part of their body. The men either wore a belly gun or had a rifle in their hand at all times. When they ate, a rifle rested upright next to them. They stayed alert, always ready to fight. That is life on the prairie.

LaFleur and Pascal took turns showing him how to "dry-fire" an empty rifle so the barrel didn't move when he squeezed the trigger. Pascal held out his hand, finger and thumb up.

"Squeeze thumb and finger together. Don't pull or jerk. If you 'pull' the trigger, it 'pulls' the barrel off target. You won't hit where you aimed. Either you miss, going hungry, or worse, you miss, letting a Redman kill you. Remember, this is part of your survival lessons."

They taught him how to load the rifle. They showed him how to measure the right portion of powder into the cap of his powder horn before dumping the cap full in the barrel. Tamp the rifle's butt on the ground twice to shake all the powder down and level at the bottom. They taught him how to place a patch and ball in the muzzle, pushing the ball down with the ramrod.

Pascal said, "Be sure to tamp it tight, leaving no gap between the powder, the patch, and ball." They showed him how to insert a percussion cap atop the firing nipple with the hammer half-cocked, so it didn't fire by accident.

The first time he fired it, he jerked in surprise thinking a cannon fired next to his ear. LaFleur gave him two red beans with a sewing thread tied around the middle. He pointed to his ears, where Nigel spotted a bean in each ear with a thread dangling.

"We use the beans in our ears to reduce the noise when we practice," Pascal said. "Only fire ten rounds at every practice and no more. Unless the Redman is chasing you, clean your rifle after using it, and reload. Then you're always ready to protect yourself. After you finish your ten shots in practice, piss down the barrel, pouring it out before you dry the barrel with a cotton patch. Pour a measure of olive oil down the barrel, swabbing it out with another clean patch. The olive oil won't turn rancid and keeps the barrel from rusting. Use the oily patch to wipe the trigger, hammer and outside of the barrel. Blow out the nipple hole to get the olive oil cleared and leave a spent percussion cap over it until you load again to keep dirt out of the firing nipple. If cleaning a rifle that way was good enough for Napoleon Bonaparte, it's good enough for an Englishman."

"I'm not English, I'm Welsh."

Pascal laughed, "Then we'll get you a tall bearskin hat like the Queen's Welsh Guards."

LaFleur showed Nigel how to start with a large target only ten paces away. LaFleur wrote messages on his slate. *When hit target each time. Make target smaller. Then smaller again. Hit small target every time at ten paces. Move to fifteen paces. Begin again.*

LaFleur pulled Nigel close, hugging him. Then he held his hand on Nigel's head, raised it, and raised it again. He wrote on his slate.

Must practice long time. Hit a deer far away. Walked before ran. Must practice. Hit target each shot. Before shoot deer.

The problem after that first day became the more time he spent at target practice, the farther he ran to catch up. And so he ran. He practiced with his rifle every morning but Sunday. Pascal denied shooting near their camp because it might attract the Redman. Nigel shot in the morning after the train moved out, and then ran to catch up. So he ran each day.

They fell into their routine of work from dark dawn to dark night every day.

Each day resembled the day before.

And the days passed.

A stop at a small ranch near the confluence of the Concho River brought another surprise.

Pascal bought an older mare for Nigel to ride.

"It's not a horse to outrun the Comanche. It's another lesson. Learn to take care of this gentle horse, to understand what she needs. Learn how to groom, feed, and care for her. One day, when you can afford a good, strong horse, you'll know how to care for it."

"But you and LaFleur have two horses each."

"*Oui,* you can't ride a horse every day, all day long. Horses need more rest. They aren't as sturdy as a mule. We ride one horse on one day, the other the next day. It keeps them fresh if we need to run. Don't worry about your mare. I won't let you ride that often when you can run."

"I know—lessons. But you wouldn't run away, leaving your mules, would you?"

"If the choice is survival or the mules, I'll try to survive."

Nigel gaped at Pascal in disbelief. "I can't believe you'd abandon your precious mules?"

"*Oui, ti-Noir.* You see, I practice what I preach about survival. I can buy new mules. I can't replace you or LaFleur. It would break my heart to have to bury one of you. But know this, I'll let crows pluck out your eyes and coyotes crunch your bones if you make some damn fool, tenderfoot mistake to get yourself killed." With that, Pascal twisted about, stomping away.

He studied Pascal's retreating back in puzzlement. *What brought on all that?*

So he ran. He practiced ten shots with his rifle each morning after the train moved out. And he ran. He rode his mare during *Anglais* lessons in the morning. And he ran. He rode his mare during *Français* lessons in the late afternoon. He remembered to pray for his slain family, but most times he fell asleep before he finished.

The day after Nigel got the mare, he stayed in the old campsite to practice with his rifle. After he broke into a lope to run to catch up, he saw LaFleur riding alone to meet him. He grew frightened that something bad had happened, wondering if the Redman got Pascal.

LaFleur stopped to write on his slate.

Rattlesnakes. All along the trail. Must be careful. Go back to water. Cut tall saplings. Slap the trail ahead where you walk. Scare snakes away.

They returned to the stream, cutting many green cottonwood saplings before returning to Pascal and the train. When they caught up, Nigel noticed that Pascal carried a long whip after all, a long black whip he cracked with every stroke.

After LaFleur and he came close, Pascal called to them.

"I've never seen such a thicket of rattlesnakes. We'll take turns thrashing the grass in front of our trail to drive the snakes away. If a mule causes a snake to strike him, the mule will panic and might even die. The worst thing is, if one panics and it pulls other mules into an area we haven't cleared, we can have a disaster. Once they panic, they'll thrash around in the area with snakes, getting more mules struck. We must keep the train in a tight line. LaFleur, you must keep your mules in the same path as the train.

"We'll have to take turns clearing the path—it's tiresome. Nigel, we're not trying to kill the snakes, we're trying to disturb them so they move away from our trail. We may have to forego any rest stops or the siesta until we move away from this snake nest. Pray that happens before dark. I don't know what we will do if we still have this many rattlesnakes when it gets dark. It's too hard to turn the mules around now that we're in them, so I'm going to go forward."

Nigel never noticed Pascal as so shaken before.

Pascal called, "Nigel, all you're to do is slap the sapling on the ground along each side of where the mules will walk. When you get tired call me, I'll spell you, then LaFleur can spell me, as we rotate from front to back to keep moving but allowing one of us to rest, while another guides the mule-train, and the third thrashes snakes from our path."

The sun peaked overhead into the heat avoided in siesta. By midafternoon, they spotted fewer snakes, but continued thrashing an hour before Pascal believed they had passed the snake nests.

"We'll find a quiet place up ahead beside the Middle Concho to camp for the rest of the day. Once the mules are unloaded, I'll ride ahead to determine if more snake nests exist in the area where we'll ride tomorrow. I've heard the old-timers tell tales of this happening along the Santa Fe Trail, but it's the first time it's happened to us."

Pascal admitted it scared him before giving a small laugh. "It is your fault, *ti-Noir*. You said you couldn't imagine a 'river of snakes' when you described the Snake River. So your strong mind conjured a 'river of snakes' on dry land."

A little shiver spiraled down Nigel's spine. "You can joke about it now, but I didn't see either of you laughing while we stood in the midst of those rattlesnakes."

"You are correct, *Noir*, but learn to laugh once the crisis has passed safely."

As his skill with traps and snares progressed, Nigel found himself assigned to find fresh meat for their meals—rabbits, prairie chickens, and now he added rattlesnakes to the list. He found it easy to catch rabbits and prairie chickens with the snares Juana Barnard taught him. He learned to run a few miles in front of the train to set the snares before running to return. When the train passed his snares, he'd recover the snare along with any game it caught.

He liked having fresh meat roasted at the evening meal to supplement the beans and salt pork side-meat. The men welcomed the change in camp meals.

Pascal said, "You must be more careful where you run. Learn to glance ahead where you'll place your feet. Don't accidentally step on, or spook a rattler into striking at you."

He admitted he never paid any attention to snakes before now. "They don't have poisonous snakes in England. I didn't know snakes got as long and fat as these rattlers."

"The word is 'venomous' snakes. Snakes have venom, not poison," Pascal corrected.

In the next camps along the way, Pascal taught Nigel how to use a six-foot wooden tent-pole to kill rattlesnakes around the campsite.

"A full-grown western rattler can strike four- to five-feet when it's upset, so don't get closer than a six-foot pole. Usually, we don't kill the snakes, but their venom can incapacitate a man for days, and maybe kill a youngster like you. You're to search the campsite for rattlers each night when we stop, killing them with the tent pole or the whip."

"I observed your use of a whip in the snake nest. So, you do use a whip," Nigel asked.

"Of course, but I don't worry about tearing the snake's skin." Pascal grinned with a wink. He continued working on repairs for a while before he spoke again.

"I don't want you using your rifle in camp. We don't need to draw attention to our camp. Never grab a rattler, even after it's dead. It has a reflex bite for an hour after death. It can still close its jaws, injecting its venom."

LaFleur showed Nigel how to step on the dead snake's neck before cutting off its head with a sharp knife. He buried the head with his knife blade, so none stepped on it by accident. LaFleur skinned the snake before teaching Nigel how to cook it, sliced, and fried in olive oil with wild prairie onions. It surprised him how good rattlesnake meat tasted when fried.

A few days later, LaFleur gave Nigel a leather belt he wove into a clever pattern. LaFleur included a knife scabbard with a large bone-handled knife from his personal kit, signing to wear the knife each day, like he and Pascal.

Pascal calculated a distance of three hundred sixty miles from Austin to El Paso. Nigel learned it converted into twenty-six days of dragging mules over that distance. They left Austin with green hills and trees along the streams, until they reached the head of Middle Concho, where several springs bubbled from a rock outcrop but few trees grew. After Head of Concho, the trail became hot and dry, with little cooling at night, or not enough to matter. Water and grazing grass became sparse with trees few and far between. The mules grew harder to handle, and more apt to bite and kick.

"This is why we go north in the spring. It's too hot here in the summer," Pascal said.

Pascal pulled the mules away from drinking too much when they made camp near the Dead Horse Crossing on the Pecos River, whose water carried a bitter mineral taste and odor.

Nigel asked, "Is it called Dead Horse Crossing because it stinks like this?"

Pascal barked a laugh. "No, but it's as a good guess as any. The Comanche gave it that name. As far as I know, no white man ever learned the true story behind the name."

The days passed into weeks, and then months. September had nearly passed, and the days became shorter. The passage of time covered his grief with scabs, but it offered him no peace.

Pascal pushed them hard the day they crossed the Pecos, covering the thirty miles southwest to Comanche Springs, where he settled for a two-day rest beside sweet-tasting water with decent grazing nearby. The mules liked the Springs' sweet water, growing a little less ornery. Nigel liked it even more because he got a break from the daily hiking or running.

He didn't like their campsite. Too far from the Springs, too far from graze, with the land almost a desert away from the sweet water, offering only different cacti or other arid plants.

"The Springs is the only water for thirty miles. Many creatures seek relief at the Springs, but few act as friends. Let them come and go from the Springs without crossing our path."

Nigel found little game, failing to find fresh meat with his snares. The only fresh meat available came from "sidewinders," the desert rattlesnake, which appeared plentiful. He wondered what they ate before he remembered what Juana Barnard had told him.

"You must learn to observe. Study the animals, learn what they eat, what they avoid. Let the natural world guide your spirit. Let it be your brother."

He decided to observe the sidewinder to learn what it hunted and who hunted it. The sidewinder didn't lie out in the full sun of the day, when it became too hot. Instead, it found a shelf the sun warmed earlier, and laid in shadow. The snake liked to lie along the bottom edge of small sandy gullies to wait for prey.

Nigel observed more small game existed than he thought. Nocturnal creatures didn't venture into the scorching sun during the day. He observed the Sidewinder becoming more active, seeking out mice, lizards and, yes, the occasional rabbit in the twilight.

He learned he must examine the ground closely for animal sign here in the desert and across the rock surfaces. He found scat differed here— smaller, almost dry, even when fresh, as though the animal didn't surrender any water, even as waste.

Pascal tolerated his nocturnal adventure because it led to survival.

"These aren't the prairies with its dangers, but it's even more dangerous in its own way. Study it, learning what you can. The Redman here is the Apache, who is as dangerous as the Comanche. The Comanche passes through in the winter going south, but the Lipan Apache lives here year 'round. Farther west, where the *Grande* turns north, there are other bands of the Apache, the Chiricahua and the Mescalero. These Redmen are different from the Comanche. The sun has rendered them into smaller, tougher, and meaner fighters. Avoid the Apache whenever you can. I don't like trading with them."

A ramshackle stage station sat north of the Springs, serving the San Antonio-El Paso Mail on its irregular runs. They built it far enough away to avoid the Redman, who depended upon its water. Water drew visitors to the only sweet water spring for thirty miles around.

Pascal wandered to the station to ask about troubles in the area. "Any hostiles raiding now? Any *'banditos'* from the south raiding in the area?"

The civilians seemed more than a little edgy, but the Army patrol said, "They had everything under control," which only served to worry Pascal. He decided to follow the stage route into the foothills, riding west alongside the *Rio Grande* before crossing into El Paso.

Pascal and LaFleur conducted a "business meeting" in camp that night. Nigel stayed awake to learn their plans. They observed more wagons in use, which made finding less bulky *cargas* for the mule-train harder to find.

"Large wagons will carry the most goods on the main east-west routes. We can't compete with their load-carrying capacity," Pascal said.

LaFleur nodded agreement.

"We'll have to seek trade going north along the *Grande* to Santa Fe or into the San Luis valley of the upper *Grande*. Next season, we could work north along the eastern edge of the mountains, or maybe even into the prospector settlements deeper in the mountains, where they have no wagon roads. The biggest obstacle is we don't know the routes in those areas and the steep hills will slow the train. However, the benefit is that supplies are scarce and we can charge more for our goods than if we delivered to a store in town."

As their business meeting continued, Pascal said, "My greatest concern is all the talk of railroads. There's been talk of plans for a *Rio Grande* rail line alongside the *Grande* up to Big Bend, then swinging north of the mountains to Comanche Springs on the way to El Paso. If we do nothing until these changes occur, we'll be wiped out because we didn't plan changes now."

LaFleur wanted to move into buying wholesale, reselling to the settlement stores, and let the stores arrange their own delivery, rather than selling small lots and doing the delivery.

LaFleur wrote many messages. *Yes, money in cartage, but it hard work. We become too old to do in a few years. I'm weary by the end of a season. We know owners of trading posts and stores in new settlements. Ask who supplies them. Ask them to trade with us.*

Pascal pursed his lips, contemplating, but admitting, reluctantly, it was a reasonable plan. "We visit these places anyway, so why not ask if they could sell on a bigger scale?"

He sighed aloud before he stood to shuffle in a circle.

"In the meantime, we need to increase our breeding stock at the rancho. If we raise more livestock, we can sell the excess stock to the teamsters. We'll have to branch out, and soon."

Nigel learned they bought their mules from a small operation at a "rancho" in Mexico, where the men often "wintered-over." It gave them a chance to rest after a long season of dragging mules while allowing them to select and train new mules for the spring trading season. Their usual schedule followed "north in the spring and south in the fall." The question became whether there was enough business to keep them going past the next few years.

He noticed the "rancho" seemed to have special meaning to LaFleur.

He asked LaFleur about it, but he signed, "W*ait and see.*"

Pascal scowled at him. "This is grown-up business. You're too young to understand."

Nigel didn't like that answer. He bristled at its meaning. *I'm not that young.*

The next day was the same as the day preceding it: up before light, fetching water, washing the pots, putting out the fire, and loading the camp kit. He practiced ten shots with his rifle each morning after the train moved out. And he ran. He rode his mare during *Anglais* lessons in the morning. And he ran.

In this heat, he ran bare-chested much of the time. With a coat of olive oil, he tanned a deep brown. He rode his mare during *Français* lessons in the afternoon, speaking *Français* in camp at night. The lessons never ended.

He remembered to pray for his slain family, but most times he fell asleep before he finished.

Chapter 11

El Paso disappointed Nigel. He had expected a grand city like Boston, based on the way every one spoke about El Paso del Norte being the transportation center. It appeared like a rambling collection of old adobe buildings. The village gave the impression of being worn out, run down. Dust covered everything, the buildings, the walkways, and the streets. He noticed few wooden buildings on the street near the ford on the *Grande*. None of those weatherworn buildings held a coat of paint.

Nigel waded in the *Rio Grande* River for the first time. It didn't look so "grand" to him. A dozen men worked on the stone foundations to hold a bridge someday. Probably not any time soon, at the rate they worked.

Nigel's geography lessons taught him everything south of the Rio lay in Mexico. He didn't know if he was a citizen of one country, but by crossing the river, he entered another country. He struggled to carry on a conversation in *Français* only to find he had another language to learn. Pascal and LaFleur had learned *español* in Spain long before coming to this continent. They spoke *en español* with the locals.

"I guess this means more lessons," Nigel muttered after a sigh.

"*Si.*" Pascal glanced at him with a wink before laughing.

They led the train along the middle of the "main street," such as it was, around a corner, to stop at an adobe-walled warehouse behind one of the wooden buildings. The business owner assigned workers to unload the mules, stacking his goods in the warehouse. The foreman and LaFleur checked the cartage bill, making sure they accounted for the entire load. While the men unloaded, Pascal tramped inside the wooden storefront to receive payment. He returned with a handful of fat cigars, handing most to LaFleur.

Pascal's good mood continued while reporting the storeowner, Señor Rafael Valencia, contracted to haul a full load of cartage north to Santa Fe. Valencia's partner had a shipment from Santa Fe north to Fort Garland, a new post. "We'll rest here a few days before we leave."

Pascal knew the village, leading them to a barn and corral for the mules, where he paid a hand a few copper coins to feed the mules dried clover for forage. After the men unloaded the packsaddles, Nigel set them upside down to allow the sweaty leather and blankets to dry. Pascal paid another man at the corral to ride south along the *Grande* with a letter to the rancho to bring more mules. Once they cared for the mules, and protected their gear, they marched to an adobe *fonda*. Pascal knew the owner, Miguel, who ordered a Mexican meal with all the side dishes.

They must have received a good price for this shipment for Pascal to be so casual with spending. Pascal probably got an even better price for the material going north. LaFleur wrote on his slate, *Money from the horses made trip profitable.*

Everything the *fonda* served became a new taste for Nigel, and spicy. At first, he thought it strange, but the more things he tried, the more he liked it spicy. He liked the round, flattened corn-meal discs, *tortillas*. They put cheese on everything, and he liked that, too. Miguel's wife, Estrada, cooked and served the table's food. She brought him a small clay pitcher of buttermilk. It cooled the spicy sting. He could get used to eating like this while loading each hand with food.

Pascal and LaFleur soon had their fill. They sprawled in their chairs, lighting cigars, before ordering a small clay pitcher of mescal. They laughed about how much food *ti-Noir* ate. It became a relaxed, enjoyable evening. After Nigel filled his stomach, they waddled with him to the barn at the corral, showing him where he would spend the night. They planned to return later, they told him. He understood their plan—drinking in the sporting houses.

So he prayed for his lost family. He prayed for them all, before he fell asleep.

They enjoyed a relaxed time the next day. Nigel helped LaFleur expand the main train-line to lead thirty mules, with ten in reserve. Pascal planned to carry four English tons of trade goods north to Santa Fe.

"Ordinarily, I wouldn't lead a train this long, but the road to Santa Fe is an old, well-established one and, unless the Apache or the Mountain Utes get upset about something, it should be an easy trip." Pascal chewed on the end of a half-smoked cigar.

"The Mexicans call this road *El Camino Real*, the King's Highway," Pascal said.

It doesn't look like any King's Highway I saw in England, Nigel thought.

"This is the primary north-south road in Mexico. It continues south for more than one thousand miles to Mexico City."

~~~~~~

While LaFleur and Nigel worked on the harnesses and trail-line, Pascal carried one of the Grimsley packsaddles to a Mexican saddler on the south end of town.

"*Buenos dias.* Señor Rafael Valencia at the warehouse suggested you might help me. Can you make twenty more like this?" Pascal asked.

"I would have to cut this one apart to see how they made the tree, and to learn the leather patterns. It will not be easy. It will take much time," Gorge, the saddler, said.

The two tradesmen haggled over price and deliver time before reaching agreement. A copy would cost Pascal less than one-third the original, which pleased him. He knew he would not have the new packsaddles available for this trip, but they would be ready when he returned in two or three months. Maybe he could get in one more trip before they took a break at the rancho in the late winter.

He would ask Señor Valencia about it. *LaFleur is right. We are getting too old for this.*

The letter Pascal sent to the rancho produced fifteen mules on the third day, and another muleteer, Antonio Ortega. Pascal introduced Antonio as one of the sons of Victorio Ortega, their partner in the rancho operation. The rancho bred mules for Pascal's use and sold mules to others. Nigel notice Pascal sent the four Indian mares along with Nigel's mare to the rancho to become breeding stock for new mules. Pascal explained they needed mares to increase the mule operation. In the rancho's breeding program, the mares became more valuable than the geldings they left at the Bar-J. Antonio returned with six geldings to serve as new mounts for the team.

Pascal laid a hand on Nigel's shoulder. "Antonio is eighteen years old. This will be his first time on the trail. Now it's your turn to give lessons. Show him how we do things in camp. Keep in mind, however, Antonio has worked mules for many years, so he can teach you how to handle the mules. Let him help with your *Español.* Learn from one another on this trip."

~~~~~~

The problem became Antonio spoke only *español*. Nigel couldn't understand him.

Pascal shrugged, "Learn to talk to each other by pointing at an object. Nigel you say the word in English, *inglés*. Antonio, you say it in *en español*. This way you will learn one another's language while you communicate."

Pascal handed Nigel a few silver coins. "Figure out how to talk to one another by buying Antonio lunch." With that said in *Anglais*, Pascal strode away, leaving the young men alone to figure out how to communicate with each other.

Nigel, always ready to eat, rubbed his stomach while he said, "Eat."

Antonio squinted at him.

Nigel's eyes opened wide. "*Tortilla*," he said, putting his hand to his mouth.

Antonio responded with his dark eyes open wide, "*Si. Comer tortilla.*"

Nigel repeated the hand-to-mouth motion while saying, "Eat." Antonio said, "Eat, eat," moving his hand to his mouth.

Antonio said "*Comer*," with the hand-to-mouth motion.

Nigel repeated, "*Comer. Comer.*"

The young men smiled at one another before Nigel raised a silver coin.

Antonio brightened, moving to lead Nigel away.

Nigel put out his hand to stop. Nigel said, "Eat."

Antonio repeated, "*Si*, eat," nodding his head up and down.

Nigel nodded, saying, "*Si.*"

Antonio nodded approval.

Then Nigel said "Yes," pointing to Antonio. After a few tries, Antonio said, "Yes" correctly. Nigel repeated the process shaking his head side-to-side to signal "No."

Antonio stared at him and said, "No," shaking his head side-to-side.

Then Nigel pointed at him to say "No" in *en español*.

Antonio laughed, saying, *"No."*

It took Nigel a couple of tries to understand that "no" was the same in both languages. With that much understanding between them, Nigel pointed away, saying, *"Comer tortillas."*

Antonio said, "Yes. Eat tortillas."

Laughing, the young men rushed to eat lunch.

~~~~~~

Pascal bargained hard with the saddler to buy a dozen old Mexican packsaddles and six used bridles. He grumbled aloud the problem with moving the big loads was the cost of the extra equipment and help.

At least, he admitted to himself, *Noir is more help in camp these days. He does most of the cooking, gets the camp set up, and knocks it down to move again. Noir is still too small to move any of the packsaddles or wrestle the mules. However, he made up for that with the fresh game he catches. I'll send him to Miguel's fonda to ask if his wife can teach Noir to cook with cornmeal and spices as they do. I wonder if Antonio knows how to cook on the trail. It would be nice to eat something other than beans for a change. The camp will smell better. I'll have to find rice to substitute for beans.*

~~~~~~

The closer they came to the day to leave, the busier and more hectic their work became. LaFleur convinced Pascal that moving at first light was not critical. He wrote a long message on paper. *We haven't moved this many mules before. We have new mules and new help. Let the first day come as it does, and get on the road when we can. Then we will work on organizing and scheduling. As you said, this is a good road. It should be a time to learn how to drag this many mules and this much weight with so few hands.*

Pascal grumbled, but relented.

Nigel thought it a sign of Pascal's respect for LaFleur that he accepted LaFleur's advice.

They loaded the mules before first light, but some of the old Mexican packsaddles needed extra lashing to hold steady on the mules. An unbalanced load makes the mule work harder because it shifts side-to-side as he walks, which causes the mule to take extra steps to maintain his balance. It also galls or rubs his hide raw, so he can't carry the next day. Two of the new mules resisted moving in the train-line, so they repositioned those two mules.

After much cussing, they moved the train along

the "main street" until they came to the ford on the *Grande*, where one of the new mules balked. Antonio, the new muleteer, slapped him smartly with a whip, keeping the train moving until they crossed the *Rio*. While Nigel stayed with the bell mare to keep her moving, which kept the train-line moving, Pascal rode to Antonio, giving a stern lecture in *en español*. Nigel didn't understand any of it, but Antonio did. He put away his whip before Pascal rode to the front of the line.

"Stay close to the train today. Let us develop a rhythm for working together. Tomorrow, or the next day, we'll return to the old routine," Pascal said.

Because they traveled north on the east side of the *Grande*, good water lay nearby for rest stops, siesta, and camps the first few days. They needed two days to settle into their routine again, as they grew comfortable working with Antonio. By the third day, even the mules settled into the routine. So Nigel ran. He practiced with his rifle each morning after the train moved out. He stood fifteen paces from his small target, striking it each time.

After the first day's practice, Nigel asked if Antonio could shoot with him.

"If Antonio doesn't know how, it's time to learn," Pascal said.

"I only fired a shotgun at varmints, but never a rifle or a pistol," Antonio said.

Nigel ran in the morning after rifle practice with Antonio. On his run, he set snares to catch fresh game. After returning, he rode his new gelding during *Anglais* lessons.

Nigel named his new horse Spotty, because of the white spots on its neck and chest. He rode Spotty during *Français* lessons in the afternoon. Nigel practiced *español* in camp in the evening and with Antonio at every opportunity.

Antonio teased Nigel that he ran like *los lobos*, fast enough you couldn't catch him, but slow enough not to wear out. Antonio didn't know Pascal already nicknamed Nigel "black wolf." Nigel remembered to pray for his lost family. Most times, he fell asleep before finishing.

During the morning rest the next day, Nigel asked why Pascal always took care with the mules around water. He noticed Pascal always moved quickly across water crossings, not letting the mules bunch together, or stop to drink.

"This is the mule's greatest failing, even worse than their stubbornness. The mule has an aversion to water. Even worse, they fear drowning. If they fall down in water, or get into deep water, getting water in their ears, they panic, sometimes dying of fright. Even if they survive, they often refuse to stand again. It is like a paralysis of fear. Avoid deep water crossings with mules. Don't let them bunch up at the edge when you lead them to drink at a rest stop or after grazing. If one mule behind wants water and it pushes another mule into the water, the mule in the water panics. It can cause the entire group to stampede away from the water. It makes no sense. Water runs downhill. It is the way they are, so we must keep that from happening to them. It is part of being a good muleteer."

This trip became Antonio's introduction to life on the trail. He knew mules and their needs, but he didn't know the dark-to-dark routine of the trail. Antonio helped Nigel with his *español*. He helped Nigel with cooking Mexican style, a welcome change in the team's meals.

Although not as tall as Pascal and LaFleur, Antonio stood stocky and strong. He could lift as a partner to either of the taller men when loading the packsaddles. They soon developed a new routine in loading, where Pascal and LaFleur loaded the first mule. Then Pascal and Antonio loaded the next mule. Antonio and LaFleur loaded the next mule before returning to Pascal and LaFleur. It made loading thirty mules a little easier, but it still left the men tired.

After six days of dragging mules from El Paso, north past the village of Mesilla, the team settled into a steady routine. Pascal called the team together during the siesta rest.

"Tomorrow is Sunday. We will rest beside the *Grande* while it is quiet. Above here, the canyon has steep sides without a usable trail. We must go inland on one side or the other. The west side has rugged mountains. On this side, the trail passes between two rocky mountain ridges, the Caballo Mountains on the west and the San Cristobel Mountains.

"On Monday, we will cross a sandy, desert trail

for six days. It is called the '*Jornada del Meurto*,' or the 'Journey of Death,' because there is no water until you reach the other side. It takes eight or ten days with a wagon with oxen, which is hard if the drovers failed to carry enough water. Mules are faster than oxen, so we can cross in less time. However, we need to carry grain to feed the mules. In that desert, there is no forage, and the animals will need food. Three mules in the train carry silage to feed the train in the *Jornada*.

"We have extra water skins and we'll use the relief mules to carry the extra water. Stay close while we are in the desert area. It is easy to wander off, get disoriented, and lost because there are so few landmarks to follow in the sand dunes.

"Antonio, you and Nigel prepare several cooked meals to serve cold, later. There is no wood for fires in the *Jornada*. Drink water often. The jerky will dry you, but you need its salts. We'll keep the mules close at night after we feed them fodder, and then let them drink. Don't let one guzzle all the water."

Pascal instructed Nigel not to run while they crossed the *Jornada*.

Pascal kept the mules moving at a steady pace. Hot, dry winds blew in the *Jornada*, carrying a powdery grit into the eyes, mouth, and nose of men and animals alike. The men wore a face scarf, or bandana to limit the powder and grit from entering their mouth and nose. They passed the desert unscathed in six days because they carried extra water. The men's shoulders visibly relaxed once they reached the other side.

On the north side of the *Jornada,* the team stopped at a flowing spring in the little village of Socorro. Pascal advised they bathe tonight while washing their clothes, getting rid of the grit. After a hot meal, the team slept well that night. The Sunday rest came as a welcome relief.

The long train stopped for water at the Isleta Pueblo ford across the *Grande* a day later.

When they ascended the trail from the *Rio Grande* canyon, south of Albuquerque, Nigel noticed the eastern mountains for the first time. When he mentioned them, Antonio told him to look behind to the west. Another line of mountains marched across the plateau's west side. Nigel marveled at the mountains "sudden" appearance, when not visible from the canyon. That evening, the sunset caused a rosy glow in the snow atop the *Sangre de Cristo* (Blood of Christ) Mountains east of Santa Fe. He understood why the mountains earned their name. Nigel found it hard to imagine snow existed on those mountains when the sun scorched the valleys. At last, he'd found the snow covered peaks Pascal promised when crossing the prairie.

The days became pleasant, not as hot, while the nights grew cooler as the days became shorter. LaFleur wrote Pascal a note, saying they must find Nigel a light jacket, a winter coat, and gloves in Santa Fe. He would need them before they returned to El Paso.

The mule-train trudged north, still five days away from Santa Fe. One morning, three Mountain Utes waited on the trail, using hand signs to signal they wanted to trade. They offered a few pieces of turquoise and silver in trade for weapons. Pascal told them he had no weapons for sale or trade. He gave each a cigar and jerky before the Utes rode away without incident.

Nigel grew visibly upset anytime Redmen visited. LaFleur wrote on his slate, *We trade with Redman. Learn to accept them. Learn each Redman tribe different. Not blame all Redman for Comanche attack. Young scout at fault. Remember your papa. Learn to forgive. Hate makes your heart hard. Don't become bitter. Remember what your mother said. Do not look back on this.*

He understood LaFleur's intentions, but he had yet to forgive.

Chapter 12

September 30 to November 30, 1853

The team traveled three hundred fifty miles from El Paso to Santa Fe. The trip consumed twenty days before reaching Santa Fe without serious problems. On the trail, each day passed like the day before. The routine of working dark to dark varied little as days became months. Santa Fe reminded Nigel of El Paso, in that both had adobe buildings, but Santa Fe seemed more organized, more colorful, and less sprawling than El Paso. A mountain stream ran through one side of the village. Santa Fe sat on a high plateau above the *Rio Grande* canyon. Warehouses, wagon yards, and stock corrals occupied the southern edge of the village, away from the canyon.

Pascal explained the obvious to Nigel, the Santa Fe Trail ended in Santa Fe. In the wagon yards, workers unloaded wagons into warehouses to sell the goods delivered from the East. Time remained for one more train filled with goods from this area, or Mexico, to return East on the last wagons before winter closed the Trail.

He reported one of these wagons carried five English-tons, more than the load the mule team delivered with thirty-mules. "I cannot compete against their load size."

In Santa Fe, Valencia's partner shrugged, telling Pascal they must unload the *cargas* themselves, or pay for workers to help. Pascal ordered the team to unload.

We know how Pascal hates to pay, Nigel thought.

They finished carrying the load into the warehouse by late afternoon, leaving them tired, hungry, and ready for bed. They strolled into the village, consisting of a large central plaza built around the Governors Palace, two small hotels, a bank, and a domed church.

Antonio and Nigel grew excited, glancing everywhere, and nudging one another to point. Pascal led them to a cantina with a view of the square, sitting on a patio for outdoor eating.

Nigel realized he missed sitting at a table to eat. It reminded him of home.

After they ate, Pascal ordered Antonio and Nigel to return to where they corralled the mules to sleep in the hay bales. Pascal said, "LaFleur and I will visit the sporting houses."

"What sports do you play there?" Nigel asked.

Pascal barked a laugh. "Ah, *Petite Noir*, you must become more fluent in *Français* before I can answer that question."

Nigel, struggling to converse in *en español*, used the time to practice with Antonio.

However, Antonio expressed his frustration because he couldn't go to the sporting houses in

Santa Fe like he did in Mexico.

The team didn't have a long rest in Santa Fe, only three days. Pascal had a contract with Valencia's partner for another thirty-mule load hauled north to Fort Garland in the Colorado Territory. During their nights in town, LaFleur and Pascal decided to divide the train in half when moving into the mountains to drag the mules to Fort Garland.

Pascal hired another frontiersman, Philippe Charbonneau. Pascal admitted loading and unloading thirty mules became too strenuous for him and LaFleur, even with Antonio helping.

Pascal held a team meeting the night before they hit the trail. He described his plan for dividing the train into two fifteen-mule segments. Pascal would lead the first segment with the bell mare while LaFleur led the second segment. Pascal thought one bell mare could lead both segments. Antonio would be a rover, moving back and forth between the two segments. Pascal assigned Charbonneau to lead the reserve mules and the pack animals in the rear. Nigel became a runner, carrying messages between the groups.

Philippe stood four inches shorter than Pascal. He spoke *Français, español,* but poor English. Philippe appeared not much older than Antonio, may be twenty-three, which confused Nigel. *How could he be a frontiersman at his age.*

Pascal and Philippe entered into a long discussion in *Français* with LaFleur adding signs.

LaFleur wrote on his slate while they discussed which trails to follow.

In response to Nigel's questions, LaFleur wrote, *Philippe knows the trails. He worked at Bent's new Post. He knows trails into the mountains in this area. We need his help.*

"Let me lead the entire train with the reserve segment. You hired me to show you the trails into the mountains. How can I show you the trails if I am in the rear?" Philippe asked.

Pascal grumbled as if he wanted to argue, but he found no fault with Philippe's logic.

The trail order changed to have Philippe lead the entire train with the reserve animals and the camp pack-mules. Pascal followed next with the bell mare and fifteen mules. LaFleur followed with the remaining fifteen mules. Antonio rode alone far behind as the rear guard, while Nigel still served as the runner.

The last decision centered on what language to use. They decided to speak *en español* because Antonio only knew that language, but Pascal ordered Antonio and Nigel to practice *Français*.

As an afterthought, Philippe asked, "Do you plan to visit Taos on the way north?"

"Yes," Pascal said. "We might spend the day if trail folks have gathered at St. Vrain's Trading Post. They may have recent information on the Redman's activities in the San Luis."

"If we follow the canyon edge from Santa Fe, it's a bit longer but less steep than the overland mountain route with this load," Philippe said.

The first night on the trail, while Philippe served the first shift of nighthawk duty, Pascal told Nigel and Antonio of Philippe's history. "Philippe Charbonneau is the grandson of a French-Canadian trapper, Toussaint Charbonneau. The elder Charbonneau married a Shoshone woman, called Sacagawea. In 1806, the Lewis and Clark Expedition hired Toussaint to translate Indian languages, but Toussaint knew only a little Mandan and some Shoshone, with no English. Worse yet, Toussaint couldn't swim, and feared water, which became a liability on the river trip.

"Lewis and Clark found Sacagawea more reliable and resourceful during the trip to the Pacific, and their return. Later, the Charbonneau family moved to St. Louis with Clark. Lewis and Clark liked Sacagawea and her son, Jean Baptiste, whom she carried on the trip west. Jean Baptiste became very personable as he grew into his early teens. After a visit to the American West, Prince Wilhelm of Austria invited him to visit Austria. While in Europe, Jean Baptiste learned German and *español* in addition to his *Français* and English. Jean Baptiste returned to the States in his early twenties, guiding other Europeans along the Lewis and Clark route. Jean Baptiste spoke Shoshone with his mother, and upon their return from the Pacific, he learned Arapaho and Cheyenne. In 1846, Jean Baptiste worked as a trapper and guide at Bent's old Fort, where he learned Comanche and Kiowa.

"In 1847, he met General Cooke at Bent's old Fort when the Mexican-American War began. The Army ordered General Cooke to find an overland route to San Diego that avoided traveling along the border with Mexico. General Cooke hired Jean Baptiste to scout for the expedition. Jean Baptiste led the expedition along the northern route of the Old Spanish Trail following the San Luis River west and down the Dolores to the ford on the Colorado River, going west to Mountain Meadow before crossing the desert to the springs at Las Vegas, and on to San Diego. In 1849, General Cooke appointed Jean Baptiste the *alcalde*, or mayor, of Mission San Rey, a coastal village. When he decided to stay in California, Jean Baptiste left behind an Arapaho woman and his child, Philippe.

"Young Philippe isn't as worldly as his father. However, he spent his formative years among the plains tribes along the Front Range and in the mountains, becoming an excellent scout and hunter. Like his father, Philippe worked for the Bent and Company trading posts and learned the easiest routes into the mountains between Taos and Fort Hall in the north. He learned *Français* from his father, and then learned *español* and English working among the other traders and trappers at Bent's. While Philippe is the son of an Arapaho woman, the Shoshone accept him as Sacagawea's grandson. He speaks Arapaho, Shoshone, and Cheyenne, with basic Kiowa and Comanche, and he can converse in trade sign language. Philippe has traveled among the tribes of the prairie and mountains with few problems. Although young, the frontiersmen in the area respect Philippe, but mostly as his father's son.

"I hired Philippe to show us the routes into the mountains from the south. If we return in the spring, I'll hire him to guide us deeper into the mountains in the north and west toward the Great Salt Lake, possibly as far north as Fort Bridger and Fort Hall," Pascal said.

"This depends upon us developing new trade as suppliers, rather than as *cargas* haulers," Pascal continued. "I do not intend to go into competition with larger suppliers in Santa Fe or Taos, because they buy supplies in bulk from the east by large wagonloads. I intend to establish trade with the smaller towns in the mountains to the north and west that are hard to serve by wagon. St. Vrain and Company does not serve these areas directly. I plan to buy trade goods from St. Vrain at wholesale prices, making a good profit when I sell in the mountains."

With this basic outline, the next day the team moved north, following the *Rio Grande* into the upper *Grande* and San Luis valleys with Philippe Charbonneau as the scout and guide.

The seventy-mile trip to Taos took four days because climbing up to Taos from the canyon edge slowed the mules. They arrived in Taos in early afternoon, choosing to forgo a siesta. While on the trail, the team spoke *en español*, but after arriving at Ceran St. Vrain's trading post, everything reverted to *Français.*

"Waugh. Pascal, my friend. You, I haven't seen in three or four years," St. Vrain cried.

"Waugh. That is because you sell the trade to everyone. I am left with the mules for company," Pascal said with a laugh.

"Who are your companions? I don't remember you traveling with any but the mute, LaFleur."

Pascal called the team to St. Vrain, making introductions.

"You know Philippe Charbonneau. The next young man is Antonio Ortega. He is the son of Victorio Ortega from Zaragoza, Mexico, where his father, LaFleur and I share a small rancho to raise mules. The young lad is Nigel Blackthorn. I call him *Noir* from the dark time in which I found him. I have adopted him, so to speak. He is my godson, or *filleul.*"

Nigel noticed Monsieur St. Vrain stood as tall and as stocky as LaFleur, but had black bushy hair with a long dark beard going to gray.

"Pascal has a *filleul,* a godson. Does that mean all those bastards you left in Europe will be disinherited now?" St. Vrain shook with laughter.

"Bah. There is nothing for them to inherit. I'm the second son. My older brother is healthy as a horse and hatching children as if he intended to populate a village."

"Come! Come!" St. Vrain waved them toward tables in the rear. "Let me get a bottle of brandy from my private stock. We will discuss what is happening in the world."

"What is this talk of brandy? I heard you stock an excellent *Français Champagne*. Why be so tight-fisted? Waugh."

"Alright. Alright, you old fox. I shall get us a bit of both. Send the young men to eat and rest while we talk."

"Food! All right," Nigel slapped Antonio's back.

Pascal handed Antonio a few silver coins before sending them to a cantina across the plaza. He said, "Return to the corral after eating. Make sure the mules are fed and watered."

Philippe went his own way upon leaving St. Vrain with Pascal and LaFleur.

Antonio and Nigel understood they would sleep in the barn beside the corrals tonight.

The men would return late.

The next morning, Pascal decided they could use another day's rest in Taos after LaFleur and he claimed a headache this morning. "We will meet the team for dinner." Pascal whispered.

During dinner that evening, Nigel asked, "What did you and Monsieur St. Vrain mean when you said 'waugh' to one another? Is that a new *Français* word for me to learn?"

"*Non, non, Noir*. It is not *Français*. It is a saying from the old mountain-men trappers. It means whatever the user means it to be. Hello, goodbye, look out, come here. I don't know where it came from. St. Vrain said the old-time trappers said it when he came here twenty years ago."

Pascal led the team to a gathering at St. Vrain's

Trading Post, where several other traders and frontiersmen joined the discussion. Pascal introduced Nigel to the group, retelling the story of finding him in the burned wagon camp. Pascal introduced him only as *Noir*.

One the men, Mr. Christopher Carson, said, "Ya are lucky, youngster. If 'em Comanch had found ya, ya'd be a Comanch slave now. If ya think ol' Pascal is hard on ya, it'd be far worse with the Comanch." The men nodded in agreement. *He had been lucky?* The other men in the circle called Mr. Carson, Kit.

Nigel understood, by the way men spoke to Mr. Carson, they respected him as a leader. Antonio and Nigel sat on the floor at the circle's edge, listening to their stories. Antonio struggled to understand their poorly spoken English. He lost track when they spoke a joke in *Français*.

From their conversations aside, Nigel understood Monsieur St. Vrain and Mr. Carson had a business together, raising cattle on land St. Vrain owned on the plateau east of Taos.

The men who spoke *Français* had no difficulty pronouncing *Noir*, but most of the frontiersmen couldn't get the *Français* pronunciation, saying it as "noah." The Spanish-speakers, like Antonio, rolled too much "r" sound for *Français*. Their rolled "r" sounded like "no-r-r-r." Nigel grew to understand your name could lead to difficulties. Now he understood why Pascal said "Nigel" would be a fight starter. He'd experienced scuffles with town kids, who thought him "strange" for being with the muleskinners.

He grew pissed at the way Philippe called, "Oh, Nigel," in a high singsong voice as if Nigel was a sissy. What got Nigel's goat was Philippe spoke *Français.* He could say *Noir* properly, unlike Antonio who struggled to say it correctly, but Philippe kept calling him Nigel in the irritating singsong voice, just to needle Nigel.

The next morning, the team departed for Fort Garland, eight days travel north of Taos. The team followed the *Grande* most of the way there, which opened into a large valley after the mountains north of Taos. When they reached the mouth of the Trinchera River, they followed it to the camp used while building Fort Garland. With the construction so new, none of the usual businesses existed outside the "fort" except a saloon in a tent, and they had no "sporting house."

The men grumbled about that fact. They asked, "What kind of military post is this?"

Pascal conducted his usual asking around in the San Luis valley. He found a large amount of surplus grain to buy at a low price. The grain created another full load for the mule-train to sell in Santa Fe. The team loaded the grain in burlap bags before loading it on the mules. Oats made the bulk of the grain, but a third was maize corn for animal feed. Pascal decided to bypass Taos on the return trip. The team arrived in Santa Fe twelve days later.

Pascal paid Charbonneau in advance to ride to

El Paso next spring when they prepared to drag the mules north using his help to get a big train to Santa Fe. Once in Santa Fe next spring, they'd decide which of the mountain trails to carry trade as they had discussed earlier. Philippe collected his pay, departing without a word to Nigel or Antonio.

With Philippe gone, Pascal used the grain as another lesson topic. "You must learn to be friendlier with the local townsfolk. Be willing to gossip in order to discover what is happening in the community."

Nigel frowned at "gossip," which his father had taught violated the Ninth Commandment. "Thou shall not bear false witness," Nigel said.

Pascal sighed. "Water flows downhill, *Noir*. Yes, people should not gossip, but it is the nature of things. If you don't let people talk, telling you what they know, they will think you are cold. People do not like to conduct business with a man who is cold and hard."

"You are confusing me. First, you said I must learn to be hard to survive on the prairie. Now you say people won't do business with me if I am hard. What am I to do?"

"You need to learn to smile, tell jokes. Smile at townsfolk, nod your head, and be sympathetic. Just listen, that is all most people want, is someone to listen to them."

"And I should say to them, 'water flows downhill'?"

"Why not, they will think you are a wise sage."

Pascal laughed and winked, and then returned to his task.

Once in Santa Fe, Pascal gained a tidy profit from selling most of the grain. He kept enough maize to carry south for the trip through the *Jornada*.

"Nigel, we'll stay in Santa Fe for a few days while I hunt for *cargas* or trade goods to haul to El Paso," Pascal said. "Practice your *español* with the locals, listen to them."

Nigel became more aware of the changing weather in the mountains as the nights grew frigid. LaFleur took him shopping, finding a heavy wool coat a pilgrim from the East sold in the summer thinking he'd never need it again. While Pascal and LaFleur scouted for trade goods, Antonio and Nigel enjoyed free run of the village and the surrounding area. Eating remained a high priority with the young men, but also exploring the canyons west of the plateau came second. Antonio learned to enjoy running. They took turns shooting each morning in a small arroyo beyond the corrals where they stabled the mules. The pair enjoyed this time because they had no work until the time came to go south for the winter.

The experienced freight haulers refused to cross the prairie in winter, so by November first, activity ceased in the wagon yards. Pascal scouted the town and warehouses, asking about what trade goods remained unsold. He bought the unsold trade carried from the East at pennies on the dollar, which saved the merchants from paying storage for the winter.

Pascal bought a dozen wagons cheap, even agreeing to four oxen thrown into one deal. The owner thought he'd have more wagons coming from the East in the spring, using the sale money to live through the winter in Santa Fe. The US-made wagons sold for a premium in Mexico. Pascal hired three workers, who removed the wheels and axles from the beds before stacking two beds in one wagon, with the wheels and axles tied on top. They placed the spare equipment, harnesses, and rigging in the middle between the two stacked wagons. The men rigged two loaded wagons in tandem allowing a twenty–mule team to pull each double wagon south. The mules didn't like being harnessed to the wagons, but mules moved faster than the oxen. They trailed four oxen south for beef stock at the rancho. The return trip to El Paso took longer than the team liked because the oxen plodded even when not pulling the wagons. The team carried extra water barrels and grain in the wagons for the *Jornada de Meurto*.

In El Paso, Pascal sold his trade goods to Señor Valencia. He sold six of the wagons separately, at three times what he paid for them in Santa Fe. Pascal kept six wagons, loading two with dry goods and supplies for their rancho. The San Antonio-El Paso Mail service offered to buy all of Pascal's mules because he had trained them to harness. Pascal sold twenty mules for a tidy profit, but kept the other mules to pull the new wagons to the rancho.

Antonio's older brother, Jesus, arrived the next day, carrying a message from his father for Pascal. Four workers from the rancho accompanied Jesus. That afternoon, Jesus, Antonio, and the four workers drove the wagons and oxen to the rancho.

Nigel enjoyed the nearby Miguel's *fonda* in El Paso during the day when alone, but ate in the cantinas when he dined with Pascal and LaFleur. At night, he "guarded" the horses while the men visited the "sporting houses." By this time, he'd learned from Antonio what "sporting" meant. Nigel, the preacher's son, thought it shameful.

Pascal, LaFleur, and Nigel stayed in El Paso a few days longer while Pascal arranged for shipments in the spring. Señor Valencia wanted Pascal to carry freight south to Chihuahua.

"That's three hundred miles of sand and bad roads without water. I'm not in the mood to try such a trip, even in the winter."

Señor Valencia wanted Pascal's service because Pascal had proven more reliable with delivery and no "lost in transit" claims.

"You should have kept your wagons and mules. I could keep several wagons busy during the winter. You would make more money by hauling freight than you got from selling your equipment," Señor Valencia said.

The price Señor Valencia offered Pascal tempted him, but LaFleur kept signaling, "No!"

They enjoyed an easy horse ride to the rancho

three days later, without mules to tend. Pascal and LaFleur talked in trade-signs about asking the Ortega family to establish a wagon freighting business centered in El Paso.

"We would have one East-West route to San Antonio, one North-South route to Santa Fe and one South-North route to Chihuahua. You and I would stay in El Paso, directing the traffic and planning the shipments," Pascal said aloud.

LaFleur wrote a note. *Mucho Trabajo. Poco Deniro* (Much work for little money).

"*Oui*, but not on the prairie," Pascal said, "However, let us ask Victorio what he thinks."

Nigel became a little bump on the log, listening to everything, but saying nothing. He looked forward to visiting the rancho.

' Pascal reminded him his lessons would begin again once they settled at the Rancho. "I expect your *Français* to improve along with your *español*."

Nigel sighed, *Will it never end?*

He practiced with his rifle every morning.

He prayed for his lost family every night.

And he ran.

Chapter 13

December, 1853 to March, 1854

Pascal, LaFleur, and Nigel spent the winter at the Ortega Rancho in Mexico, fifteen miles southeast of Zaragoza on the *Rio Grande's* south side. Zaragoza is fifteen miles downstream from El Paso del Norte, Mexico. In this region, the *Rio Grande* formed a wide canyon with the river sixty- to eighty-feet below the plateau on each side. The rancho served as a horse ranch to breed stud burros with mares to yield mules for the cartage trade. They also bred horses for sale. Pascal set its size at 100 *Caballeria* in Spanish terms, but Nigel failed to relate to the number.

The corner marker for Ortega Rancho lay one-eighth mile in-land, south of the *Grande*. The property line ran three miles southeast, parallel to the *Grande*. It extended six miles south into the hills. It measured eighteen sections in the English system, or eleven-thousand five-hundred acres. Flatter land near the canyon's edge rose steadily to a rocky ridge hiding a higher valley below the southern mountains. The rocky ridge divided the property into two pieces, with two miles of land between the *Grande* and the ridge and a larger section extending four miles south of the ridge.

They kept their stock in the high meadow, using the grassy slopes on the plateau in winter. To a passerby, the rancho appeared supported by agriculture from the fields.

The rancho used the land closer to the river to grow corn and grain for the animals but converted one-half into pasture in the cold months. An *acequia* system irrigated the crops grown on the lower section of the plateau with water diverted from miles upstream. The rancho worked at being self-sufficient, raising its own chickens, pigs, goats, milch cows, and beef cattle. The Rancho's gardens grew vegetables year round because greens like cabbages, peas, and beans withered in the heat of the scorching summers near the edge of the Sonora desert. The ridgeline shielded the rancho from the worst of the desert's heat and winds.

Nigel followed Pascal around the rancho to run errands or doing whatever task Pascal assigned. Today, Pascal supervised the construction of new stone gate-channels on the *acequia*.

"After the Texas Revolution in 1836, the Mexican government made it difficult for non-citizens to own property. Before the Revolution, the Texans bought large sections of property, and then claimed the Mexican land for themselves as the Republic of Texas. Now, Mexico treats *Yanquis* and foreigners with suspicion when it comes to owning property or a business within Mexico," Pascal said in response to one of Nigel's endless questions.

"What are *Yanquis*?" asked Nigel.

"Anyone from north of the border, even when the first border lay along the Arkansas River at Bent's old Fort. The word has come to reflect the ill feelings between the two countries. Foreigners, including the Spanish, treated the people of Mexico roughly, in response they do not trust foreigners. LaFleur and I applied for Mexican citizenship. Because we are French Catholics, they approved our citizenship request. They considered us better than *Yanquis,* of course."

"What does being Catholic have to do with it?" Nigel asked.

"Catholicism is the State religion of Mexico. In the early days before the Texas Revolution, you could not enter Mexico if not a Catholic. Austin and his followers pretended to convert in order to buy Mexican land in Texas, and then stole it from Mexico by revolution."

"If you are a Mexican citizen and you own the rancho, why is it called Ortega?"

"There are many legal obstacles that kept me from owning property directly," Pascal said, as he continued to unload flat stones from the pack train Antonio and Nigel had led from the mountains where other workers cut and finished the stone into usable shapes and sizes.

"I had to arrange a 'marriage of convenience' with a Mexican citizen whose name appears on the land title."

"Are you saying you married Señor Ortega? Such a thing doesn't make any sense."

"*Non, Noir.* Do not take my words so exact. A 'marriage of convenience' is a saying. I had a little money, but I cannot buy land. Victorio Ortega could buy land, but he had no money. We decided to share our burden by owning the land together. For legal reasons, his name is on the land title, and we call it the Ortega Rancho. But I, clever Pascal, have a promissory note from Ortega giving me controlling interest in the land and a majority share of the profits from its operation. The note is quite legal in Mexico, so we are joined by a contract, like in a marriage."

Pascal stopped to stare at the *hacienda* on the ridge before he grunted. "If you survive your apprenticeship, you too may own a piece of this pie someday. God's will be done," he said as he crossed himself.

"Amen," said Nigel, from habit in response to the prayers he learned from his father.

Pascal showed Nigel where to stack the stones he carried to the sluice gate that Pascal rebuilt to improve the water flow in the *acequia.*

"I met Victorio Ortega five years ago," Pascal continued speaking *Français.* "I would buy his mules each winter. I asked others about him, learning others considered Victorio an honest, hard-working man trying to better his family's station in life by raising mules. The Ortega family contributed neither money nor lands to the 'marriage,' allowing me to easily convince Victorio this might be his only opportunity to have his own rancho."

"Antonio and the other workers call you *el patron*. What do they mean?"

"As I have become your godfather, I've become a godfather to Victorio and his family. I brought the Ortegas a prize beyond their wildest dreams. They honor me with that title."

They continued working for a while, with Pascal giving instructions in Spanish to the workers laying the stones in place. "There is a lesson to be learned here, *ti-Noir*," Pascal said.

"A lesson? How surprising," Nigel mumbled.

"What? What did you say?"

"Oh, nothing important. Go ahead. I'm listening."

"I am away eight or nine months a year. While I am gone, Victorio manages everything. He is the '*jefé*,' the boss man who gives the orders. When I come here each winter, I do not take charge or tell him what to do. We sit together after dinner with a cigar and a brandy or two. We talk about the year past, and then we talk about the future years. If I see something I think needs work, like this *acequia*, I suggest it to him. Victorio tells the workers he asked Pascal to help rebuild the *acequia*. He says, "Work with Pascal. Follow his instructions." This way, he is always the '*jefé*,' never losing his men's respect. It costs me nothing to treat Victorio as an equal, and we stay loyal to each other, and to the land. It is to our mutual benefit."

"Why choose land this far from El Paso? Why not some place closer, or in Santa Fe?"

"Between the Texas Revolution and the Mexican-American War, the people in Mexico City considered land along the border tainted by the *Yanquis*. Years ago, the Spanish King gave away this land as favors to friends and nobles. The original Spanish land grant for this land belonged to the grandee Don Jose Castaneda y Medina. His great granddaughter, Dona Maria Josefa Bazauxi considered selling a 'little piece of land' along the *Rio Grande* to a Mexican national at a reasonable price to keep the *Yanquis* away."

Pascal continued working with the stones while he studied the other Ortega workers widening the water channel leading to the Ortega land.

"Land in Santa Fe costs too much," he said. "What made this a bargain is it came with water rights to the Zaragoza *Acequia Madre*, the primary irrigation canal we are repairing. It provides water for all the landholders along the *acequia* system to irrigate the fields near the *Grande*. This water allows the Ortegas to grow corn and beans to feed their extended family with enough to sell to the neighbors. The Mexican people have a saying about an *acequia*. *El agua es la sangre de la tierra.* The water is the blood of the land."

Pascal and Nigel returned to the *hacienda* for their noon meal and a short siesta. They considered the rancho's *hacienda* a work in progress. On the ridge's crest, it gazed upon rancho land on each side. They constructed the *hacienda* in the typical square, with tall adobe walls on four-sides and watchtowers at the northwest and southeast corners. The large entry gate opened on the south wall, requiring visitors to ride past the west wall before entering to the gate. The married workers at the *hacienda* lived in *jacales* (huts) along the northern slope below the hacienda, where they received water from the hacienda's cistern each morning.

The rancho's working section, the upper valley, included the breeding pens and corrals. The living quarters for the *vaqueros (cowboys)* lay beside a wide meadow at the ridge's southeastern end. They built a cooking facility and cistern-water tank at the *cocina de campaña* (camp cookhouse) beside the meadow. The unmarried men lived in a bunkhouse, or *cuatel,* next to the *cocina.* A twenty-foot square, vine-covered patio joined the two adobe buildings. In the *cocina,* they built a six-foot wide stone fireplace for cooking or roasting. It heated two ovens on the patio side. To reduce the dust, or mud when it rained, they covered the patio with a raised wooden deck. The patio contained long tables and benches for the *vaqueros* and workers to gather for meals or parties.

The Ortegas built two large tile-roofed buildings for the *establos* (stables) for the saddle horses, but unlike barns Nigel visited in England or Wales. They used tile roofs on key buildings because cedar wood was too scarce. Clay, used in sun-baked *Mexicano* tile, was plentiful.

Victorio, whose father had been a stonemason,

created a quarry in a rocky outcrop at the base of the southern mountains. They used this stone to construct the foundation of the *hacienda* and a large granary, or *granero*, for the *maize* (corn). Both buildings had tile roofs to keep the inside dry. Pascal allowed Nigel to shoot the rats around the *granero* in the evening after everyone had eaten. His skill improved to where he hit rats on the run.

Over the years, as the rancho improved and prospered, Pascal said a growing problem became others desired it as "a plum ripe for the picking."

"Victorio has an ace up his sleeve," Pascal said. "Victorio's older brother, Enrico, had the good fortune to have survived the Mexican-American War, receiving a battlefield promotion to lieutenant for bravery. Rico, as the family called him, rose to the rank of a *Federales* captain. He serves at the *Presidio del Norte,* twenty miles downstream from Zaragoza. Rico keeps the more nefarious interests from finding a way to steal the Ortega Rancho from his family. The process is quite simple and very traditional. Rico pays bribes to the key officers and to local and state administrators to alert him if anyone makes inquiries. In return, he is one of Victorio's partners in the rancho's operation." He slapped his hand on the table as if he scored a point.

"Paying bribes is the cost of doing business in Mexico," Pascal said.

"Victorio has become a respected leader in the community, as the years passed, and the rancho prospered. He arranged with the *Alcalde* (mayor) of the little village of Zaragoza to find a harness maker to live in the town, as well as a saddle maker at my suggestion. The rancho could make its own leatherwork, but it created better neighbors to allow local merchants to prosper from work at the Rancho. In a similar move, Victorio supported the present *majordomo* (manager) of the Zaragoza *Acequia Madre*, even though some suggested Victorio take control because of the improvements the Rancho's workers performed. This subtle move gave Victorio a strong ally in the *majordomo*, and it cost him nothing to be kind.

"He allowed the rancho blacksmith to do small jobs for the villagers or neighboring ranchos for a small fee. Victorio and the blacksmith split the fee because the Rancho provided the equipment and supplies plus paying the blacksmith a worker's wage while providing him a *jacal* for living quarters."

Pascal framed this story as another object lessons for Nigel.

"You will attract more bees with honey than vinegar. The real lesson is if you are courteous to your neighbors, it could repay your effort in unexpected ways, and if done in friendship, what little it cost is often returned in multitude."

As Pascal had said, Nigel observed Victorio had a full-time job running the rancho operations. The *vaqueros* tended the stock of horses, mules, and cattle from which the rancho provided new mules.

Each crew trained mule teams to assist in their work. The stone workers led several mule trains into the mountains to return with cut stone for building a dam spillway, lining the *acequia's* sluice gates, and fireplaces in the *hacienda* and *cocina de campaña*. Other crews descended into the *Grande's* canyon, or ventured farther downstream, to return with cottonwood trees for corral fences, for strengthening new adobe construction in the *hacienda,* and for the *jacales* built for married workers. The woodcutters also harvested hardwoods for finished furniture and doors. The rancho had two furniture craftsmen, and they trained apprentices. The field workers trained mules in harness to pull farm wagons or plows. In addition, Victorio recruited and trained family relatives and selected local men to work the land or learn to drive the new wagons. Children of the rancho apprenticed in the trades to have a way to earn a living outside the rancho.

The rancho's workday started at sunup, which meant an hour's extra sleep for Nigel. It also meant a breakfast with eggs three or four times a week, which he enjoyed. He didn't mind letting someone else cook or gather firewood. Nigel found the evening meal much more formal at the *hacienda* with the Ortega family than the meals at the *cocina* with the cousins and the vaqueros during the workday. They stayed so busy it didn't seem like a "winter rest" to Nigel.

The Ortegas served meals at the hacienda in the formal style of the landed gentry in Mexico. The formal dining room had high-backed chairs along the walls. The primary serving table lay along a wall near the *cocina* in the next room. The family and guests didn't sit at a table but held their plates on their lap, raising the plate to their chin when eating. In their tradition, they served wine, fruit juice, or water following the meal. The meal consisted of several courses, with garden vegetables first, then beans, or occasionally yams, then meat followed by more vegetables. Servers carried a separate plate from the *cocina* to the serving table for each course. The cook staff included dishwashers to wash dishes between courses when a large number of guests attended. The family of the married *vaqueros* or the field workers at the rancho served as cooks and servers. The formal meals became the only times the men and women at the rancho sat together. Usually, the men conducted the business of operating the rancho while the women conducted the operation of the household, the kitchens, and *hacienda* gardens. The *hacienda* created its own village.

Pascal, LaFleur and Nigel made occasional visits to El Paso for supplies or equipment through the winter. The Ortega men considered it a favor to ride to El Paso with *el patron* because they could visit the *cantinas* and *bordellos* in the "big city."

After his recent visit to El Paso, Pascal reported to Victorio.

"I met one of St. Vrain's men driving a load of

hand-painted tile north to Santa Fe. I gave the drover a coin and a letter for Charbonneau, instructing him to present the letter as a loan request to St. Vrain. I directed Charbonneau to buy any freight wagons still available in Santa Fe, bringing them south when he came. I also instructed Charbonneau to arrive in El Paso by March fifteenth to organize a mule train drive north to Santa Fe and on to Fort Bridger.

Pascal's gentle persuasion convinced the Ortegas to attempt one season of freighting. They'd use the wagons and Rancho stock for the new Ortega wagon-freighting business.

Chapter 14

March to April, 1853

On March twelfth, Pascal's team arrived in El Paso, ready to move a forty-mule train to Santa Fe, which consisted of thirty loaded with packsaddles and ten mules in relief.

Victorio, leading four teams of new wagons, arrived in El Paso the next day to meet with Señor Valencia. The Ortega family decided to haul freight between El Paso and Chihuahua one time. If it went well, the family would work with Señor Valencia until Pascal returned in the fall.

Captain Enrico Ortega led a supply detail to the *Federales* regional headquarters in Chihuahua, allowing Victorio's wagons to follow his military supply detail. Rico planned his return to coincide with the Ortega wagons. His presence assured, with his unit's help, they'd train the Ortega teams, making them ready to work the *El Camino Real* to Chihuahua on their own.

Pascal warned a large salt lake lay along the trail, making fresh water scarce most of the two hundred forty-miles on a desert trail. He suggested limiting the runs on that route during the summer, when it became too hot and dry.

Señor Valencia vented his frustration that

Pascal didn't plan on returning until fall.

"Most freighters are careless with the trade goods, taking too long to deliver," Señor Valencia said. "You are the only reliable muleteer I've used. Your pack train is faster than any wagons, especially those pulled by oxen. Bah, oxen are only good if eaten."

In a low voice to Nigel, Pascal said, "Saying 'careless' is another way of saying those drovers stole. They claimed the *cargas* fell, damaging it, or it fell off while traveling. Actually, they steal it so they can sell it to make more money. They are but common thieves." He spat, grinding his boot on the spot, putting his curse on those who stole.

Pascal placed an arm on the man's shoulder, speaking in soft words, to assure Señor Valencia about the reliability of the Ortega family. To guarantee their performance, Pascal promised to pay for any freight lost by the Ortegas on their first trip south this season.

"If you like their work, and the Ortegas make a decent profit, they will expand to Santa Fe next year," Pascal said, patting the man's shoulder. "I will use them to re-supply my trade goods once they establish a regular schedule along the North-South route of *El Camino Real*."

"I tell you, if you can find a faster route to Matamoros from here, we'll make more profit by importing directly from the Gulf rather than going by road through lower Mexico to Vera Cruz. Consider making a new route, if you can," Señor Valencia suggested.

Charbonneau arrived two days late. He blamed the delay on crossing the *Jornada*.

"I know now why my father didn't like to work with mules. They are even worse when pulling a wagon than when in-line for a train. Each wants to lead, and none follows. No more wagons," Philippe said before cursing under his breath.

Nigel noticed Pascal rubbing the back of his neck while pinching his lips together. He recognized the signs of Pascal's frustration from his own experiences with the Frenchman. The delay had irritated Pascal, but he must have chosen not to argue with Philippe about it.

"We'll go north to Santa Fe before going to Fort Garland," Pascal spoke to the assembled team. "After Fort Garland, we'll use the pass at La Veta before continuing across the prairie along the Arkansas to La Junta. Then east to Bent's new Post at Big Timbers on the prairie."

Pascal added an additional two muleteers this season. Benito Perez y Reyes was a year younger than Antonio and a little taller but much heavier. Reynaldo Sanchez y Reyes was two years older than Antonio, at twenty-one, and taller than his cousins, but slimmer. The new men were nephews of Josafina Ortega y Reyes, Victorio's wife, and Antonio's mother.

The Reyes cousins had grown up in the same little village in the mountains about fifty miles south of the rancho. They responded to Victorio's call for workers because their small village held little future for them. The Reyes cousins had worked with Antonio and Pascal over the winter using mules to move cut stones from the mountains. They learned how to load and drag the mules without whips. They had yet to learn the drudgery of dragging mules daily, but as the days passed, they learned working mules on a long trail became exhausting, unending work from the dark before dawn into the dark past sunset.

Nigel had worked with the cousins during winter. He liked them. They joined in the regular rifle practice each morning before doing the day's work assignment. Victorio and the vaqueros practiced shooting until they satisfied Victorio with their accuracy. Nigel noticed Victorio used one of the Beecher Bible Sharps Pascal bought in Fort Atkinson last season. Nigel wondered when they'd allow him to use, and then carry, one of the heavy 52-caliber Sharps.

When the team crossed the *Rio Grande* leaving *El Paso del Norte*, Nigel studied a new building on the *Estados Unidos* (United States) side. He cocked an eyebrow at a flowing irrigation canal along the *Grande's* north bank with a stout wooden bridge across the canal.

I'm sure that acequia ran there when we came south, but I lacked the understanding of its value when I first came to Mexico.

"The *Yanquis* named their little town Franklin, building it on higher ground of the north bank so it doesn't flood during the heavy spring runoff from upstream," Philippe said.

Nigel thought it resembled a haphazard collection of wooden buildings without any plan. Ten miles north of town, construction moved forward on new buildings for the Army Post at the base of a large hill. They erected a stockade from large pines cut from farther up the hillside. These buildings replaced the older adobe buildings first built too close to the *Grande*. Spring flooding destroyed the original adobe buildings the previous year.

"One of the workers told me the Army has named this Fort Bliss. The men stationed there will find it anything but bliss," Philippe said.

Even Pascal chuckled at his comment.

Three days later, thunder preceded heavy rain, announcing a late spring cold snap as the team proceeded north from Mesilla. The thunder echoed between the Caballo Mountains on the west and the San Cristobel Mountains on the east. The crack of lightning sounded like cannon fire. They experienced a wet and cold trip through the *Jornada*, with a constant north wind.

"It is unfathomable that this area is even more miserable when wet and cold than in the summer, when hot and dry," Pascal said.

Another two weeks passed before it began to warm. By then, the team climbed from the *Rio Grande* canyon leading to Santa Fe and higher altitudes. The team found the mountains cold at night. Even in the cold, it surprised Nigel to find wildflowers blooming in wet spots among the rocks and hard caliche clay at the canyon's rim.

The area greened in the spring, where it had lain brown and dry when they rode this way last fall.

Nigel continued learning to cook in a Mexican style. He and the Reyes cousins took turns preparing the evening meal. The extra men working the train gave Nigel more time to run ahead, setting snares for small game.

He ran every morning after target practice, and again in the evening before eating.

Nigel didn't trust Philippe, avoiding the man. He resented Philippe's complaint that he was a hopeless sissy who created a constant danger to the other men because he couldn't work the mules, lift the packsaddles, or shoot a Sharps to defend or hunt.

Philippe often made sarcastic comments to Nigel or one of the cousins when they shot target practice each morning after the train started.

Philippe doesn't believe I can teach the cousins to shoot with accuracy.

"LaFleur and I suggested the young men learn accuracy with the small-bore rifle until they can hit their target on a regular basis. When they are accurate, the cousins will learn to use the heavier, Sharps rifle faster and easier," Pascal said.

Nigel snorted. *Philippe wouldn't dispute something Pascal said.*

The team used the same travel organization as last season, with Philippe in the lead with the camp mules and the relief animals. Pascal followed with the *marina* and a sixteen-mule train while Reynaldo keep the line in order. LaFleur followed next with another sixteen-mule train while Benito maintained the line's order. Antonio helped where needed on either train. Nigel worked as the camp cook and runner for relaying messages.

Nigel failed to understand why Pascal used such a large team on the trail this season.

When he asked, Pascal said, "We need more people trained to work the pack trains, and they provide LaFleur and me relief from the heavy lifting."

Español became the primary language when moving, but evenings in the camp, Pascal pushed the cousins to learn enough *Français* to understand instructions. The rest of the time, he encouraged the cousins to practice English with Nigel, so the cousins could speak with the *Yanquis* during trading sessions.

The first leg of the season up to Santa Fe went slower than Pascal liked, taking eighteen days. The first week found them sore in the mornings, including the mules. It took all of them a while to get their muscles and joints used to the daily routine. They welcomed a rest in Santa Fe.

Philippe tended to go his own way in Santa Fe. Nigel and the cousins didn't miss him.

The cousins liked to stick together and, except when the young men visited the sporting houses, they took Nigel with them. Benito said visiting the sporting houses is what makes all the sweat on the trail worth the effort when they joked with

Antonio after returning to the mule corrals. Pascal's team set up their small camp beside the corral where they furnished water.

On Sunday, the cousins went to the San Miguel Chapel for Mass, while Nigel visited a little Methodist church.

The minister, Reverend Mark Sanders, invited Nigel to his house for lunch after services.

That's not a lunch. It's a small snack, really small. I'd been hoping for a big dinner.

The team left Santa Fe at dawn Monday morning, heading for Fort Garland.

"We will bypass Taos because it adds three or four days to the trip," Pascal said.

Nigel noticed Pascal appeared in a hurry. He even used the relief mules to carry the *cargas* for Fort Garland, which left the train-mules loaded fully with trade goods to sell, once they went into the mountains.

Fort Garland came at the end of an uneventful six days, with a Sunday rest day.

Boring, Nigel thought, *this is no fun at all.*

The men didn't ask to spend an extra day in Fort Garland, because it still lacked a real saloon, or a sporting house.

Pascal is pushing us to keep moving, like he has a schedule to keep. It's not like him.

The team crossed La Veta pass in the cold with three inches of snow on the ground. Nigel struggled to believe spring had arrived.

They pushed on to the prairie near the tiny

village of La Plaza de los Leones on Cucharas Creek. Normally, it'd be an easy three-day trail from there to La Junta on the Arkansas River where the Santa Fe Trail turns south toward Raton Pass.

Not this time, however.

Philippe sighted a large party of Comanche moving across their trail farther east. After Pascal, LaFleur, and Philippe discussed it, Pascal decided to wait in the deep draw, out of view from across the prairie.

Pascal sent Philippe to scout south and east of their position to find if the group of Comanche he saw earlier continued to move northeast.

Pascal sent Nigel to a small rise nearby to warn the camp if any Comanche came in their direction. He served as "lookout" because he couldn't load or move the mules, if forced to run.

Pascal decided to take an early siesta break, unloading the mules while Philippe scouted.

Later, LaFleur wrote to Nigel, *Pascal planned if Comanche attacked in number, he'd abandon the trade goods, running with the mules. If the mules became troublesome, they would abandon the mules, trying to outrun the Comanche, or at least find a better defensive position.*

Nigel glimpsed Philippe returning at an easy pace. He left the high ground to tell Pascal that Philippe returned, and then he returned to his post, still carrying his "peashooter."

LaFleur signaled for Nigel to come return to

camp once Philippe had reported. Nigel recognized the men's relaxed posture, taking it to understand the Comanche had moved away, and failed to notice them.

Philippe ragged at Nigel, "How many Comanche will you kill with that peashooter?"

"The first one," Nigel responded as he scooted by, "And mayhap, the second when I bash his skull with it."

Philippe barked a laugh, readying a retort, but Pascal cut him off.

"Let us eat, resting a bit longer. We will load again in an hour to move out." He shifted to face his guide, "Philippe, I want you riding alone quite a ways in front, a little north of our trail."

"Noir, I want you out front where you can just keep the train in sight. If you see Philippe riding hard, or you see Comanche riding our direction, fire your rifle.

"Antonio, you will take the camp mules and relief stock way to the rear, just keep us in sight. If you see us turn, running toward you, turn around to head southwest. That should give us a five to ten minute head-start to escape. The Redman will stop at the *cargas* to see what plunder they've found, which might allow more time to escape."

Pascal stopped talking for a few minutes, staring out at the prairie before he said, "Philippe, once you hear Noir's shot, break off, heading in another direction. You should be able to survive on your own. You can join us when you are able."

Philippe nodded his agreement.

"*Noir*, after you shoot, ride hard to catch up with me, you are lighter than the men, so you will be able to run with your horse longer than the rest of us. Ride for me, I'll not abandon you."

Pascal took a long drink of water from his waterskin before he continued. "We will not be able to fight off a band of twelve or more Comanche. I have told this to *Noir* before.

"Now I will tell you all. It will hurt my purse to lose the entire train, but it would hurt my soul even more to lose one of you. If we are attacked in surprise, I want you to abandon the train and try to survive. Your survival chances are better with two or more together, but do not risk yourself to try to rescue one already captured. My orders are to run, hide, and survive. Meet at Fort Union or Santa Fe. *Comprender*? Understand?"

Pascal gave each of the men two twenty-dollar gold pieces. "This is to help you survive until we can get together again. South of here seven to ten miles is the Purgatoire River. Follow it southwest toward Raton Pass. You will see the Santa Fe Trail up there. Follow the Trail south to Fort Union on the Mora, or on south to Las Vegas on the Gallinas, and then ride west to Santa Fe. Just follow the Santa Fe Trail."

Then he added as an afterthought, "Find St. Vrain if I do not return. He will send you south to El Paso, but he will expect you to work, too."

They had a cold camp that night with two nighthawks on guard through the night.

Pascal waited until full daylight before moving, but Philippe left camp in the dark.

Nigel rode at a trot to get in front of the train. There would be no target practice or running this morning. These undulating plains made distance deceiving. What appeared flat prairie could hide a large herd of buffalo in a depression, or a raiding party of Comanche.

The team continued east for the Purgatory River, halting for their usual noon siesta.

Philippe rode back to where he caught sight of Nigel on guard during the siesta break, sending an "all-clear" sign by holding his arms straight over his head before crossing them atop his head, twice.

Nigel relayed the "all-clear" sign to Pascal. After the signal, Benito rode up to Nigel with a canvas sack of jerky and hardtack biscuits.

"Is it like this all the time? *Los indios* ready to kill us?" Benito asked, his face pale, his brow creased.

"No. This is the first time they spooked us like this. Philippe said he spotted a large band of Comanche riding east toward their summer camps on the Canadian River."

"Are you scared?"

"Sure. I'm so tight I had a hard time pissing a while ago."

Benito burst out laughing, "*Si, compadre!* Me, too." With that, he remounted, riding to the siesta camp.

The team rode into La Junta the next evening,

camping close to the village. Philippe reported the townsfolk in La Junta never noticed any Comanche, so the Comanche must be in a good mood for time being.

The next day, a man named Brooks rode in from Bent's new Post to report a large buffalo herd grazed north of the old fort ruins. "The Comanche camped at the west side and the Cheyenne camped at the east. The two tribes are ignoring each other while they're busy killing buffalo and preparing stocks of cured meat and hides after the long winter," Brooks said.

"Can we ride to Big Timbers?" Pascal asked.

"You might could go east if you stayed well south of the Arkansas, but I'd return to the mountains. Don't go north across the prairie for the next couple of weeks," Brooks replied.

Pascal nosed around La Junta to ask if people needed any trade goods, because the wagons from the East had yet to reach this far following the Santa Fe Trail.

Hours before dawn, Pascal shook Nigel from his bedroll in darkness.

"Get dressed, bring your personal gear. Philippe, you, and I are riding to Bent's Big Timbers Post. We're not taking the train with us. They will wait here for us to return."

After he dressed, Nigel gathered his gear from LaFleur's packsaddle. He joined Pascal at the horses. "What are we doing?"

"I want to push hard. Get to Bent's in one day of

hard riding. I've been concerned about your safety before, but after we wandered into the middle of those Comanche the other day, I realized we'd be hard put to survive. This season, we are going places I haven't been before. I don't know what we'll encounter. It'll be more dangerous than usual. I think you shouldn't come this season."

"W-W-What do you mean? A-A-Are you just going to leave me here?"

"*Non.* I'm not abandoning you. I'm taking you to live with young Bent and his family at Big Timbers, east of here. Bent has two sons and a little girl. I think George Bent is about your age. You'll be safe until I return in the fall. I'll ask if you can stay with Bent's boys."

"I don't want to be safe. I want to come with you and LaFleur. Please, don't leave me behind. Please!" Tears pooled in his eyes.

"Oh, *Noir*, do not cry. I'm doing what is best for you, for your safety. You are too young to be here."

"Is this what you had in mind bringing the extra men? You planned leaving me all along."

"*Non, Noir.* I hoped with extra men we would be safer, but the cousins are too green yet. They grew frightened the other day. I'm not sure they'd have been much help in fighting, if it had come to it."

"They are becoming better shots. I'll keep teaching them. They'll be better shots if I stay."

"Yes, you have taught them to shoot well, but it is not the problem. They got so jittery the other day they couldn't load their weapons. They have no experience. They are too green yet. They'll panic in a real fight, and worthless when we need them. They need a season to be dependable.

"*Noir,* you may not understand, but this is why Philippe rides you hard. He says you shouldn't be here. He thinks LaFleur and I would endanger the whole team to protect you. He believes you'll panic at the wrong time, getting us killed."

"I won't panic. I can kill Comanche. I want to kill them." Nigel's tears streamed along his face.

"Your time with the Comanche will come. It is too soon for you yet. Please understand."

"I won't understand. I don't believe you. You're just trying to be rid of me."

"I understand you are hurt, but I must do what I think best for you. Right now it means you stay here on the prairie this season, while we go into the mountains to learn new trails. We will return to the rancho together in the fall, like we do at the end of each season."

Pascal reached out for Nigel, "Come, give me a hug."

Nigel pulled loose, saying as he ran, "You don't care about me at all."

They rode in silence the rest of the morning. They rode hard to get to Bent's new Post. They wanted to avoid contact with the Comanche or the Cheyenne who also hunted in large numbers along the Arkansas River Valley. Pascal led three extra horses and a pack mule.

Nigel wondered why the extra horses for such a short trip.

During a rest for the horses, which they watered

from the Arkansas River, Pascal said, "William Bent married a Cheyenne called Owl Woman. She is one of Gray Cloud's daughters. She died in childbirth a few years ago. Gray Cloud is an important medicine man for the Cheyenne. He lives with Black Kettle's band up on the sandy creeks north of Big Timbers.

"Black Kettle is a new Chief among the Southern Cheyenne. They made him one of the senior chiefs in their ruling council this year. The Cheyenne like and respect young Bent. They traded at the old Fort often. The Cheyenne call Bent, 'Little White Man.' You can learn many things about the Redman this summer, if you accept their way."

"I do *not* want to learn their ways. I want to kill them for what they did to my family."

"The Cheyenne didn't kill your family. The Cheyenne don't like the Comanche any more than you do. If you learn nothing else this summer, learn that all Redmen are not the same."

"I'm surprised you didn't say 'water runs downhill,' learn to accept what cannot change."

Pascal grunted, "Huh. So you use my own words against me. It would be a good application, however. What did Juana Barnard tell you? Let nature be your guide, learn from what you see in nature. Learn from this and become stronger by doing it."

Pascal sighed aloud. "Let us ride." Philippe remained silent.

Nigel didn't think he'd have withstood any of

Philippe's smart remarks.

They reached Bent's Big Timbers Trading Post near dusk. Mr. Bent welcomed them. Philippe off loaded the packsaddle from the mule before unsaddling the horses.

Pascal and Mr. Bent spoke on the trading post's porch.

Nigel observed that Mr. Bent kept shaking his head "no," shrugging his shoulders.

Nigel noticed Pascal grew more agitated, waving his arms. Then a woman stepped onto the porch, standing next to Mr. Bent. She entered the conversation, pointing at him, nodding.

After a while, Pascal tramped to us. "We have problems. There have been troubles with the whites this winter. The Cheyenne are angry. They talk of rejoining the Northern Cheyenne, joining their Dog Soldiers. Bent is worried enough to have sent his children east on the Santa Fe Trail during the winter to live with kin in Missouri, going to school there. They're gone a month.

"Peacemaker Woman, *Na-no-mo-ne'e*, a daughter of Black Kettle, is trading here today. She returns to Black Kettle's camp tomorrow. Bent is their Indian agent. He asked her to ask Black Kettle to calm people for a while. He says it is just as well we're going west into the mountains this season. Bent expects a hostile season on the prairie."

"Good. I don't want to be here. It appears I'll be safer in the mountains with you."

"*Non, Noir.* Peacemaker Woman wants to take you with her to meet Black Kettle. She wants you to spend the season with her at Black Kettle's camp. The Comanche will not attack Black Kettle. Peacemaker Woman said the trade goods and horses I brought along makes you an important guest for Black Kettle."

Pascal stopped talking for a minute, shifting to glance at Philippe.

"Philippe, she wants you to come along, if you're willing. The Cheyenne who traded at the old Fort liked your father. They know you from when you worked with Bent. She thinks if you come, it will help calm their feelings that whites are no longer their friends."

Philippe stared hard at Pascal for a long while. Finally, he said, "My father did not get along with the Northern Cheyenne when the Arapaho camped with them. Mother never spoke of it. She was jealous J.B. spent so much time with the Southern Cheyenne, thinking he had another wife here with the Southern Cheyenne. I know their language. I can talk to them."

Philippe stood silent a while before glancing at Pascal, "Are you coming along?"

"*Non.* Peacemaker Woman wants this to be a visit by 'friends.' She says her father will be more open with people who are known to the Cheyenne."

"What about him?" Philippe said, nodding his head toward Nigel.

"Peacemaker Woman says *Noir* will not be a risk. She says it is not unusual for children to spend a season with another band. It will show there are no hard feelings between the whites and The People. Black Kettle knows me. I think he trusts me as a trader. She says if *Noir* comes to them under her protection, *Noir* will be as safe as she is in her father's camp."

"Under these conditions, I cannot refuse to go. When do we leave?"

"Peacemaker Woman planned to leave at first light in the morning."

"You're joking?" Nigel exclaimed. "You expect me to live with ... these ... these ... heathens? You'd just leave me there?"

"Speak soft, Nigel," barked Philippe. "You speak of my mother and me when you say 'these heathens' with such a tone."

"*Noir*, you must understand," said Pascal. "It is a matter of honor with the Chief. If he gives you his protection, you'll be safer there than with us."

"What will I do there? How will I live? How will I talk to anyone? You cannot just leave me there!"

"You are a spoiled, whiny brat," snapped Philippe. "You've had it too easy. You'll live in a tipi, a *vee'e*, like the rest of The People. You will eat with them, and learn to like it, or go hungry. You're fortunate to meet Chief Black Kettle. I have seen him, but I have not met him. He doesn't come to the Fort. Bent rode to meet him. Live this summer with The People and you will understand how foolish are your threats to 'kill them all.' You will learn you are a puny weakling who couldn't survive without the protection of others. It is time for you to grow up."

What he said hurt, but Nigel wouldn't let Philippe see him cry.

Nigel glanced at Pascal for help, but he put his hand on Philippe's arm, shaking his head.

"*Noir*, think of this as a rite of passage. In the Redman's way, each youngster must prove himself as a man, as a 'brave.' This is your time. You must grow up."

Bent's Post

Chapter 15

May to July, 1854

Nigel rode into the Cheyenne camp beside Philippe and Peacemaker Woman. The scene filled him with dread. They passed three Cheyenne men riding away as they rode into the camp, but no one seemed excited or bothered by them riding into camp. Several mounted men followed them from a short distance away. The camp spread along the stream's west side near a cottonwood grove, but their tipis set apart from one another. It appeared as if a street divided the tipis, leading to the stream. The stream had sandy banks with small sand islands in the water.

A large herd of horses roamed across and downstream from the camp. He scowled as naked little children ran and played. He wondered if anyone watched them. Juana Barnard had said if he visited a camp ask a woman working on skins how they cured their skins. There must be three dozen women working on skins in the camp. Hides hung drying everywhere.

Buffalo hides? They must be buffalo hides from the big hunt Bent's man spoke of.

Every item appeared strange and threatening. The camp reeked of smoke and cooked food, but the odor spoiled Nigel's appetite. The sights equally fascinated and frightened him.

Peacemaker Woman stopped in front of a large tipi, dismounting. Nigel shifted to dismount but Philippe touched his arm, giving one quick shake of his head. A short, heavy-set man stepped from the tipi with a red trade blanket wrapped around him. He never raised his head to glance at the two on horseback, but spoke soft words to Peacemaker Woman. Nigel guessed this must be Black Kettle. His creased face appeared angry, fierce. Nigel wondered what would happen to him when Philippe left him alone in this camp.

Nigel didn't understand Peacemaker Woman's words, but she cried. The fierce man opened his blanket, welcoming her into his arms. They talked in quiet murmurs for two minutes after he wrapped her in the blanket within his arms. Black Kettle barked a guttural command, bringing several women from his tipi to embrace Peacemaker Woman. The women chattered to each other as the man refolded his blanket around himself, studying the women with a slight smile. He never gave Philippe and Nigel a thought. Nigel glanced about, noticing people gathering but not coming too close. Black Kettle barked another command, silencing the women.

Black Kettle faced the two on horseback, and spoke. Philippe answered him. Nigel thought from Black Kettle raised brows, he questioned Philippe.

Black Kettle faced Nigel asking *en español*, "You are son of Pascal, the Mule Man?"

"*Si, el jefé!*" (Yes, Boss man), Nigel responded, not knowing what to call Black Kettle.

"Come, sit by my fire. We will speak of these things," Black Kettle said *en español* again, but nodded at Philippe.

Philippe shifted to dismount, nodding at Nigel to dismount.

Peacemaker Woman held the tipi flap open while Black Kettle stepped inside. She motioned for Philippe and Nigel to follow, which they did. Peacemaker Woman came in behind them, sitting next to Nigel.

Nigel noticed the women behind Black Kettle preparing bowls of food.

Black Kettle spoke in Cheyenne, and Peacemaker Woman translated for Nigel.

"Black Kettle welcomes both of you to his camp. He asks you to share a meal with him. Eat a little of everything even if you don't like it. You insult him if you refuse to share his food."

Black Kettle took a drink from a bowl before passing it to Philippe. After a long drink, Philippe passed to Nigel. Nigel sipped it. It tasted like watery berry juice. Nigel finished it.

Peacemaker Woman nodded approval.

Black Kettle accepted another bowl from the women, dipping his fingers in to shovel it into his mouth. He said words, passing it to Philippe. Philippe scooped a couple of finger loads of food into his mouth before passing the bowl to Nigel. Nigel accepted the bowl, raising it to his mouth, sniffing. It didn't smell tasty, so Nigel dipped in his fingers before sucking on them.

Oh! Puke! This is awful, thought Nigel.

Nigel noticed Peacemaker Woman motioning to eat more, so Nigel took another taste on his fingers. He had to keep from gagging as he swallowed.

Nigel noticed Black Kettle whispered words to a woman, after which, she left the *vee'e.*

The next bowl Black Kettle handed to them held roasted meat.

Philippe took several pieces before handing Nigel the bowl.

Nigel took it all, stuffing it in his mouth in a noisy manner.

Black Kettle said guttural words.

Peacemaker Woman said, "Black Kettle says you eat fast like a hungry wolf."

Philippe spoke in Cheyenne. He and Black Kettle conversed for a few minutes.

Peacemaker Woman whispered, "Philippe said your common name is Black Wolf, but it is not your true name. Black Kettle said it is right to keep your true name hidden. It is the Way of The People. He is pleased you are learning the Way of The People."

Philippe said more words, and Black Kettle nodded his approval. Philippe left the tipi.

Philippe returned with trade goods from the mule. He laid them before Black Kettle.

Peacemaker Woman translated, "These gifts of friendship are from Mule Man. One horse and the mule outside are yours, gifts from him. He wants his son to learn the Way of The People this season. The little wolf's true father came from across the great water to teach the Cherokee. Comanche killed his true father. Little wolf wants to learn to kill Comanche, avenging his father and his family. Mule Man wants him trained as a Cheyenne to know the Way of The People, and learn to kill Comanche."

While the men spoke, Nigel noticed a woman came into the tipi, sitting next to the flap.

"It is a good thing to kill Comanche. It is good to avenge your father," Black Kettle said *en español*. "You will need many summers to become a Cheyenne brave. I welcome you to the *Wotápio* (Cheyenne-Sioux) camp. Be at peace with the *tsé tsé he's tâh ese* (The People)."

With that said, Black Kettle waved to the new woman. She moved to sit beside him. He reverted to the guttural words, while Peacemaker Woman translated to him.

"This is Yellow Blossom. The Comanche killed her husband when they tried to steal our horses. She has a son like you. He husband's brother, Tall Bear, protects her, but he is not her husband. She needs help raising her son. Tall Bear is to teach him. Tall Bear will teach Black Wolf. Take a few of these gifts to Yellow Blossom's tipi."

"The little wolf can run all day long. He is to run every day. He has learned to set snares for food like a woman and cooks for old Pascal. Teach him to hunt like a man, letting the woman set snares and cook," Philippe said.

"When a man travels without a woman, someone must cook. In this camp, Yellow Blossom will cook," said Black Kettle as he stood, wrapping his red trade blanket around him again.

Yellow Blossom rushed to the flap, stepping outside to hold it open for Black Kettle.

Philippe, Peacemaker Woman, and Nigel stepped from the tipi behind him. Yellow Blossom stood behind Black Kettle.

Philippe spoke in Cheyenne to Black Kettle, nodding to Peacemaker Woman, before he mounted his horse. He glanced at Nigel, speaking in *Français*, "Try to grow into your name this summer, little wolf. Mayhap one day I will have some respect for you."

Philippe reined his horse around to ride from the camp in a slow walk.

Nigel waited alone with the Cheyenne.

Black Kettle nodded at Yellow Blossom. She opened the tipi flap for the chief to reenter his tipi.

"Yellow Blossom speaks a little Spanish, but no English. You need to learn Cheyenne soon," said Peacemaker Woman as she led the horses away. "I will go with you to Yellow Blossom's *vee'e*, helping you get settled and to meet her son, Running Elk. Black Kettle will give you two buffalo robes to sleep on. Use one of your bedroll blankets to sleep under on the buffalo robes. I suggest giving your spare blankets to Blossom. She can use them for trade. It will help her regain status she lost when her husband died. Share your trade goods with her and her son. They are your family now. They'd not understand if you did not share with them."

"What about my rifle? My black powder? My knife? Do I share everything?"

"No. Those are personal things. Running Elk will have things that are his and won't share them. Your rifle, your horses, those things are yours. If you have some spares, you may want to share them with Running Elk. He will not be any more pleased with this arrangement than you. You two must learn to live together. Blossom and Running Elk will teach you our language. I will be in a vee'e near Black Kettle's, if you have questions, but do not expect me to hold your hand. You must change, adapting to our way."

"That's it? Learn to adapt? I'm on my own?"

"The whole camp knows who you are. You will never be 'on your own' until you leave, when Philippe returns in the fall. You may think you can sneak away, doing something with no one knowing. It will not happen. Someone will notice, know where you are, and what you have done. See the little ones playing over there, running around everywhere? The whole camp watches to make sure they aren't hurt. It will be like that with you. You are not alone. You are one of The People now."

Peacemaker Woman glanced away, and then said, "Here comes your first test. The young man coming is Running Elk. Let his mother talk to him first. While she does, I will tell you that Blossom and I were best friends when young girls. If she thinks things are bad for you, or you need help, she will tell me."

"Does Running Elk speak Spanish? Are you and Blossom all who understand me?"

"That is why you must learn our language. You have learned *Français* and e*spañol*. You can learn this language too."

"Will the lessons never end?" Nigel said aloud, while looking to the heavens.

"Another thing. Tall Bear has no sense of humor. He will seek for an excuse to strike you to show he is in charge. Do not provoke him. If he strikes you, stay down. Don't glare like you glared at Philippe. Tall Bear'd take it as a challenge, beating harder. Learn to mask your face."

"I'm supposed to let him beat me? Just like that?"

"No, not like that. It is the man's way to show he is in charge. If you don't challenge him after the first time, he'll not bother with you again. It is why I'm telling you to stay down—don't look at him if he hits you. It means you accept his leadership, and there is no need for him to do more."

"What if I don't accept his leadership?"

"He will kill you." She turned to leave.

"One other thing. Blossom said he likes to visit her often. You know what men and women do?"

"You mean like making a baby?"

"That is the best example of what I mean. Tall Bear is her guardian since she lost her husband. He is allowed to take the husband's role whenever he pleases. It pleases him to visit her often. Most men would not take advantage of a woman, but Tall Bear does. Stay away when he comes to visit.

That presents a serious challenge to him for you to try to interfere. If you think he beats her during his time, let me know because Black Kettle won't allow it. Running Elk is not allowed to interfere. If you come to me, I could tell Black Kettle."

Peacemaker Woman turned to Blossom and Running Elk to say words in Cheyenne before she left the group standing there.

Nigel jammed his cold hands into his armpits, trying not to let them see his fear. Sighing, he stepped to Running Elk, offering his hand while saying *en español*, "I am Black Wolf."

Running Elk glared at Nigel, slapping the extended hand away.

Yellow Blossom said *en español*, "The People not touch in greeting like *blancos*."

"How do I say hello to him?" Nigel asked *en español*.

"You say Running Elk." She pronounced it in Cheyenne, "*mo'e-he-koma-estse*."

Nigel repeated "*mo'e-he-koma-estse*" several times trying to get it to sound right.

Running Elk said his name slow as if speaking to a child, "*mo'e – he – ko-ma – es-tse*."

Nigel repeated it.

Running Elk nodded approval.

Blossom pointed at Nigel saying his name, Black Wolf in Cheyenne, "*mo'oh-tavo-nehe*."

Nigel repeated "*mo'oh-tavo-nehe*" several times.

He noticed they swallowed some sounds like saying, "Oh-oh" in English where you inhale the first "O" sound, giving it a guttural quality.

Pascal's pronunciation lessons served a value after all.

Running Elk said words to Blossom. She asked, "Who gave your name?"

Nigel thought about it before answering. "A man of the Great Spirit."

Blossom translated that for Running Elk. Running Elk replied in Cheyenne.

She translated his answer, "A strong name comes from man of the Great Spirit."

Blossom said, "Let us unload your things to put them in our tipi. Learn a new word, *vee'e* is tipi. I will show you how to mark your horses, so others know they are yours. You are rich to own so many horses when you are so young."

Nigel thought about what Peacemaker Woman said, remembering Pascal's "marriage of convenience" with Victorio, where they shared what they had to gain more together.

En español, Nigel asked, "Are we a family? Is Running Elk my brother?"

Blossom responded, "*Si*," before translating to Running Elk, who frowned.

"If we are family, then one horse is yours. One horse is for Running Elk."

Blossom leaned away, staring at Nigel. "You mean that? Not say if not true."

"I mean it. If we live together, we must give strength to one another. It is what a family does. I can only ride one horse at a time. I don't need three horses."

Blossom translated to Running Elk and, for a

moment, he pulled away, shocked, and then set his face again. He gazed at Nigel as if he became a trick to resolve.

Nigel handed Running Elk the reins of the other two horses before stepping away.

"After his father died, we not have horses. Running Elk not hunt with young men. Tall Bear promised me a horse, but he only wants my mare. Be careful. I tell Tall Bear that Black Kettle said this gift for you staying here. He not question Black Kettle."

Nigel said, *"Comprender,"* but he didn't really. *What was it women had to make men desire it so?*

After they carried Nigel's bundles inside, Blossom said, "Horses no use bridle. You keep here. We use a nose rope, a *jáquima* (Hackamore). No iron bit. I tie thong on hair by ears with my knot. People know our horses. You and Running Elk guide horses across water to the graze."

Nigel struggled to understand her message in her partial *espanol*, "These horses have iron shoes. Will it help identify them?"

"No. I ask Digging Badger. Pinchers to pull nails. No shoes best."

"Should we hobble them so they won't wander in the night? I have hobbles."

"Not the Way of The People. Young braves keep ponies close. Training for young braves. Running Elk train this season."

While she put Nigel's things in different piles, she glanced at him.

"I say to you. He proud. His own horse. Not from

Tall Bear. Not go fast with gifts. Not buy his friendship. Be insulted."

"I have some gifts for you, too. Does that I mean I should not give them to you?"

Blossom, laughing, reached across, ruffling Nigel's hair with her hands.

"Oh, no. A man can't give a woman too many gifts."

And they laughed together.

I'd forgotten how nice it is to be around a woman. I remember mother or my sisters acting like that.

Running Elk led his mother's and his horses as they crossed the stream. As he followed with his horse, he shivered for a moment realizing no one here knew "Nigel." With The People, he must learn to think of himself as Black Wolf. When they returned to their *vee'e*, he said, "I want to run before it gets dark. I will return soon."

"Run? Run where?" she asked, her eyebrows pinched together. "Something bad?"

"Training. Did no work today. I need to stretch my legs by running."

"Running Elk go with you?"

"He can, but he doesn't have to. I'll run for an hour before washing in the stream. When will we eat?"

"Come back eat. Not come Tall Bear here ...."
She lowered her head as if embarrassed at Tall Bear being with her in that way.

"*Entender.* I'm to stay away. Peacemaker Woman told me."

Blossom said something to Running Elk, who

glared at him.

Black Wolf took off his shirt before grabbing his "possibles bag," rifle, and shot pouch.

Blossom grabbed his arm, pulling him toward her, asking in her broken *español*, "Why gun? You hunt?" She squinted, gazing into his eyes.

"I'm training to be a man. My rifle goes everywhere I go."

Blossom translated for Running Elk. He gave a quick nod of understanding and approval.

Running Elk grabbed his wooden lance.

The young men left the camp at an easy trot.

Black Wolf washed the sweat and dirt in the stream when they returned from running. Running Elk squatted on the bank, studying him. They trod in silence to Blossom's *vee'e* before entering. She'd prepared a stew of some kind that smelled like what Black Kettle served, and it tasted just as bad. He thought it smelled rotten. Blossom had also roasted a rabbit on a stick. He and Running Elk shared the rabbit, while Running Elk and Blossom finished the stew.

Running Elk said Cheyenne words to Blossom, rose to his feet in a swift, smooth motion before slipping from the *vee'e*.

In the unexpected silence, he asked, "I can set snares for rabbits or prairie hens. Would you like me to do that tomorrow?"

Blossom smiled at him, shaking her head.

"Woman set snares ... cook food. You shoot a deer ... we sing. I skin ... cook the meat. The Way of The People. Young men make sport ... tease you if set snares near camp."

"What do I do? I work with mules. I carry water, set snares, tend the fire, and prepare meals three times a day. I'm supposed to help, am I not?"

"No woman's work in camp. Must not in camp. You do when you and Running Elk hunt. Leave the camp ... stay the night."

"What do I do?"

"Learn to speak like us. Learn to walk in woods ... not scare animals hiding ... birds not stop singing. Learn to smell if animal nearby. Learn to shoot a bow. Learn to throw lance. Learn to hunt all animals. Ride your horse, walk him until it cools down, and wash him in the stream. Run. Even if his name is Running Elk ... said you ran far ... tired when he returned."

"That's it? I'm just going to take it easy until Philippe returns?"

"Running Elk friends ... they curious ... come see you. Young men wrestle ... no anger. Teaches you to escape ... if captured ... defend the camp."

Blossom sat in silence. "Tall Bear hunt buffalo ... come tomorrow ... next day. He visit in two to three days. He take Running Elk ... practice with bow and lance. Black Kettle said he teach you ... teach Running Elk. Tall Bear only visits my mare ... not teach Running Elk. He must teach Running Elk and you ... face Black Kettle. Tall Bear hard ... mean to you. Don't fight him. Try best. Tall Bear say The People you no good ... white boy weak. You try hard."

A voice called from outside. The *vee'e* flap opened, allowing Peacemaker Woman to enter carrying two buffalo robes. Peacemaker Woman said words in Cheyenne to Blossom before facing Nigel to repeat it *en español*.

"These robes are from Black Kettle. Leave them with Blossom when you ride with Far Walker's grandson."

"Black Kettle observed you and Running Elk this evening. It pleased him that you run, even if you have many horses. He noticed you carrying a rifle, asking if you thought you weren't safe in his camp. I told him at Bent's you always carried your rifle. You wanted to be ready for the Comanche. He laughed, saying to tell you the Comanche won't visit here."

"I'm used to shooting target practice in the morning before I run. Is there somewhere near where I can practice?"

"I'll ask Black Kettle. Don't shoot until Black Kettle has approved, telling you where to go."

While they spoke, he studied Blossom and Peacemaker Woman fashioning the buffalo robes into a space by the *vee'e* edge, using a rock to drive wooden stakes into the ground to hold the robes in place.

Blossom and Peacemaker Woman continued in Cheyenne, while he unrolled his bedroll. It had three blankets rolled in a *ghuta percha* waterproof square he used when it rained. He remembered what Peacemaker Woman had said about giving away extra blankets, so he asked Blossom *en spañol,* "Would you like my extra blankets?"

Blossom smiled, lowering her gaze while blinking her eyes before reaching for his arm. "You ask me ... share blankets, young wolf?"

"I meant them as a gift." His eyelids flew wide as his jaw dropped, realizing what she meant. "Oh, no. I didn't mean it that way." His face burned with the flush of embarrassment.

At this, both women laughed aloud. Blossom reached across, scrubbing his hair.

"We tease, young wolf. Learn to laugh ... a lesson. Tall Bear never laughs. No stone face in my *vee'e.*" She tickled his ribs.

He sat on his blanket, removing his moccasins and leggings.

Blossom grabbed them, scowling before showing them to Peacemaker Woman.

"Who make?" Blossom asked.

"I did. The silent one showed me how to make them."

The women laughed, chattering in Cheyenne, while pointing at parts of his moccasins.

Peacemaker Woman spoke in Spanish, laughing. "Mule Man too cheap to buy anything."

He flushed in embarrassment again, nodding.

Blossom pulled apart his moccasin, making comments.

"Moccasin is *tse-he-sto'ke-ha-no-tse.* I make moccasins *tse-he-sto'ke-ha-no-tse.* Let none think I make such." She wrinkled her nose as if they smelled before she ruffled Nigel's hair.

"Sit on my blanket. I show you mine," she said,

batting her eyes with a flirty smile.

Peacemaker Woman and Blossom giggled like young girls.

He knew they teased him, but he enjoyed it.

Blossom showed him her moccasins, showing what to do to make them last longer.

It grew late, so he stretched on his buffalo robe bed, saying prayers for his lost family.

He fell asleep during his prayers.

Black Wolf awoke before first light, as he did in Pascal's camp. Blossom and Running Elk still slept. He dressed in silence before pulling on his rebuilt moccasins and leggings, lacing them tight. He took jerky from his "possibles bag," moving in silence past the flap to outside. The camp lay quiet. The fires from the previous night smoldered, creating a thin layer of smoke over the camp. It carried a strong smell. His stomach roiled. A dog noticed him moving, barking twice. A light fog rose from the stream, mixing with the smoke to create swirling, hazy curtains in the light breeze. The sky hinted at brightening as the stars faded.

A woman came from a vee'e, yawned, glancing at Black Wolf before lifting her skirt to squat, pissing in the grass behind the *vee'e*. She scratched her bare butt, stood, lowered her dress, and returned inside. She didn't try to hide herself, or go behind a bush or anything. Although too dark for him to see her parts, she lifted her dress in front of him without any concern that he gazed upon her relieving herself.

What am I doing here? Is this what I'm supposed to learn?

He stood, shaking his head in disbelief, when someone touched his arm. He jumped in a startle. He never heard the old Cheyenne man who stepped behind before touching him.

The old man muttered Cheyenne words at him, motioning for him to follow.

He followed the old man to the camp's edge where sat an old *vee'e* painted with shapes of different animals. The old man sat at a small fire, pointing for him to sit, saying words in Cheyenne. He repeated the words, *"ha-me-sto-o'este,"* motioning with his finger to sit.

Black Wolf said, *"ha-me-sto-o'este,"* pointed to the ground, sitting.

The old man nodded before saying the word again, *"ha-me-sto-o'este."*

Black Wolf repeated it. The wizened old man nodded approval.

The old man roasted an animal larger than a rabbit on a stick over the fire. He pointed to himself saying what sounded like "wolf" in Cheyenne.

Black Wolf didn't understand, but pointed to himself, saying, *"Mo'oh-ta-no-nehe."*

The old man nodded, pointed to himself. *"He'hes-ko-nehe."* (Old Wrinkled Wolf)

Black Wolf repeated the sounds and glottal stop.

The old man nodded, saying it again. *"He'hes-ko-nehe."*

He repeated, *"He'hes-ko-nehe."* The old man

222

nodded approval.

The old man said, "*Mo-tse-ske*," pointing to the knife on Nigel's belt, saying again, "*mo-tse-ske.*"

Black Wolf repeated, "*mo-tse-ske*" a couple of times.

Old Wolf reached his open hand.

He handed *he'hes-ko-nehe* his knife, while wondering if he should have.

He'hes-ko-nehe tested the blade, smiled in approval, and sliced several pieces of meat from the roasting animal. He used the *mo-tse-ske* to hand Nigel a hot slice of meat, and said, "*me-se-estse*," (eat), putting a piece of meat in his own mouth.

Black Wolf repeated "*me-se-estse*" before he ate the meat. The greasy meat had a strong gamy flavor he didn't recognize.

Old Wolf smiled, pointing at the roasted animal. He said, "*xao'o.*" He motioned for Black Wolf to repeat it. The first sound came as a guttural "ch."

Black Wolf said it five times before Old Wolf approved.

They sat across the fire from each other.

Old Wolf pointed at different things, saying Cheyenne words, then motioning for him to repeat the words, over and over again. After a dozen words, Old Wolf started over again, testing if he remembered the new words.

He signaled Black Wolf to repeat words, while he sliced the roasting animal.

Black Wolf pointed at roasting animal, saying, "*Xao'o?*" while spreading his hands.

Old Wolf laughed. *"Xao'o,"* he said, pointing to hide hanging from his *vee'e*, a white-striped black hide with a bushy tail. He laughed aloud, *"Xao'o."*

Old Wolf's twinkling eyes reminded him of Pascal's when he pulled a trick. Black Wolf grinned, laughing aloud, and shaking his head.

Old Wolf sliced another piece handing it to him while grinning.

They ate all the meat on the roasting animal.

Old Wolf broke off a hind leg, gnawing the remaining meat, before he threw the carcass to a dog waiting nearby. He wiped his greasy hand through his hair before wiping the greasy blade on his hide shirt, and then handed it to Nigel.

"Merci. Je va a'dormir," (Thank you. I'm going to sleep.) in clearly spoken *Français.*

"W-w-what? *Vous parl le Français?* (You speak French?)"

Old Wolf replied in *Français,* "Voila! Do you think I'm an ignorant savage?"

"Why did we spend all this time learning those words, if you speak *Français*?"

"I couldn't find my knife in the dark. I saw you had one, so I invited you to bring your knife. Then, I tried to discover if you are an ignorant savage who cannot speak Cheyenne."

Old Wolf laughed aloud before he entered his *vee'e.*

He sat there, staring at Old Wolf's *vee'e*, feeling every bit the fool, but he barked a laugh.

Black Wolf learned something else that morning. The People woke up in stages. The young braves and the warriors came outside soon after Nigel. They appeared to have a set of tasks assigned to them like scouting, guarding, and hunting. The little children tottered outside next, followed by older women who lit cook fires while keeping an eye on the little ones. When the sun rose, more women ventured outside with the older children. Several women directed the children to collect wood for the fires while others carried water skins and large gourds to the stream. The camp came to life at an easy pace. The different scents increased with the sounds of people strolled about, talking. They served the morning meal by the time the sun's ball lifted from the horizon. After the morning meal, another old man rode a horse to different parts of the village shouting announcements, much like a town crier did in the Wales countryside.

The People listened before returning to their work.

Black Wolf stepped into Blossom's *vee'e*, grabbing his bridle. He waded across the stream to search for his gelding. He found it, slipped on the bridle, and walked the horse away from the rest of the herd. From the sun's angle, he guessed the time later than his usual morning run. He led the horse by its reins, pulling her along beside him as he ran, letting them exercise together. Blossom and Running Elk had risen, dressing when he left the *vee'e*.

Running Elk had gone with friends when Black Wolf returned.

Blossom said, "I have tasks. Lessons first." She worked on his moccasins for an hour, while he repeated phrases to learn to talk to her, Running Elk, and others in the village.

He ran again that evening. Running Elk and two friends ran with him. He ran a little faster than usual. By the time, he turned to return to camp, Running Elk's friends gasped for breath. Halfway to camp, the first one quit and, in another hundred steps, the other stopped running. He slowed so Running Elk, who gasped hard, could reach the camp. He ran straight to the stream, jumped in, and relaxed in the cool water for a few minutes. He stood, leaving the water to stroll around, cooling down and drying off before entering the *vee'e* to eat.

He glimpsed Running Elk tease his friends because they hadn't kept up with them. The teens ate their evening meal together. He practiced speaking with Running Elk until he grew tired of the repetition, going outside to join his friends.

Black Wolf realized The People didn't go to sleep early. They liked to sit in groups by their fires, talking, or telling stories. As the children grew sleepy, they laid on blanket pallets. The adults soon followed, letting the fires burn to embers.

In the habit of going to bed and rising early, he continued that practice. He rose early the next morning, strolling to Old Wolf's *vee'e*, but didn't find the old man. He returned to Blossom's tipi to retrieve his "possibles bag," grabbing some jerky for breakfast. He didn't think he'd miss the strong coffee and gruel LaFleur fixed in the morning, but he'd welcome it now.

He waited until it became light enough to see where he stepped before his morning run. He decided if Running Elk's friends joined them for the evening run, he'd better limit morning runs to stretching, not pushing hard.

He arrived at Blossom's *vee'e* while she fixed a morning meal for them. She prepared a different version of the same old stew. It didn't taste any better, but he was hungry.

It did not taste so bad, but it had a terrible smell. *Did she let this spoil first?*

Peacemaker Woman visited to report Black Kettle ordered Black Wolf to ask Tall Bear to supervise his target practice. Tall Bear must find a place for him to shoot and not hurt anyone.

By observing Peacemaker Woman's posture and motions as she repeated the orders, he guessed she wasn't any happier with the idea than he.

While they stood there, Tall Bear strode close. He *was* the tallest man in the camp.

Blossom lowered her head, saying, "Say his name, Tall Bear, *Na-ka hais-tah.*"

Nigel repeated the words Blossom said but Tall Bear ignored him.

Tall Bear gave Peacemaker Woman a sneer before saying, *"ma'a-atano'e"* to Black Wolf, pushing him toward the *vee'e.*

"Get your rifle," Peacemaker Woman said *en español.*

Black Wolf returned with his "possibles bag,"

shot pouch, and rifle.

Tall Bear reached his hand to take the rifle, but Nigel pulled back.

Tall Bear slapped Black Wolf with an open hand before he moved or said anything, knocking him to the ground while Tall Bear held his rifle.

Black Wolf rose, grabbing for his rifle.

Tall Bear backhanded him to the ground.

Black Wolf rolled to sit up on the ground, but noticed Peacemaker Woman standing behind Tall Bear motioning for him to stay down. He glanced above for a moment, but long enough to glimpse Tall Bear standing ready to beat him with the butt of his own rifle.

Tall Bear barked words at him that he couldn't understand. Tall Bear shouted the words louder a second time, sounding angry.

Running Elk whispered, *"hee-he'e,"* yes, in Cheyenne.

Black Wolf repeated, *"hee-he'e,"* and Tall Bear stepped away.

With a sneer on his lips, Tall Bear uttered surly comments while studying the rifle before he threw it on the ground in front of Black Wolf. Tall Bear pointed to Peacemaker Woman, who repeated *en español.*

"Tall Bear says your rifle is a toy for little children. It isn't a rifle for a man. It fits you."

"I still want to practice. Do I ask his permission?" he asked her in *español.*

Peacemaker Woman said, "Say, 'me target practice'," before saying the phrase in Cheyenne "*eo-ne'ame.*"

He repeated "*eo-ne'ame*" as Peacemaker Woman had said.

Tall Bear grunted words in Cheyenne.

Peacemaker Woman repeated it *en español,* "Tall Bear says he won't waste his time with a child's toy, but he'll show you where to practice. Tomorrow, you and Running Elk will learn to use bow and lance in The Rabbit Society of The People. Follow him now."

Black Wolf scrambled to his feet, hurrying to catch up with Tall Bear and Running Elk, who trotted behind Tall Bear. When the three strode from camp, another Cheyenne man caught up. He spoke with Tall Bear, pointing at Black Wolf. Tall Bear barked words at Black Wolf as the other man held out his hand. Black Wolf noticed Tall Bear watching him over a shoulder as he continued striding away.

Black Wolf handed the second man the rifle. The man studied the muzzle, laughed, and said words to Tall Bear who just grunted. The other man returned his rifle as the group continued walking at a trot for fifteen minutes.

Tall Bear stopped when they came to a shallow arroyo in a small depression more than a half-mile from the camp. Tall Bear pointed into the arroyo.

Black Wolf jumped down to find five pieces of dead branches about one-inch thick. He set them against the bank, returning to the top of the rise. While on top, he spread his gear from his "possibles bag" to set up for practice shooting.

First, he loaded, going through the complete loading ritual. Blowing through the primer nipple to assure it's clear, measuring black powder in the horn-cap, and pouring the powder from the horn-cap into the barrel's muzzle. He stamped the rifle butt on the ground, settling the powder, before inserting a cloth-patch and ball in the muzzle, and then driving them down with the ramrod. He pulled the hammer to half-cock, inserted a percussion cap on the firing nipple.

He grew a little nervous with the Cheyenne men watching him. Black Wolf aimed the rifle, and fired, hitting one of the small sticks he'd set up.

Tall Bear grunted words causing the other man to laugh. Tall Bear said words to Running Elk before swiveling to return to camp. Black Wolf tried to ignore Tall Bear leaving and continued loading. When he got ready, he shot again, hitting another small stick.

The second Cheyenne man spoke to him in Spanish.

"Does the white-man have a name for that small rifle?"

Black Wolf shied away, surprised that someone else spoke *español*.

"*Si*. They call it a "peashooter," because the ball is about the size of a pea."

"You shoot straight. Can you teach Running Elk how to shoot straight with your rifle?"

"*Si*. I will need your help explaining things to him. Do you want to help me now?"

"*Si*. I am called Digging Badger. Say what you

want. I will say it to Running Elk."

Black Wolf handed his rifle to Running Elk. He pointed to the parts as Digging Badger said each name in Cheyenne. Black Wolf and Running Elk each repeated the word several times.

Black Wolf said *en español*, "It will be easier if Running Elk practices before he loads," holding out his hand. Running Elk returned the rifle.

He knelt, saying, "Tell Running Elk to study how I hold the rifle." He cocked it before he squeezed the trigger, letting the hammer fall with a loud snap. Next, he removed a small copper coin from his "possibles bag" before saying to Digging Badger, "*Por favor*. Lay it flat on the end of the barrel when I am ready."

Black Wolf took his position, cocking the hammer before he said, "Set the coin."

Digging Badger needed two tries to lay the coin flat on the octagonal barrel without it sliding off. With the coin in place, Black Wolf squeezed the trigger, but the coin did not fall from the barrel even after the hammer fell. He explained the importance to Digging Badger.

"Until you can click the trigger without the coin falling, there's no need to load the rifle. This part of practice is slow, but it guides you to shoot straight. It is more important to shoot straight than shoot fast and miss."

Digging Badger nodded. He repeated what Black Wolf had said to Running Elk who screwed up his lips and nose in frustration.

Black Wolf loaded his rifle. He asked Running

Elk to kneel, handing him the rifle before pointing to the target sticks. He instructed Running Elk how to cock it.

Running Elk fired immediately. His shot kicked up dirt at the top of the arroyo, far to the right of the sticks.

Digging Badger knelt next to Running Elk, pointing his arm, and speaking soft words. When Digging Badger finished, he patted Running Elk's shoulder while he stood.

"I told Running Elk when you shot, barrel didn't move. When he shot, barrel jumped before rifle fired. I told him to listen to Black Wolf. Practice as you teach him. When he shoots a stick, we go hunting together. Until he shoots straight, he practices with Black Wolf. I leave you now. Don't stay too long." He placed his hand on Black Wolf's shoulder before he trotted away.

Black Wolf held up ten fingers before pointing to Running Elk. He guided Running Elk into a good position before cocking the rifle. He placed the coin on the end of the barrel. Running Elk jerked the trigger, causing the coin to fall.

He set the rifle aside to teach Running Elk to squeeze, using only his trigger-finger and thumb. He used the proper squeeze to pinch Running Elk's finger. Then Running Elk squeezed his trigger-finger and thumb on Black Wolf's finger making each one press equally.

After a few times squeezing Black Wolf's finger, Running Elk learned to stop jerking his trigger-finger, squeezing with constant pressure between thumb and trigger-finger.

Once Running Elk smoothed his trigger pull, Black Wolf returned to the rifle to practice shooting again. Pascal called this "dry-fire" because it didn't use powder. By the last two of ten dry-fires practices, Running Elk squeezed the trigger without the coin falling.

Running Elk wanted to shoot the rifle now, but Black Wolf signed "tomorrow" in the trade language. He signed Digging Badger said to practice as Black Wolf showed him. Running Elk frowned, but nodded he understood "tomorrow."

Next, he taught Running Elk how to clean the rifle. Running Elk found pissing into the barrel hilarious. He pointed at Nigel's pants, saying Cheyenne words while laughing.

Blossom had prepared a meal for them when the pair returned to her *vee'e*.

While they ate, Running Elk spoke to Blossom. They broke into laughter.

Blossom laughed, before asking *en español*, "You piss in rifle barrel?"

Black Wolf's face burned in embarrassment. He couldn't speak, stammering, while nodding. *No woman ever asked him about pissing.* It wasn't something women asked men, in his minister's son world.

Blossom asked in her limited *español*, "Why you do that? Rifle shame you?"

Nigel stammered once more, but squeaked, "Men don't talk to women about doing that."

Blossom laughed, mussing his hair, a sign she wanted him to talk to her.

"Why not? It natural. All do it, even mothers," she said.

He attempted changing the subject, to ease his embarrassment.

"Mule Man said it cleans burnt powder from the barrel. Mule Man said *los francés* army did that in the war to clean their guns quickly. It removes the spent powder."

Blossom burst out laughing, repeated his words to Running Elk. They sat laughing for several minutes. Blossom made another comment causing them to laugh some more.

Blossom faced him with an open-mouth smile showing her amusement.

"Dream Blue Coats shoot rifles. Stop shooting. Use 'pizzle' … piss in barrel. They forget. Piss at the enemy. Shoot own 'pizzle.'" Blossom laughed so hard, she struggled to talk.

It offended Black Wolf at first, because he thought they laughed at him, but when he thought about it, he admitted it'd be a funny sight. He grew puzzled by Blossom's calm talk of a man pissing and saying "pizzle." *White women don't talk like that, do they?*

He couldn't imagine his mother, or his sisters, ever saying those words aloud, let alone saying them to a man. It confused and embarrassed him to think about saying such to a woman.

After the midday meal, she worked him in Cheyenne, teaching him phrases. "I want food. I want water. I want sleep. I want run. I want ride horse. I am hurt. I not understand. Enemy comes. Need help. Go bring help. Warn people. Wait for me. Come to me. Follow me. Do as me. Yes. No. Stop. "

Why is Pascal always right? Will my lessons never end?

Running Elk and Black Wolf visited the arroyo to practice the next morning, but didn't shoot the rifle. He helped Running Elk develop smooth motion when he aimed the rifle before pulling the trigger. He showed his new brother how to use the sights pieces to align on a target.

Tall Bear came that afternoon, leading Running Elk and Black Wolf to a meadow across the stream to practice with the bow. Running Elk hit the target, a buckskin pouch stuffed with grass, about every third time he shot. His arrows fell close to the target, even when he missed.

Black Wolf struggled to pull the bowstring back very far. As a result, his arrows didn't reach the target.

Tall Bear grew bored watching the young men practice. He stood and barked words at Running Elk before he strode across the stream, heading toward Blossom's *vee'e*. By observing the glare on Running Elk's face, Black Wolf understood his brother didn't like Tall Bear's visits to his mother's *vee'e*.

Running Elk handed his own bow to Black Wolf, while he retrieved their arrows.

Black Wolf didn't want to practice any longer.

He thought Running Elk tried to return the favor of shooting lessons Black Wolf had given his brother.

Running Elk said, "*ma'tse-ske*," and made a motion like pulling the bow.

Black Wolf pulled the bowstring on Running Elk's bow, becoming surprised at how far he could pull it. He loosed an arrow past the target.

Tall Bear made a fool of me. Again.

Running Elk grabbed the bow Tall Bear had given Black Wolf, pulling its bowstring. Running Elk failed to pull it, too. The bow had dried, becoming too stiff to use as a weapon.

Black Wolf grew angry at Tall Bear's tricks. He said in Cheyenne, "I want ride horse."

Running Elk shook his head, "No. Follow me."

He led Black Wolf to Old Wolf's *vee'e*, where the old man sat outside whittling on a bone. Running Elk handed Black Wolf's bow to Old Wolf.

Old Wolf grunted before bending it. He broke Tall Bear's old, useless bow over his knee. Before he threw it in the fire, he retrieved the bowstring. He pointed at the bowstring saying, "*ma'tano*," motioning Black Wolf to repeat the word.

Old Wolf struggled to rise, entered his *vee'e*. He returned a few minutes later with two bow staffs. He strung Tall Bear's bowstring on one of his bows, handing it to Black Wolf.

He struggled to pull it all the way back to his nose.

Old Wolf held out his hand, recovering the staff before he removed the bowstring. He placed the bowstring on the second bow, handing it to Black Wolf.

Black Wolf pulled this bow back to his nose with effort.

Old Wolf spoke to him softly in *Français*.

"Use my bow until you get stronger. Come to me each morning when you rise. I will teach you to make your own bow, *ma'tse-ske*, bowstring, *ma'tano* and arrows, *maa-he*, that shoot straight. You must bring me three turkeys you shot on the wing before you leave us. This is the last time I'll speak *Français*. You must show us you aren't an ignorant savage."

Old Wolf resumed whittling. The People prized his totems, earning him many gifts.

Running Elk slapped Black Wolf's arm, saying in Cheyenne, "I want ride horse," before they raced to the herd across the stream. The two young men rode until the sun sank to set. They walked their horses to the herd, wiping them with tufts of grass to dry their coat.

They returned together to Blossom's tipi to eat their evening meal.

After the evening meal, Blossom worked on Black Wolf's new moccasins and leggings while they practiced Cheyenne phrases. Running Elk left to visit with his friends after the evening meal, and stayed late.

Black Wolf prayed for his lost family as he lay on his blanket, drifting to sleep.

And another day had passed.

Black Wolf worked with Old Wolf each morning, even after he'd made a new bow and several arrows. Black Wolf ran to a different area each morning before the sky brightened, setting snares before he ran. He returned with the game he caught for Old Wolf's fire. Old Wolf complained he'd grow fat with the extra food. One morning it rained, and he caught no game. Old Wolf grumbled in mock bitterness, complaining how he'd starve because Black Wolf failed to bring fresh game.

Old Wolf told great stories, and when he used a Cheyenne word Black Wolf didn't understand, Old Wolf complained before saying it in *Français*. He'd slap the back of Black Wolf's head, saying "ignorant savage" in *Français*.

And the days passed.

Running Elk and Black Wolf took turns firing the rifle every other morning. Running Elk became a good shot with the target rifle.

Digging Badger visited to observe on occasion. One day, he carried a couple of sticks of wood and a thong. He told them to stop, while he walked down to the arroyo. He drove the tall stick in the ground, then tied a thong around the other stick and hung it so that he could keep it swinging at a steady pace. Digging Badger sat off to one side pulling the thong, making the target swing. He said, "Shoot."

Black Wolf said, "You are too close. We might hit you by mistake."

Digging Badger laughed, "Even if you did, a pea

won't hurt me."

He didn't like shooting this way, but Digging Badger acted so calm, they commenced shooting. The youngsters needed several shots to learn the timing of when to fire. After several days of that practice, Digging Badger threw the pouch used for an arrow target up in the air, catching it when it fell.

Black Wolf gauged where he thought the pouch stopped rising, hitting it on his third try.

Digging Badger noticed what Black Wolf had done. He tied a long thong onto the pouch, throwing it in an arc before pulling it to him with the thong. Digging Badger wanted them to hit the pouch in the air, but he allowed them to shoot it when he pulled it across the ground.

Soon, Digging Badger came to the bow practice with Tall Bear, playing the same game while the young men loosed arrows. The other boys joined them in loosing arrows at the pouch while Tall Bear and he tossed the pouch back and forth.

The Southern Cheyenne had formed a training program for the youngsters as they approached their ceremony of the man. They learned the basics of traditional hunting skills. As best as Black Wolf understood they called it The Rabbit Society. Neither the men nor the boys liked him asking questions.

Black Wolf practiced his timing, and rarely missed with either bow or rifle. Running Elk became equally as good. By now, four young teens went everywhere together.

Running Elk's friends, Spotted Horse and Red Knife, often joined in their adventures.

They wrestled each other, they ran, they practiced stalking animals, they raced their horses, and teased the girls. That was all The People expected of boys their age.

The warm sunny days of spring passed.

The days became weeks.

One morning, everyone in the camp rose at first light. The women stripped the *vee'e*, loading their belongings on a travois made from the *vee'e* support poles. Blossom explained the time had come to move the camp. The horses had grazed all the grass in the meadow. Wild game became too hard to find.

"We will move the camp north to find water, good grass for the horses, and more game meat. Maybe we find buffalo. After many suns, it becomes time to move again," she said.

Blossom sent Running Elk to bring in their horses. She told Black Wolf to wrap his things in his buffalo robes, tying them tight, before carrying them outside.

Running Elk and Blossom had removed most of the *vee'e*'s hide cover when Black Wolf carried his robes and personal gear to the growing pile of goods outside the *vee'e*.

"How did you move like this when you had no horses?" Black Wolf asked.

She smiled her gentle welcoming smile and patted his arm. "Now you know why Black Kettle had you stay with us. We needed help. He shamed Tall Bear for not giving us ponies. He knows what happens in his camp. He keeps it peaceful."

Blossom showed them how to tie the vee'e poles to make the travois and how to tie the hide *vee'e* sections on the poles. Black Wolf's gear filled one travois and theirs filled a second.

Running Elk asked his mother to ride his horse, while the teens strode alongside the horses pulling the travois. Blossom moved about talking to other women on horseback.

Black Wolf noticed Digging Badger lead four young braves in front to scout ahead.

Blossom said, "Their job is to keep us from being surprised by our enemies, the Comanche, Kiowa, or Pawnee, while we are spread like this."

Looking behind the column, he glimpsed a herd of horses, smaller now because they used so many horses to move the camp. Black Kettle had assigned Tall Bear to lead the young braves driving the small herd.

Blossom pointed to unmarried and seasoned warriors who rode on each side, again to prevent a quick strike by their enemies. Black Kettle's band spread in a line almost a mile long, traveling at a child's pace compared to Pascal's pace when moving mules. He thought they would be lucky to make twelve miles this day, but they were in no hurry.

While he considered this band moving their village, he understood why Pascal became careful when the train traveled across the open prairie like this. They had no place to hide if attacked in the open prairie.

Pascal lacked mounted scouts to warn or protect him as Black Kettle did. Black Wolf straightened in surprise. *Charbonneau!* That is why Pascal hired the man. He scouted the land to avoid the Redman when possible. Black Wolfe still didn't like the man, or his attitude, but he gained an understanding of why, and what Pascal attempted to accomplish this season.

About the time of Pascal's usual afternoon rest, excited voices pointed to Digging Badger on a small rise. The village knew this meant they'd come to the next camp. He had grown accustomed to walking daily while helping to keep the mule-train moving, so he knew what to expect on this type of working day. The clouds to the southwest worried him because they had grown taller and darker as the afternoon wore on. By the time they reached the rise where they had seen Digging Badger, the wind whipped about them followed by a crack of thunder. Black Kettle's band moved into a shallow valley where a stream meandered along its center. Leafy cottonwoods grew where the stream turned. A series of beaver dams upstream formed sparkling blue pools. The grass in the area grew thick and lush following the spring rains.

Pascal would have picked a spot like this.

Lightning flashed with a sharp crack, followed by a loud clap of thunder. The People froze in place. He twisted around to behold the horse remuda scattering with Tall Bear and his braves in pursuit. Several people had shift their gear to unload their travois, letting the poles loose to set up their *vee'e*.

Black Kettle shouted for everyone to stop setting up their *vee'e* while the wind grew fierce. He motioned for those on the rise to join them quickly. People used a piece of *vee'e* hide to cover their belongings and another piece to cower beneath when the sudden rain pelted them.

It grew darker, as if the sun had set, before the clouds lightened to a strange greenish-gray color. The wind created an eerie howl and round pieces of ice fell from the sky.

Blossom, Running Elk, and Black Wolf huddled together under a thick buffalo hide as the rain and falling ice thumped them. Blossom instructed Running Elk and Black Wolf to sit on each corner, pulled the upper portion across to cover them while she sat on the other end to hold it down. The fierce wind tugged at the hide from every direction while they clung to the hide. People wailed in fear before the howling sound faded and ice balls stopped falling. The heavy rain continued for another hour, and by then, true night fell. The storm left The People in the camp wet, cold, and unhappy. Many claimed the storm as a bad omen, wanting to move on.

Black Kettle walked among them, calling to his people.

"Don't try to set up *vee'e* in the dark. Wait until morning. Sleep under the *vee'e* hides tonight. I'll decide if we need to move tomorrow at first light.

Rest and eat now. Stay away from the water. It is rising and moving fast. Keep the children close. Wood is too wet for fires tonight. Rest and eat now."

His presence and words calmed his people, but they remained wet and unhappy.

Huddled together, Black Wolf asked, "The People acted afraid of lightning and thunder. I know it frightened me. I thought the men acted more afraid when the lightning cracked nearby."

Blossom spoke in a whisper, "Don't let the men hear you say that, even if it were true."

She sat silent a while before whispering *en español,* "Don't speak of lightning, *'vovo'ho' kase'ha,'* and thunder, *'ho'o-tse-o-tse.'* These symbols have special meaning to us. They are messages from the spirits. Sometimes these signs mean good luck. Other times they are bad omens. The men will call off a hunt or an attack on the enemy, if there is a storm like today. It is a bad sign when the black winds howl and, *'ao'estse-to-no-tse eame-h-ne-ton-estse,'* ice falls. The spirits have sent us a message. Tomorrow, Old Wolf will tell us what it means. Never speak of this with The People. The whites need not know what the spirits tells us or when."

She said no more that night. Her wide-eyed gaze told him she too was frightened.

He said prayers for his lost family. His thoughts shifted, unsettled. In the past months, he'd blamed all Redmen for his family's loss, but The People knew nothing of their death.

He couldn't grant forgiveness, but focused his blame on the Comanche alone.

He said prayers for his new family.

Heathen or not, they represented all the family he had this summer.

~~~~~~

Old Wolf advised Black Kettle to move in a day or two, after the stream bank dried enough for people and horses to cross without bogging in the mud. The scouts reported upstream, above the beaver dam, the storm uprooted many trees. Old Wolf advised people to stay away from the area. Of course, Old Wolf's warning made everyone curious and many, including Black Wolf, Running Elk, and Blossom, rode to survey the area.

The storm destroyed a hundred-foot section of trees along the stream, tearing trees from the ground by their roots, tossing them willy-nilly. The storm left a sixty-foot wide swath from the ridge, across the stream, and onto the prairie. It resembled the destruction of a huge buffalo herd stampeding across the valley, crushing everything along that swath. Black Wolf failed to imagine what had caused it. Black Kettle's people surveyed the damage in silence. They reached a general agreement that they'd be happy to move today.

Under Black Kettle's leadership, the *Wotápio* band moved farther north two days later, after waiting for their goods to dry. The People grew anxious to move, leaving bad memories of the strange damage upstream. The storm had soaked everything. The village spread items to dry in the warm sun. The area resembled a gypsy camp he once visited in Wales, not the orderly and well-organized camp he first visited.

~~~~~~

Blossom spread her *vee'e* hides to dry before they repacked to move the next day. She told Running Elk and Black Wolf to set their belongings out to dry. While searching the supplies LaFleur sent with him, he found two ten-inch Green River knives, and two iron 'trade' tomahawks. When they ate, Black Wolf gave one knife to Running Elk and one to Blossom.

When he unwrapped the iron tomahawks, both Cheyenne hissed at the weapons.

He failed to understand what caused their angry reaction. "What is wrong?"

"The handles are wrapped and marked by Comanche. If you won these in battle, it would be a mark of pride. If your father gave you those, it would be acceptable for you to use them. You are too young. It would be an insult to Tall Bear to use those."

"I don't understand. Why would Tall Bear be insulted?"

"It shows he is not a strong enough warrior to take such prizes to give to you."

"It is not about Tall Bear. They are mine. The Mule Man took them in trade."

"All the more reason you must not use them. You appear as friends of the Comanche."

"If I rub out the markings, removing the leather so not like Comanche, can I use them?"

"Do you have a hard tool to scrape the design or cover it with a sign of The People?"

"Yes, the file I use to sharpen it. I can scratch a mark of The People atop this."

"I will show you a common sign for a wolf. If you mark it like that, I will cut a piece of wet hide to shrink tight, covering the wooden handle. I will ask Peacemaker Woman to come up with a good reason for showing them now. That way others will not wonder why you have not used one before now."

"My birthday is next week. Can we say Mule Man said not to unwrap his gift until my birthday? That is why I am using them now."

"What is a 'birth' day?" Blossom asked with her eyebrows bunched in confusion.

"It marks the day I was born. It makes me another year older. We give small gifts."

"The People mark periods by the moon. Running Elk become a man during Facing Into Moon, four moons from now. It is proper in the year you become a man your father gives a gift, such as these tomahawks. We will ask Peacemaker Woman to tell Black Kettle. He will ask to see them, and then he will return them to you, with his approval. Tall Bear will have no say."

Black Wolf worked each night after their evening meal that week to file out the Comanche sign. He used the file's sharp edge to create the wolf mark Blossom had shown him. Blossom used a piece of hide to make a sleeve with laces, fitting each wooden handle. When the hide dried, shrinking, the laces along the front improved the grip. Running Elk examined them carefully before approving.

The next day Peacemaker Woman told Black Kettle about the gift. As expected, he asked to see the tomahawks. He made a comment about the wolf sign, saying, "Black Wolf has become a Cheyenne." He returned them to Black Wolf, as predicted. Tall Bear didn't learn about the tomahawks until later, when he could say nothing.

Four days after the big storm, Black Kettle's band relocated to a small creek feeding into what the whites called the Republican River, twenty miles farther north on the prairie. Black Kettle told his people they planned to move the horse pasture area each day so they could remain longer in this camp. He told them they would cross the Republican River for the next camp, crossing it after the spring flood receded. Black Kettle said in a moon they would continue north, crossing the South Platte. They planned to camp beside the Northern Cheyenne to hunt buffalo in the land between the two branches of the Platte.

"After the rendezvous, Black Kettle will travel south again, arriving in the Big Timbers area by the end of the Fall Moon. Black Kettle wanted to establish a winter camp in the area along the Arkansas near Big Timbers," Blossom said.

The village settled into its routine after leaving the "bad omen" area, allowing The Rabbit Society to resume daily practice. Black Wolf grew concerned the fathers of his friends, Spotted Horse and Red Knife, never came to practice. One evening, Black Wolf asked Blossom about it.

"It is the Way of The People to separate father and son for this training," Blossom said. "Often the mother's brothers help train her son. If those uncles aren't available, the father's brothers are asked. Sometimes a father and son are too much alike causing the lessons to become a contest where no one wins. The People found the son learns better from an uncle or from another friendly man."

"Another 'friendly' man? How did Tall Bear get assigned to Running Elk?"

"Black Kettle hoped it would teach Tall Bear more consideration of others. It may not seem like it to you, but Tall Bear has improved. I think Digging Badger is responsible for that. Tall Bear has always respected Digging Badger, and allows Digging Badger to give him counsel. Of course, Digging Badger is the Bowstring leader."

Yellow Blossom paused, glancing away, "We must stop talking about this."

"I am sorry. Did I say something wrong? I did not mean to upset you."

"I would not discuss these things with Running Elk, even though I know it bothers him. I speak with you like a man of my family. It is not right for us to talk like friends. Now that you speak our language, you should talk to others besides Old Wolf."

Noticing his reaction, she laughed. "Yes, I know you and Old Wolf get together many mornings. You must spend time with Running Elk in the evening, speaking with the young people your age, particularly the young women. They ask about you often."

"Is that where Running Elk goes at night?" Black Wolf asked. "What do I talk about?"

"Ask Running Elk if you can go with him in the evening when his friends meet with other young people. The villagers are curious. They want to talk to you. It would be rude to come close, asking personal questions. If you are among the young people, they will ask you questions. Answer them as you have spoken with Running Elk and me. Glance at people's face, but look away, never stare. When you answer their questions, smile. You are becoming a handsome young man if you don't appear so grim or angry. Learn to smile more, and joke or tease with the other boys, you'll find the girls will do the talking." Blossom tickled his ribs with both hands. "Relax, smile, and answer their questions. Let them get to know you," she said.

"You make life sound so easy. Relax, smile, talk to people."

"Ask Running Elk about it tomorrow. I think you may be surprised."

After The Rabbit Society practice, Black Wolf asked, "May I join you this evening?"

"I wondered why you didn't asked to join me," Running Elk said. "I thought when your Cheyenne became better you'd ask to come with me at night."

At first, the other young people remained quiet when Black Wolf accompanied Running Elk. However, their curiosity got the better of them, and the usual banter carried on. The young men wanted to know about his rifle.

"What is it like to shoot every day?" became a common question.

"What animals have you killed with your rifle?"

"What Indians, other than Comanche and Kiowa, had he seen?"

"Did you fight with them?"

"Did they try to steal your mules?"

The young boys agreed mules made good eating, but not as good as horses.

One of the other boys wanted to know why Black Wolf used his "wolf's red knob" to piss on his rifle to clean it.

Black Wolf did not understand what they asked.

"What is my 'wolf's red knob'? I don't understand?" Black Wolf asked.

They looked at each other for a few moments before Spotted Horse answered, "When a dog or a wolf mates, its pizzle sticks from its sheath. Those animals have a red knob on the end of their pizzle. The wolf has a bigger red knob than a dog. We thought you were named for the wolf because you have a big red knob on your pizzle, like the wolf."

Black Wolf grew so embarrassed he sat open-mouthed, gasping, saying nothing at first.

"I never studied a dog's pizzle. Never been close enough to a wolf to study its pizzle. I didn't know those animals had a knob on their pizzle." The topic shocked the minister's son.

"Sometimes a dog will get stuck in the female because his knob is too big. Has your knob ever been stuck in a female?" Red Knife said.

The boys joined in laughter at that question.

Black Wolf lacked understanding. "All pizzles are the same, aren't they?"

The other young men laughed, slapping one another's arm or back.

Black Wolf experienced a flash of understanding. *His father thought Christ-loving Christians should follow Christ's example of circumcising a month after birth. He had Nigel circumcised as an infant.*

Nigel had no comparison until now to recognize the difference in his pizzle. He never understood what circumcision meant, because he had never gazed at another man's pizzle to notice the difference. Speaking about your pizzle, or another man's pizzle, let alone a dog's pizzle, never ever occurred in the Reverend John Blackthorn's home. Nigel's mother was as strict as his father was about profanity. She forbade any mention of body organs or functions.

Black Wolf never had gazed upon an uncircumcised pizzle any more than the Cheyenne had gazed upon a circumcised pizzle like Black Wolf's. No wonder they thought it funny.

Three young women strolled past, causing the young men to follow them. They dropped the earlier subject as they followed, striking up a discussion with the young women.

Later in the week, Black Wolf and Running Elk asked Tall Bear if he would teach them how to throw the tomahawk.

He grumbled, as usual. "You don't throw away your tomahawk. You use it to strike your enemy when he is close. Throwing is not important. You want to feel your enemy's blood hot on your skin when you kill with a tomahawk. You want to feel his last breath on you so that his spirit fears you, as his body did in life."

Black Wolf noticed changes in his posture and face, as if saying these words aroused Tall Bear's angry fighting spirit.

Tall Bear shoved both young men, shouting at them. "You are children. You think this a game. The buffalo herds grow smaller and harder to find. White men kill them for their skins."

Tall Bear knocked Black Wolf to the ground with the butt of his lance before he handed it to Running Elk. "Show me you are ready to become a man. Kill this white man now while he is small. When this white man is grown, he will kill you."

Digging Badger, observing Tall Bear's outburst, trotted close, speaking soft words to calm Tall Bear. "Black Wolf has Black Kettle's protection. If you harm Black Wolf, I must kill you. You are our finest warrior. I need you to protect us from our enemies. We must not fight among ourselves. Black Wolf is not our enemy. You know Mule Man does not kill buffalo. He trades with us. He honors agreements. He refuses to sell bad whiskey or guns to any. He trades metal and food. Mule Man is not our enemy. Leave these young men to me. Don't be angry."

Tall Bear stalked away, still angry. They observed him riding from the camp.

Digging Badger helped Black Wolf regain his feet. "Are you hurt?"

Black Wolf shook his head to signal no, but Tall Bear's outburst left him a little shaken.

Digging Badger placed a hand on each teen's shoulder. "It does not have to be that one must kill the other. One day, when you are both men, we shall sit and talk about this. Black Wolf, you are not our enemy. The white man has made many promises. They have not kept one promise. Each time they take more of our hunting grounds, leaving us with nothing. If they would stay away, we would not fight them. These are the problems of men. They are not the problems of The Rabbit Society, not until you are men."

Digging Badger faced Black Wolf. "Do you trust Running Elk with your life?"

"Of course. He is my brother," Black Wolf replied.

Digging Badger then faced Running Elk, "Black Wolf trusts his life to you. Do not dishonor the trust of your brother."

Digging Badger asked, "Do you trust Black Wolf with your life?"

"I trust Black Wolf will not kill me," Running Elk said.

Digging Badger faced Black Wolf, "Running Elk trusts his life to you. Do not dishonor the trust of your brother."

Digging Badger straightened before saying, "Tall Bear is right about one thing. In battle, do not throw your tomahawk or your knife. Use it to kill an enemy close to you. I know it's fun to try throwing the knife and the tomahawk. I will not stop you from throwing them, but do not do it when you practice with the other weapons. If you want to throw, throw the lance."

Digging Badger shifted away but returned, "I know young men test who is the bravest by throwing knives at one another, testing who flinched in fear. I don't like the game. If I catch you two doing it, or you get hurt doing it, you'll find I'm worse than Tall Bear when disobeyed."

With Digging Badger's stern warning ringing in their ears, the two gazed at one another in amazement.

"I would not have struck you with the lance," Running Elk said.

"I know. Tall Bear is angry. I understand his anger. When I think of my sisters stolen by the Comanche, I want to kill them. Black Kettle is right. We have many years of practice before we can kill our enemies."

"That means we must practice more," Running Elk said, grinning.

"We can still throw the knife and tomahawk, if alone," Black Wolf said with a grin.

"Yes," said Running Elk, sharing the laugh.

The days passed.

~~~~~~

The four young men, Running Elk, Spotted Horse, Red Knife, and Black Wolf, became accomplished horsemen. They tried every conceivable trick from horseback. Their antics often became a source of amusement for the women. Blossom expressed her amazement none of them received more serious injuries than scrapes, bruises and sprains.

The days passed.

It surprised Black Wolf to learn most Cheyenne warriors rode a hand-made saddle when hunting or riding in a raiding party. Cheyenne constructed a saddle from two pieces of wood tied in the front to form a small "tree" with an identical arrangement in the rear to form a raised cantle. The saddletree resembled an upside down "V," making the Cheyenne saddle lightweight. They covered each "V" with wet deerskin that shrank, molding to the "tree's" shape. The seat formed from a piece of wet deer hide, draped like a hammock between the trees. Successive layers gave the hammock strength. Warriors spent many hours carving the wooden tree to fit their favorite war pony before applying the first layer of deer hide to the tree. The Cheyenne saddle used a cinch strap tied under the horse's belly like a Mexican saddle. The saddle allowed the rider a brace against the cantle when stabbing a buffalo or an enemy with their lance. The Cheyenne covered the saddle with a blanket when riding. However, when performing tricks on horseback, the Cheyenne didn't use a saddle.

The youths became accomplished hunters. Their teenaged rivalry spurred them to outperform one another. Digging Badger encouraged their competition. He varied the training to hold their interest. He had Tall Bear continue working with the teens on using the lance. Tall Bear had powerful arms and shoulders. He drove a lance into a buffalo's heart, bringing the huge animal to the ground with one killing blow. Tall Bear thought the young men not ready to hunt buffalo because, being smaller, they lacked the strength to kill a buffalo.

Digging Badger continued teaching them basic hunting skills. The young men learned to move quietly in the woods, so the birds didn't fly away in a burst, warning of their presence. The proof of their practice became hunting. Digging Badger sent the young men in pairs, or as individuals, to learn to survive alone for days at a time. The tests grew more difficult with each trial. Black Wolf grasped a fun game had turned serious because it became part of the ceremony leading to manhood for the Cheyenne youths.

While he contemplated during these exercises, Black Wolf thought of Pascal's lessons in survival he drilled into Nigel during those early days. Those lessons drifted away during his summer with The People, yet he knew his lessons would never end if he wanted to survive.

The days passed.

The days became weeks.

The weeks became months.

The prairie grew hot with long days.

Chapter 16

August to October, 1855

The people in Black Kettle's camp accepted Black Wolf. Blossom made him a buckskin *neh-pe-so'h-est-o-tse* (breechcloth) similar to what Running Elk wore. In the summer sun, Black Wolf tanned deeply and wore his long black hair in a single braid past his neck, like The People. From a distance, Black Wolf resembled any of the young men. They spent the summer learning hunting and fighting skills like other young men of The People. The men's ability to hunt and fight made Black Kettle's band strong and respected.

As Black Wolf learned to speak the language of The People, he grew to understand the value of his training, growing at ease while living among The People in Black Kettle's camp.

The weapons training progressed from bow and arrow to the lance. Digging Badger joined the training often when Tall Bear taught the lance. Spotted Horse and Red Knife joined the lessons while one of their uncles attended. When the young men improved their skills, they practiced from horseback. At first, they practiced with the bow on a horse standing still. As their accuracy improved, then they learned to shoot the bow from a moving horse. The young men used this time to improve their horsemanship, learning how to mount by jumping on a running horse, moving between running horses, and loosing arrows from under the horse's neck. Several young Bowstring braves rode across the practice field, showing their riding skills while letting the youngsters observe their skills.

Black Wolf gaped in amazement as the young braves performed a running mount by holding onto the horse's mane, lifting their feet off the ground before touching their feet down using the horse's momentum to vault their body onto the back of the running horse. The finest example of this skill came when, mounted on a running horse, the men would slide from one side, let their feet touch the ground before vaulting to the other side. They touched their feet on the ground again before vaulting to straddle the galloping horse without it ever breaking stride.

The Rabbit Society youngsters fell from their horses often. Their spectacular falls created great amusement among the braves and the village. Many bumps and bruises occurred. Black Wolf learned The People expected the youngsters to get up and ride again without complaints. He observed people coming to the practice field to watch the youngsters learn horsemanship. Everyone laughed and joked. They offered good-natured teasing for those who fell. The entire camp shared a relaxed time as their youth progressed toward manhood. Nigel never considered the Redman living in a family unit, or being a people with a sense of humor. In some ways, Black Kettle's village resembled the small village where he was born, except this village had no roots, but roamed across the prairie.

By mid-summer, Black Kettle's band joined a "rendezvous" with the Northern Cheyenne in the land between where two rivers joined. A large band of Arapaho joined the buffalo hunt. Black Wolf found the Cheyenne and Arapaho languages similar, and the two nations remained peaceable with one another.

At this time, Black Wolf dressed in a *neh-pe-so'h-est-o-tse* (breechcloth) and leggings like Running Elk and the other Cheyenne. He learned enough Arapaho language to speak with those who visited in Black Kettle's camp. One or two asked about his eye color. He told them his name, saying he used the wolf spirit totem. The Arapaho nodded in understanding.

Northeast of the North Platte River, the land of the Lakota nation extended into the Black Hills, more than three hundred miles away. An alliance existed between the Lakota and the Northern Cheyenne, which they extended to include the Southern Cheyenne and the Arapaho. They formed the alliance to join in a common defense against the white settlers encroaching on their traditional hunting lands. The Redmen grew weary of retreating to make room for the whites. They became angry that buffalo herds shrank smaller each year.

Along the South Platte, Black Kettle led his men in a buffalo hunt. The men let Running Elk and Black Wolf follow along to guard the men's ponies. Black Kettle's skill impressed Black Wolf when the leader rode into a small herd to drive his lance deep into a cow that ran twenty yards before she collapsed. Black Wolf noticed Peacemaker Woman among the women who descended upon Black Kettle's kill. The women's skill fascinated Black Wolf with their quick and efficient skinning and butchering of a downed buffalo. Peacemaker Woman helped another woman load heavy meat sections onto the mule Pascal gave to Black Kettle. They returned the meat and hides to the camp, where other women worked to preserve the hides and meat. The entire camp held a ceremony to celebrate the harvest of buffalo for the long winter ahead. They built a bonfire that night where both men and women danced in celebration.

The *Hisiometä'nio* (Ridge People) band camped near Black Kettle's camp, Black Wolf noticed many braves of both camps dressed in a similar fashion. These men guarded the camp, led the hunting parties, and patrolled the area to prevent raids by their enemies, the Comanche and the Pawnee. The story spread that these men had raided the Pawnee earlier. He spoke enough Cheyenne that after the men returned, he gathered they had a successful raid.

Black Wolf questioned Blossom about it.

She glanced about to notice if any stood nearby, signing quiet. Blossom motioned him into the *vee'e* before speaking *en español*, "I knew you would ask one day. I told Digging Badger he should discuss it with you. He said it is not your place to know. I will tell you this much, but you must never say anything to anyone."

Blossom continued speaking *en español* to prevent others from overhearing her. "The white man and our enemies have attacked The People for many seasons. The People grow weary of fighting and running. Many years ago, The People split into two groups to allow each group to follow one of the great buffalo herds that live to the North and South. This allowed more hunting and grazing areas for each group, but it also allowed our enemies to attack the smaller bands. The People selected strong men as our soldiers. These men protect their band from the enemy. They help provide food and shelter. They formed secret societies within each band. Years ago, the Kiowa and Comanche killed most of our society in a battle. The problems with the white man are forcing us to reform the men's society. They do not want their enemies to know who they are or what they do to become powerful, so the enemy cannot learn how to defeat them. The *Hĭ-má'tanó-hĭs* or "Strong Bowstrings" protect Black Kettle's band. A white man should not know about these things. In the next few weeks, The People from North and South will meet with the Arapaho and the Lakota, to decide what course to follow with the white man. They built a separate ceremonial ground for this, and they will not allow you to go there, or listen to what is said. It is for The People alone to know. Ask no questions about this with anyone except Digging Badger, and only if alone with him. The People trust you. To talk of this openly would break that trust. Please do not dishonor us."

With that statement, Blossom fled from the *vee'e*, acting as though they'd never spoken.

Trees covered most of the land between the two forks of the Platte. A large grove stretched from bank to bank at their confluence. Plentiful small game existed in these areas, leading the young men to make a great adventure of hunting these areas. The youngsters crawled on all fours to stalk deer and turkey. It sharpened their hunting skills while giving them an excuse for being away all day. Black Wolf learned deer used turkey to alert them to danger. If the turkeys flew or hid, then the deer became alert and hid also. Thus, the young men studied the tracks on the ground to find common feeding areas within the grove for hunting turkey and deer. Digging Badger used his lessons for this purpose, hunting.

Black Wolf hunted in earnest for a turkey to fulfill his pledge to Old Wolf, as the young man promised two moons ago. He discovered getting in range of a turkey became more difficult than bringing it down with an arrow. The turkeys grew into crafty birds in the wild and easily spooked. Black Wolf slinked through the undergrowth hoping to come within range of a flock of turkeys feeding within the grove. Running Elk crawled behind Black Wolf while Spotted Horse crawled next, bringing up the rear.

He continued the habit of carrying his "possibles-bag," even when not carrying his rifle. While crawling on all fours, his "possibles-bag" dragged on the ground between his arms and legs, leaving a furrow in the dirt. The turkeys leapt into flight after a noise popped behind him, where Running Elk and Spotted Horse laughed.

"What are you doing? That is the closest I've come to a turkey," Black Wolf grumbled.

Running Elk grew silent, glancing down as if shamed, but Spotted Horse continued laughing. The young men resumed pushing and shoving.

"What is so funny that you interrupted the hunt?" Black Wolf asked, upset by their noise.

Running Elk motioned for him to study his tracks in the dust where he had crawled.

His path showed the imprint of his left hand somewhat covered by the imprint of his left knee. He made a similar track where his right knee imprint almost wiped out his right hand imprint. However, in the middle of the two paths lay a wide furrow in the dust.

Spotted Horse burst into laughter. "I told Running Elk that Black Wolf's pizzle dragged the ground to mark his territory." Spotted Horse and Running Elk laughed aloud at their joke.

Black Wolf laughed in spite of being upset they had spoiled his hunt. He didn't bother telling them his "possibles-bag," hanging from his chest, made the furrow.

Instead Black Wolf asked, "Is that all you think about? Your pizzle?"

"No, it is not all," said Running Elk, "I dream about lying beside White Fawn."

"I thought Blossom said the young men were not supposed to lie with the young women until they completed the ceremony to become a man?"

"Do you always do everything you are supposed to, Black Wolf?" Spotted Horse asked.

"Yes, he does," Running Elk said, wrestling Black Wolf to the ground. "Even if I cannot lie with them, I ask them to stroke my pizzle. And don't you tell Mother I said that."

"I don't tell on you to Mother," Black Wolf said before twisting to roll on top of Running Elk, "Besides, you aren't supposed to stroke your pizzle for worldly pleasure."

"I don't stroke it. I let the young women stroke it for me," Running Elk said, laughing after Black Wolf released him.

Spotted Horse broke into laughter again, pointing at the bulge in Black Wolf's breechcloth. "I think the Wolf's red knob speaks for itself. We should find a young woman who wants to stroke his wolf's knob."

The laughing young men raced to their horses, returning to the camp to eat.

On their return, Spotted Horse teased, calling Black Wolf, "Wolf who drags his pizzle."

After a few days, Running Elk, Spotted Horse, and Red Knife shortened Black Wolf's new name to "pizzle dragger," and then "dragger." They only used it when alone, but one night, Running Elk called to Black Wolf as he left the *vee'e*, "Wait for me, Dragger."

Blossom laughed and glanced at Black Wolf, "What's your new name? What's it about?"

Black Wolf ran from the *vee'e*, hiding in shame. Later, he confronted Running Elk. "Don't call me Dragger again. Do you want to explain to Mother what it means?"

"You're right. I don't think she'd find it funny. I'm sad that Mother heard, but you have a bigger problem. You must tell the others not to call you by it any more. I will ask them to stop because I started it," agreed Running Elk, "But I think it's too late. Many people have heard the story."

In shame, Black Wolf covered his face with his hands, wondering what The People think of him.

A few days later, Black Wolf and Running Elk hunted in the same area at first light. They crawled through the underbrush being as quiet and stealthy as they knew how. They almost crawled over a young doe lying in the grass, chewing her graze. When the doe bolted, the pair rose as two bowstrings twanged in unison. The doe fell with two arrows in her, but rose struggling to run when the two loosed arrows to strike her again. The two young men gaped at one another, wide-eyed at their triumph. Each whooped a loud cry and then again. They stood reliving their hunt, when Digging Badger and another warrior appeared at the meadow's edge. They glanced at the kill before smiling at one another, knowing the joy the young men shared.

Digging Badger unstrung his bow while the other man gathered their horses. "We heard those mighty war cries, worrying that the Pawnee attacked," Digging Badger said with a laugh.

He placed his hand on Running Elk's shoulder. "I promised to take you hunting when your aim was true. I think with this you can come on the buffalo hunt. I am pleased with you both."

Digging Badger told the other man to return to his patrol, saying he'd rejoin him after he taught the young men to gut and clean the deer. He sent Running Elk to fetch their horses, but he changed his mind, thinking they'd do better carrying the whole deer to Yellow Blossom.

"Let her use all the organs before skinning the hide." When Running Elk returned with his horse, Digging Badger said, "Stay mounted. I'll lay the doe across the pony's rump. Your mother deserves the honor of receiving your kill. Let the other women see how she is honored."

Digging Badger turned to Black Wolf. "I noticed your arrow in the doe's heart. Blossom will notice also. She will know both of her sons have honored her. The next time, you will carry the kill to her."

"I understand. Running Elk is getting ready for his ceremony of the man. He must show The People he is ready," Black Wolf said.

"Both of you have done well. You will bring strength to The People when you are ready," Digging Badger said when he sent the young men to the camp. He returned to his duties.

Late in the summer, Black Wolf had almost exhausted his supply of black powder and percussion caps, which curtailed their target practice. This meant more time for practicing with the traditional weapons of the Redman: the knife, tomahawk, lance, and bow and arrow. When no one else came around, Running Elk and Black Wolf practiced throwing the Green River knives or the tomahawks. They learned which grip worked best to throw each weapon, becoming consistent in making either the knife or the tomahawk drive deep into a tree from a dozen paces.

Early one morning, while working on new arrows with Old Wolf, Black Wolf summoned the courage to speak to him about the changes occurring within his body.

"May I ask you questions in *Français*? I don't know the Cheyenne words for what I want to talk about," Black Wolf said.

Old Wolf nodded while continuing to work on the *maa-he*, or arrow shaft.

"Pascal told me of mating. He has shown me how the burro stallion mounted the horse mare to make a mule. He said the parts of a human are not that different. Man is smaller than a burro, so his pizzle is smaller." Black Wolf remembered Pascal at the time, giving little Nigel a conspiratorial wink, and saying, "except for a *Français* man, of course," and laughed aloud.

"He said a woman has a cleft between her legs

like the mare's cleft. The male plants his seed in the female's cleft that grows inside her to produce a little one, whether mare or woman. This was the simplest explanation he could give. When I grew older, he'd explain the important part, convincing the woman to let you gain entry into her sweet flower. He said it's the sport, whatever it means."

Old Wolf worked on his arrows, listening, and nodding on occasion.

"I watched a woman here raise her dress, exposing her cleft, while she squatted to piss. My sisters would rather be boiled in oil than allow a man to watch them do such. I have seen women here expose their breast to feed a baby. I never gazed upon a woman's teat before. She didn't care that I watched her. I fail to understand why The People have no shame at exposing their bodies."

Old Wolf wagged his head from side to side. "You sound like the old *Français* priest who came years ago to teach us about his Christ. I learned this language from him before he grew weary and returned to his people. He too grew upset and angry that The People went naked on occasion, letting other people see their naked body."

He pointed with the arrow shaft. "I ask you what I asked him. Are your women so different, they do not piss? Did you not suckle your mother's breast as a baby? The priest said their women hide when they do these things."

Old Wolf stopped talking while he examined an arrow shaft.

"I ask you, as I asked the old priest. What is the

shame they must hide when they do what is natural? What shames white women to hide?"

"It is not the white's way to let any part of a woman's body be exposed to another person or be seen in the light," Black Wolf said, thinking of his mother and sisters.

"It is the Way of The People to accept what is natural. It is natural to see a baby suckle the mother's teat, whether woman, or mare, or buffalo cow. A horse, or a buffalo, drops its chips and pisses a stream where it stands. Why should The People hide in shame for doing what the other animals do naturally?

"The People, by custom, do not drop their chips or piss around the camp, so others do not step on it. You know we set aside places to use while in camp. It is rude to enter into one of those areas when it is in use or to watch the other person. It is rude to stare at a woman suckling her babe. Our women do not expose themselves around the camp, so as not to offend others or arouse the men. The women have not spoken of your being rude, so you have not offended anyone while observing them. If these things happen again, glance away and leave."

"You sound like my true father. Don't gaze upon temptation. Walk away from it."

"Is it bad?" asked Old Wolf with a straight face.

After a few moments, Black Wolf said, "Pascal tells me 'water runs downhill,' when something is natural. He says I must learn to accept those things I cannot change. I guess this is one."

"Was this all you wanted to ask?" Old Wolf said as he worked on another arrow.

"I cannot understand why Running Elk, Spotted Horse, and Red Knife talk about their pizzle so often. It is bad enough that my pizzle gets stiff whenever it wants to, but do they need to lift their breechcloth, waggling it at each other? They talk about stroking their pizzle or having one of the young women stroke it for them. They say they want to lie with the young women. My father said it is a sin to lie with a woman."

"The People do not understand 'sin.' The People understand good and bad, and try to be good because it is best for this clan, and for all The People. The old *Français* priest who lived with us seemed to think everything The People did is a 'sin.' I fail to understand how he kept track of all those things, or how he had time to think about them. To ease your mind, The People do not encourage the young ones to lie with one another until married. You will learn our discouragement if her father catches you."

Old Wolf worked the arrow shafts as he talked.

"I am surprised you don't speak of The People allowing a man to have more than one wife. The priest thought it the worst sin." He barked a laugh, then winked. "Well, not quite. The worst sin came from the widow woman we had cooking for him. She stroked his pizzle in the night. She admitted lying on top of him while he pretended to sleep. He tolerated her advances, but one night, she tried to arouse him to active coupling by

272

suckling his pizzle. He groaned in pleasure, reaching for her. When he realized what she did, he screamed like a little girl, before throwing her from his *vee'e*. He left us a few days later, returning to his people."

Old Wolf chuckled to himself when he told this tale. Black Wolf knew from the burning sensation, his face bloomed red with embarrassment.

Black Wolf muttered, louder than he intended, "Pascal would love your story."

"Yes, he did. We laughed about it one evening. It is hard for me to believe the Mule Man wore the Black Robe. I learned more about your Christ from Mule Man than I ever did from the old priest. If Pascal had been the messenger, we would have considered his entreaty to follow your Christ. Pascal liked to sit, smoke a cigar, and sip brandy. I liked his brandy better than the bad whiskey some traders sell us."

Old Wolf sat quiet for a few moments, and then asked, "Did Little Charbonneau say your true father came to teach the Cherokee the way of your Christ? Was your true father a priest?"

"He was a man of God," said Black Wolf, thinking of a way to say it. "My father came from a different clan than the priest. It would be like the Arapaho are different from the Cheyenne, but do not fight each other."

"And you, will you become a priest?" He used the Cheyenne word for "shaman."

"No, I do not think so. My father claimed listening to God's word gave him peace in his

273

heart. I am angry. I want to kill the Comanche. I want to avenge the death of my mother and father. They stole my sisters."

"It is easy to say those words. It will be harder to do, even when you are a man. I say this with care. Study Tall Bear. He is a fierce warrior, but his heart is hard. Tall Bear hates our enemies so much there is no joy in his life. Then study Digging Badger. He is a fierce warrior, one day he will become our war chief. He takes pride in the success of the little ones, finds joy, and seeks comfort for The People. He slays our enemies but takes no joy from it. His heart is open and he laughs at life. Think on this.

"I will ask one more time, is that all you wanted to speak about?" asked Old Wolf as he worked feathers into the shaft of the arrow he held.

"There is one other thing," Nigel whispered as he ducked his face.

"I'm confused about what I'm supposed to do. One evening, Rising Fawn asked me if she might examine my 'wolf's red knob' before it got too dark to tell if it was red. It shocked me. I didn't know how to respond. Rising Fawn lifted my breechcloth, touching me. She stroked around my 'red knob.' I knew I ought to tell her to stop, but I couldn't believe she just reached to me, pulling my pizzle in the light to examine it."

"I wish I had that problem," said Old Wolf chuckling. "The women just giggle now when I try to use them."

"What happened when Rising Fawn touched me

is what I wanted to ask about. It felt so good while she stroked it. I grew rigid as a hot flash erupted from my 'red knob.' That never happened before. Rising Fawn giggled before she wiped her hands on my leggings, slipping away to talk to her friends. I don't understand what happened."

"You spoke earlier of the stallion planting his seed in the mare. You are the stallion—that is your seed. I do not know about the white man, but it is natural among The People that as a boy becomes a man his pizzle often grows stiff. If you do nothing with it, it aches in the night. It feels good to rub it, stroke it. It feels better when a woman strokes it, and better still if she suckles it. It feels best when she lets it into her 'cleft.' We encourage young people to wait until they are married, but what Rising Fawn did is not surprising. If you did not want her to touch you, tell her to stop the next time. If you stay with us another summer, the young girls will sneak into your *vee'e* at night, or you will prowl around their *vee'e*, howling like the wolf."

"Why would they want to do that? What do they do it for?"

"Did it feel good when she stroked your pizzle?"

"Oh, yes. It was wonderful."

"Did it feel even better when it spit your seed?"

Though it embarrassed Black Wolf, he said, "I have never felt anything like it before."

"Do you think the woman does not enjoy having her cleft stroked, or suckled, or taking your hot pizzle inside her? You must learn to do your part, returning the pleasure she gives you. A woman is not a mare for servicing. I know white men do that with women, but it is not the Way of The People."

"Should I have touched Rising Fawn? Is that why she avoids me now?"

"No, not without her permission. If she doesn't tell you to stop or slap your hands away."

"I don't understand. I don't think white people touch one another, even when married."

"That may be why they are so unhappy," said Old Wolf as he laid aside the arrow.

Looking at Black Wolf, he continued, "I think you need to ask your mother to help you understand what is happening. Her lessons will make more sense to you than anything I say. I can tell you how it is for the man, but you need to know how it is for the woman. Ask her to explain about the woman's cycle with the moon. You need to understand and avoid a woman when she is in her moon cycle. It also has to do with having babies, so you need to learn how to make babies or how to avoid making babies."

"You are making no sense. What does the moon, *ta-a'e-ese'he,* have to do with mating? Having babies? I know enough to know the women have one. Why do I need to learn about babies? I couldn't talk to Blossom about such things. I'd be too ashamed to tell her about my pizzle, or speak of a woman's cleft, or ask about mating with her."

"Your mother is the one to tell you these things. She knows men have a pizzle. Her lessons will help you understand the role of the woman in mating. Learn how to treat a woman with respect. You must learn to talk to women. Ask Peacemaker Woman if you're afraid of Yellow Blossom."

"I am not afraid of Blossom."

Old Wolf smiled, "We shall see." He selected another wood shaft to make into an arrow. "Now I have a question for you about this," Old Wolf said after a few minutes.

"What do you want to know?"

"The young men have given you new names. What the whites call a 'nick-name.' One is the 'wolf's red knob.' They don't say it around me, but I understand most of the women know about it. Many are amused by it. Do you know about it."

Nodding while hiding his face, he asked, "Have you heard the other name?"

"Pizzle Dragger. Yes, I heard that story too." Old Wolf laughed aloud. "That is the best story since the old *Français* priest left us."

He turned as red as Black Kettle's ceremonial blanket, moving to run away in shame.

Old Wolf held Black Wolf's arm. "Do not be ashamed. The men say it to mean Black Wolf is already a man, with a man's pizzle. The women pretend they are offended, but I am not so sure. I have seen several women gaze at you when you walk away, like they are curious about what they see, and not just the young ones either. Yellow Blossom knows."

"Dear God! How long has she known? Is she angry with me?"

"I think she has known for a while. She is not

angry with you. She was furious with Running Elk and Spotted Horse for telling everyone the story."

"My real question," continued Old Wolf, "is your 'red knob.' What happened to the skin on your pizzle? Other whites used their pizzle to piss, but they had skin like us. Where is yours?"

"It is hard to explain. They cut it off as part of becoming a Christian. You see—"

Old Wolf interrupted, "What? It was cut off? The old priest never mentioned such. I would never consider following your Christ if they cut the skin off my pizzle. That is a strange ceremony." He leaned away, "How can the whites call us 'ignorant savages' when they do those kinds of ceremonies?"

"No, you do not understand," Black Wolf said.

"You have already endured such? You have passed a test of manhood few men of The People would accept. I think the men must understand what your 'red knob' means. It is not a wolf's sign, but the sign of a manhood ceremony. I'm happy now I didn't agree to baptism by the old priest. I don't want the skin cut off my pizzle, even if it is old and shriveled."

After several tries, Black Wolf gave up trying to explain circumcision, which had been done when a baby. He didn't remember any pain. After he considered it, he understood why Old Wolf rejected the idea. *Why would that be part of any Christian ceremony?*

It would really hurt to do it now. Shivers ran down his spine.

Chapter 17

Late October, 1855

Black Wolf hiked away from their camp later that afternoon before running from sight. He loped to the grove where he had seen the turkeys that fateful day. Once he neared the grove, he dropped to the ground to let his breathing grow quiet before crawling to the grove.

When he returned to the camp, he sought Old Wolf, only to find Black Kettle and Digging Badger with him. Digging Badger signaled for him to approach.

"I have brought you a turkey, as I promised," Black Wolf said, handing it to Old Wolf.

"Only one?" Old Wolf grunted, "You still owe me two more."

"If you are giving them away, I will take two," Black Kettle said with a slight smile.

"He works hard to learn what our young men already know, but he will need another season to become one of The People. Even so, I would take him on the buffalo hunt tomorrow," Digging Badger said.

Black Kettle grunted aloud, "Ummp! I am not sure. I do not want him dragging his wolf's pizzle near the herd, making the wolf's scent to scare the buffalo away."

The men burst into laughter, while Black Wolf hung his head, embarrassed.

Black Kettle reached for Black Wolf, slapping his back two times before saying, "Have the Mule Man teach you to laugh loudly like he does, *'tah-pe'a-ta-ma-o'o.'* It is good for a man to laugh. Better when he laughs at himself."

The men turned to their talk after Digging Badger signed for Black Wolf to leave.

They assigned Black Wolf and the other young men to keep the buffalo herd from scattering as they drove the herd toward where the warriors killed them along the herd's edge. Two young braves thought they found an easy kill when a large calf peeled away, running into heavy brush. They rode their horses into the brush but raced out, being chased themselves when a large bull charged from the brush. A hunt of this scale meant work for the whole Tribe. Each band at the rendezvous helped in the hunt. The People seemed in a much better mood after the hunt, as if it signaled a good omen.

During the next week, they assigned Black Wolf the duty of patrolling the horses at night. He understood they intended this task to keep him away from the ceremonial ground when The People discussed the problems with the white man, who continued to spoil their traditional hunting grounds.

Why do the white men sign treaties if they

cannot keep their promises? There is so much land here, why can't they learn to share? I wondered before but now I understand why Pascal doesn't kill any buffalo when we ride the trail. The Redman needs the buffalo to survive. They treat those who kill buffalo as a threat. Pascal and his survival lessons—it is always a matter of survival.

"But, whose survival?" he said aloud. "Who decides who survives?"

Black Wolf became thoroughly confused. *Is this why Pascal sent me to live with The People? Philippe said, 'If I learned to live with The People and survive, I might grow into a man one day.'*

It makes my head hurt to think about all this.

As the Cheyenne Harvest Moon, *'o-en ne-ne-ešе 'he,'* waned at the end of August, the rendezvous concluded. The different bands meandered their way toward their traditional winter camps. None spoke of what the alliance decided. Black Wolf knew better than to ask. Black Kettle's band moved farther east before shifting south, avoiding the same trail on which they traveled north. The *Hisiometä'nio* (Ridge People) band moved west then south so they'd not drive game away from one another's route by being too close together.

In the eastern distance one day, a heavy column of smoke rose. Black Wolf asked Digging Badger about it while they rode along the flank of the moving column.

"It is a fire in the dry grass. You must learn to

be careful with fire in the dry moons," Digging Badger said.

"Mule Man was always careful with his fires. He feared a fire in camp," he said.

"The Pawnee, and sometimes the Comanche, use a fire to trap their enemy if they catch them in a dry area. They set fires all around to burn their enemy, killing those who try to escape."

"I have not encountered the Pawnee. They sound as bad as the Comanche. We should kill our enemies."

"Yes. I know we have told you, but it easy to say words. It is harder to kill them. Let your actions be your words. When you have counted coup, and then taken your first scalp, no words are needed."

Black Wolf nodded in silence.

The Cheyenne Fall Moon, *to-no e ve eše 'he*, grew fatter each night as Black Kettle's band continued winding their way south toward Big Timbers. The days didn't grow quite as hot while the nights became cooler. The youths took advantage of a rocky waterfall several hundred yards downstream from the camp, finding a deep hole for swimming.

Black Wolf remembered in Wales calling it "skinny dipping," to swim without clothes. His father had forbidden him from doing it when they crossed the great prairie. The Cheyenne youngsters enjoyed it as great sport.

Black Kettle allowed the women to visit the swimming hole in early afternoon, ordering the men away. The teens tried to sneak in twice, but

Digging Badger stationed his patrols around the area to prevent them from sneaking close.

Black Wolf spent afternoons hunting. He had killed the two turkeys he promised for Old Wolf plus two for Black Kettle. Running Elk, keeping their rivalry alive, killed two turkeys for Blossom. Today, he sat hidden, patiently waiting for an antelope to come within range. He used a trick Tall Bear had shown them to bring antelope close. Tall Bear said when the antelope is close wiggle a rabbit hide or a bird's wings on the end of a stick. The antelope grows curious, coming closer to see what it is, and then you loose an arrow. The trick worked for Running Elk, but not this afternoon.

He admitted, grudgingly, Tall Bear might be good warrior, but he's not a good leader.

Black Wolf always carried his rifle along when leaving camp even when he carried his bow and quiver across his shoulder. He knew he couldn't kill anything worth eating with his target rifle, but served to show he was a man. He crossed the stream at the camp, heading north when he left, but as he rode, he circled east and then south.

Digging Badger cautioned him to be vigilant for Pawnee when he rode alone, but he never noticed another Redman. He failed to notice any game on this ride, which surprised him.

While he circled toward the camp, he walked his horse. He returned from the downstream side, above to the swimming hole. The meadow above the hole had no trees on this side. The broad meadow, sloping to the stream, held nothing but dried, yellow-brown grass two to three feet tall. On a distant ridge, he noticed Digging Badger's patrols. As often happens, what appeared as soft rolling plains hid an arroyo feeding the stream below, getting deeper as it dropped to the stream.

He wanted to take a fat *'va-ot-se-va,'* a deer, for Yellow Blossom. *Mayhap I can find a deer in there.* He searched for tracks or droppings to show recent passage by a *va-ot-se-va*. While examining the ground, he found marks in the dust showing a man crawled into the arroyo. From lessons with Juana Barnard, he had learned to scan the back trail. With careful scrutiny, he spotted the back trail leading over a rise above the stream. As she taught, he staked his horse to one side with a rope, so it didn't wander, or scare the game away.

After he entered the arroyo, he found several moccasin prints where "they" sat in a circle. Black Wolf knew Spotted Horse made a game of sneaking past the patrol to watch the naked women swim. *This is just dumb.*

Black Wolf squatted, studying the signs, when the hair on his neck rose and tingled. *Something is not right. What am I missing? What is the danger?* He glanced about without moving. *Dear God! The women! These tracks are Pawnee. The Pawnee are trying to steal our women. I must get help.* He crawled from the arroyo.

Black Wolf jumped onto the meadow before standing at the arroyo edge, waving for the patrol he observed earlier. They surveyed the other direction, probably distracted by Spotted Horse's games. He readied to shout a war whoop by taking a step back, raising his hands to call.

An arrow nicked his chest in its passing.

In a reflex action, Black Wolf shifted, raising his rifle, cocking as he raised it. He shot the charging Pawnee in the face without aiming. The Pawnee continued running with his tomahawk raised. Black Wolf raised his rifle to block the tomahawk, screaming in terror.

The running Pawnee bowled him over, falling on top of him, dying. The man's tomahawk sunk into the ground, nicking Black Wolf's head. The Pawnee's blood covered Black Wolf's face, running down his chest. He lay still, too frightened to move, when four other Pawnee appeared, running from the arroyo toward him.

Black Wolf closed his eyes, too frightened to move, realizing he had pissed himself.

Dear God! Let them kill me, so I don't face the shame of pissing myself.

The first two Pawnee ran past, shouting words to the last two, who stopped to lift their dead companion, carrying him away. One grabbed Black Wolf's rifle, taking it with him.

Black Wolf listened to them rustling in the grass while running away.

One of them shouted words before a horse whinnied.

No. It is bad enough I pissed on myself, and they stole my rifle. They aren't going to take my horse, too. Now, by God, I've had enough. No more!

He rolled to stand, grabbing the tomahawk that

had been in the ground beside his head, to throw it as hard as he could at the Pawnee pulling himself onto the back of Black Wolf's horse.

The Pawnee's trade tomahawk resembled the one he practiced throwing, but he must strike at a greater distance.

Black Wolf screamed as the tomahawk struck the Pawnee's chest, knocking him from the horse.

Without thinking, he screamed, charging the downed Pawnee while drawing his Wolf's tomahawk from his belt. His horse reared, stomping on the ground. As he rushed close, the Pawnee rolled from under the horse's hoofs, regaining his feet. A full-grown man stood.

The Pawnee snarled, shouting words before he charged with his knife raised.

The running man bowled Black Wolf head over heels before the Pawnee landed on top.

Black Wolf used his tomahawk haft to block the Pawnee's attempts to stab him.

The Pawnee straddled him, grabbed the haft, and yanked the tomahawk from Black Wolf's hands with a twist.

The Pawnee rose on his knees, screaming a war cry, ready to plunge his knife into Black Wolf.

The Pawnee's body jerked, his back arching away when an arrow head protruded from his chest, splattering blood.

The Pawnee's knife dropped away.

Black Wolf realized the arrow head would strike him in the chest if the Pawnee fell on top of him. He twisted, shifting hard to roll the Pawnee aside.

In a flurry, a fleeting shadow jerked the dead Pawnee from his chest as a Cheyenne pony thundered past, its rider's lance carrying the Pawnee away.

Black Wolf rolled onto his stomach to glimpse the mounted Tall Bear, shaking the dead Pawnee from his lance.

Shouted war cries and whoops filled the air as the Cheyenne patrol killed the running Pawnee.

They had conducted daring raid in the middle of the day, and close to their main camp. Black Wolf lay there trembling—his body shook without control. He sat up before he glanced at his chest covered in blood. Some of it must be his. He searched to find where he bled.

A pair of big hands jerked him to his feet.

"*Ha-aa-he,*" Tall Bear grabbed Black Wolf's upper arms. He said, "*Ha-aa-he,*" again, using the traditional greeting of Cheyenne men, often said while grasping one another's arms.

"Are you hurt? Is this your blood? Is this the blood of your enemies?" Tall Bear asked, wiping a big hand across the blood on Black Wolf's face.

Black Wolf stood there confused, still in shock. He gazed at Tall Bear. *Is he wearing a smile?*

Tall Bear grabbed a water gourd from his saddle, offering it to Black Wolf.

While he drank, Black Wolf cast a glance at Tall Bear striding to the first *ho'ne-he ta-ne-o'o* (Pawnee) before rolling him face up.

"*Me'es-evo-tse ho'ne-he* (baby wolf) is growing teeth. This one will wander lost in the afterlife.

You shot out his eye," said Tall Bear. "You have counted coup with two *ho'ne-he ta-ne-o'o* (Pawnee) while making your first kill. Come take his scalp now. Do it quickly. Don't think about it—do it. You will ride into Black Kettle's camp at the front of his warriors."

Black Wolf wanted to vomit. He didn't want to take the scalp but knew he must.

And so, he did.

Without urging, he released a long wolf howl, holding the scalp high, and then sat down heavily, shaking.

He became aware of others washing blood from him while he sat, dazed.

Digging Badger led Black Wolf's horse close to them.

He grew aware that Tall Bear and Digging Badger spoke to him. One of them wrapped a blanket around his shoulders. The two men helped him stand before lifting him on his horse. Tall Bear tied the scalp on Black Wolf's tomahawk, placing it in his hand. Digging Badger led Black Wolf's horse to the camp.

The ride passed in a daze. Black Wolf rode into camp between Digging Badger and Tall Bear. Later, he remembered the trilling calls of the women and the men's war cries.

Yellow Blossom's tears flowed as she washed him, bandaging his cuts. He had a long scrape across his chest where the first arrow just missed. He had a cut on his head just above his ear where the *ho'ne-he ta-ne-o'o* (Pawnee) tomahawk had nicked him. He had several cuts on his fingers and forearms where he had fended away the second *ho'ne-he ta-ne-o'o* (Pawnee) with the knife. He had a deep plunge cut in his thigh but had no idea when it happened.

Peacemaker Woman prepared a poultice for his leg wound to draw out the poisons. Blossom tied his cloth bandages in place by strips of a checkered cloth. He thought he resembled a court jester with the checkered pattern.

Blossom wrapped him in a blanket, forcing him to lie still. He fell asleep.

Black Wolf awoke in early evening with Running Elk sitting beside him. Running Elk held his hands over his face as he said, "I have shamed myself and our mother. While I played games like a child, you hunted like a man. I sat in camp while you fought our enemies. I promised Digging Badger I would protect you. Tall Bear beat me hard when he returned to camp. The elders may send Spotted Horse away from the camp as punishment. His family has turned their back on him. Black Kettle must decide his fate. They have delayed our ceremony of the man for two more moons. We will seek our totem in the cold. It will be hard to survive alone in the winter. It is part of our punishment."

Running Elk sat rocking back and forth for several minutes.

"I will beat you with a stick in the morning after

the sun is above the rim," said Black Wolf. "You are still my brother. We shall protect one another."

"I accept your punishment, my brother. I will call our mother."

Blossom entered with an iron pot on a stick, setting it in coals at the *vee'e* center.

She gazed at her sons before rapping her bone spoon on Running Elk's head.

"What am I to do with you two? Neither has the brains of a *hoh-kee-he-so*, a mouse."

She hit Black Wolf with her spoon "What were you thinking? Trying to attack five *ho'ne-he ta-ne-o'o* (Pawnee) warriors by yourself. Why didn't you signal the patrol, or call for help? Even Tall Bear says he would not have attacked five *ho'ne-he ta-ne-o'o* (Pawnee) without sounding a warning to bring help before attacking. I know you want to show us you are brave. You need not prove yourself until you are a man. Don't be so foolish again." She rapped his head with her spoon.

"I did not mean to frighten you. It happened so fast, once they attacked I had no time to do anything other than fight," Black Wolf said.

"Digging Badger said he rode to you," she said. "He saw the *ho'ne-he ta-ne-o'o* (Pawnee) strike you several times with his knife. He thought you wounded, so he risked loosing an arrow, thinking you wouldn't survive if the *ho'ne-he ta-ne-o'o* struck with his knife again. Digging Badger said he feared Tall Bear wouldn't arrive in time."

"I don't remember much of what happened after the first *ho'ne-he ta-ne-o'o* (Pawnee) loosed an arrow at me."

"Tall Bear said you were so covered in blood, they must have thought you dead when you played *oo'keh-ev-a'se-he,* the possum. Tall Bear thought you dead before you rose to throw the tomahawk. It surprised him when it knocked the *ho'ne-he ta-ne-o'o* (Pawnee) from your horse. He thinks your horse kicked him when he was on the ground. When the *ho'ne-he ta-ne-o'o* stood, Tall Bear hollered for you to get down. He said you ran at the *ho'ne-he ta-ne-o'o* with your tomahawk like a man of The People does when facing his enemy."

"He was stealing my horse. I couldn't let him take it," Black Wolf whispered.

"That is so," Running Elk said.

"Be quiet, both of you. I will beat you both in the morning," Blossom said, in tears.

They sat in silence for ten minutes. After a deep breath, Blossom ladled soup into a *he-toh-ko* (dish) for Black Wolf.

She handed a *he-toh-ko* to Running Elk, saying, "This is more food than you deserve."

"Do you know if they found my rifle? One of the *ho'ne-he ta-ne-o'o* grabbed it as he went by," Black Wolf asked.

"Yes. It is here. Tall Bear brought it to me. He said he did not think it could kill anyone. He said he spoke the truth when he said the rifle fits you. You are both stronger than you look."

In the morning, with many people watching, Black Wolf beat his brother with a stick. The stick broke after five or six hard swats. Yellow Blossom handed another stick to Black Wolf, motioning him to continue the beating. Then Yellow Blossom took a stick to both of them, but after a few swats at each, she stopped, covered her tear-streaked face, and entered her *vee'e*.

The camp people who cheered the action turned to shuffle away.

Tall Bear appeared, grabbing both by the arm, marching them to Black Kettle's *vee'e*.

Black Kettle sent Spotted Horse away for ten days, during which time no one from this band would help him in any way. If he came close enough for anyone in the camp to glimpse him, they would attack and kill him. As Running Elk had feared, they postponed his ceremony of the man until the Big Hard Face Moon, *ma' xe hé' kon en eeše' he*, in mid-winter, which is a brutal time to survive without shelter and food during the required ten days. Those young men would be hard pressed to survive. Black Kettle set a severe punishment.

"When I first saw you and learned your name, I said that name is too strong for this boy, he will be killed trying to live up to his name," Black Kettle said. "The spirits guide us, as does your name. They have made you stronger. You are welcome in the camp of the *Wotápio*. We will tell others of The People. They will know you saved our women from the *ho'ne-he ta-ne-o'o*. They will welcome you. If the Mule Man will give you away, both Digging Badger and Tall Bear asked to adopt you. They will make you a warrior of the *Hi-ma'tano-his*. You would no longer be a white man, if one of them adopted you. Think on this."

Digging Badger, who had been standing behind Black Kettle stepped close. "Those on patrol learned a lesson. They let themselves be distracted with the women and the games. They failed to observe the Pawnees, and I punished them. I want you to know I would have you as my son if you grow weary of walking the grasslands with the Mule Man."

Digging Badger motioned to one of the braves, who led a horse to Digging Badger.

"This pony is one we captured from the *ho'ne-he ta-ne-o'o*. It is yours because you killed one of them. Your luck held in your fight with *ho'ne-he ta-ne-o'o*. Only the one who killed you could claim your scalp, so they didn't bother when you lay on the ground. Do not try that trick with the *se'se-no-vo-tse-ta-ne-o'o* (Comanche). They would scalp you where you lay."

Black Kettle and Digging Badger strode away.

Tall Bear turned Black Wolf to face him, "I set you on a difficult path. I made it hard for you. You are stronger than I knew. Your Wolf spirit is strong medicine. I would welcome you in my *vee'e* as my son if you choose to live with The People. The women believe the spirit of your wolf's pizzle gave you strength, and many want to learn about the wolf's red knob. As your father, I must tell you to be careful, but as another man, I tell you to remove your *neh-pe-so'h-est-o-tse* (breechcloth) and *he'ko-ne-hos-ese* (lie down with a hard pizzle). Let the women have their way with you. Enjoy it—you earned it. Be careful with the married women, unless the husband allows you into his *vee'e*. If he asks you to spend the night, he is offering you his wife. That is the safest way. Try not to make too much noise if that happens. Do not shame the husband for his gift."

With that, Tall Bear strode away, leaving the two youths standing alone in the camp.

The young men gazed at one another in amazement. They had never known Tall Bear to be so civil. "I think he smiled," Black Wolf said before the brothers joined in laughter.

"I will tie our sign on this horse to mark it as ours. I'm sore from yesterday, but I want to visit my gelding, checking if it is unhurt. Would you walk with me?"

"I would like that," Running Elk said as the two strode to the stream, only vaguely aware of The People shifting to watch them swagger past, smiling after them.

"I am thinking we ought to go by the *vee'e*. Many people brought food last night or this morning. We should honor their gifts by eating all," Black Wolf said, laughing.

At the *vee'e,* they promised Blossom they'd not run until Black Wolf's leg healed. They also promised to return soon to let Black Wolf rest.

"*Hee-he'e nah-ko'e,*" (Yes, Mother) each said, laughing, as they walked to the stream.

Red Knife visited that evening as they sat in

front of Blossom's tipi. His father had beaten him hard. "I hope I have your courage. Digging Badger said after you knocked the *ho'ne-he ta-ne-o'o* from his horse you charged him with your tomahawk, screaming a war cry. Your wolf totem is strong."

"I think each of us has a strong totem," said Black Wolf. "The knife is the weapon of The People. The Elk is known for its strength and endurance. Together we are strong."

Some of the young women began to drift their way. Running Elk called to Rising Fawn who waved at him. Yellow Blossom came from the *vee'e*, telling the young girls Black Wolf needed his rest, before she sent them away.

The youngsters bleated in unison, *nah-ko'e* (mother!).

"Do not play that game with me. You think I have not listened to the whispers about the magic of the wolf's pizzle? Not tonight, my young bucks. The season for rutting has not begun for you two. Go inside," she said.

~~~~~~

The next morning Blossom asked her sons to walk with her. She handed each a hide-wrapped bundle of food, telling each to carry a gourd of water. Blossom sought a quiet spot upstream near the water but within sight of the camp and the patrols.

"I have delayed this talk far too long, not wanting my sons to be grown too soon. Now there is no more time. You think you know everything we are going to discuss today but I want both of you to pay attention," Yellow Blossom said while she opened the bundles of food.

"We needed this talk when I first heard the stories of the wolf's red knob and Pizzle Dragger."

Black Wolf hung his head red-faced with embarrassment.

The two youths tried to complain but she shushed them both. She ruffled Black Wolf's hair. "You attack five *ho'ne-he ta-ne-o'o* like a true man but hide like a *me'es-evo-tse* (baby) when I say 'pizzle.'" Blossom spoke with them all morning.

Black Wolf recovered his shock of hearing a women use the terms she did. He failed to imagine his English mother having such a conversation with him. He did not think his true father would have either. He never imagined his true father doing such things with his English mother.

Now he gained an inkling of what Old Wolf tried to tell him about the moon. Neither boy knew women of marrying age bled from their cleft each moon cycle. Running Elk said he knew the young women went away for a week when they came to marrying age. He thought it a ceremony of the woman like the boys had a ceremony of the man. Bleeding that way didn't sound like it would be comfortable to Black Wolf. They learned her "season," the bleeding, stopped when a woman carried a baby. It was how women knew the man's seed had taken root.

"I don't understand," Black Wolf said. "If the

man uses his pizzle to plant the seed, why doesn't the seed produce a baby every time?"

"It is fortunate it doesn't work that way. We'd have more babies than food. It is hard on a woman to have babies season after season. Their bodies grow weary and the woman dies. We studied the moon to understand how it guides the woman's season. The medicine women, like Peacemaker, have thought on this, deciding a woman must pace her rutting with men.

"In the seven days of her season and the seven days following her season, a man's seed does not ripen. The next seven days are when women are most ready for a man's seed. In the last seven days, a man's seed is not likely to ripen."

"What does this have to do with the moon?" Black Wolf asked.

"In this camp, most women begin their season as the moon becomes full and are least fertile when the moon is in its cusps. We're most fertile when the moon is dark," she said. "The moon cycle is not always easy to follow, and sometimes the joy overtakes reason. Medicine women, like Peacemaker Woman, have found a combination of medicine plants that disrupts the seed, keeping it from ripening. These clever women have tracked these things for more seasons than you can count. They found plants to help the seed ripen. These medicine plants let a woman decide when she is ready for another baby, no matter how many times a man plants his seed."

"But why would a woman want a man to keep

planting his seed if she doesn't want a baby?" Black Wolf asked. "If she does not want the baby, don't lie with the man."

"I don't intend to embarrass you," Blossom said. "Did it feel good when Rising Fawn stroked your pizzle until your seed spurted?"

Black Wolf hid his face in his hands, his face burned with his blushing.

Running Elk nudged him, laughing at his embarrassment.

"Don't laugh, my son," she said. "I know you and Morning Star have done more than stroke each other. You played your suckling fawn games more than once."

Running Elk's mouth shut as his head hung.

She lifted Black Wolf's head. "I know Tall Bear told you to remove your *neh-pe-so'h-est-o-tse* (breechcloth) and *he'ko-ne-hos-ese* (lie down with a hard pizzle), letting women have their way. That's foolish talk by a man who thinks his pizzle is the answer to all problems. After Running Elk becomes a man, Tall Bear is not welcome in my *vee'e*. Black Kettle has told him."

The two young men remained quiet, avoiding their mother's gaze.

"Now, I am serious about this. I have talked to the young girls mothers', telling them you are too young to understand the game you're playing. Both of you must leave them alone. Now for you, Black Wolf, I hear that some men may invite you into their *vee'e* so you may share their wives. It is the Way of The People to honor a guest with that gift. I have never liked to share, but it is the Way of The People. Don't let their attraction swell your head, thinking you're a real man. Once the women learn you don't know what to do with your great red pizzle, it'll soon end. Don't expect it to continue.

"Think on what I have said."

With that, she ordered the young men to gather their bundles, carrying them to camp.

~~~~~~~

The Fall Moon, *to noe ve eše'he*, (September) waned and faded. The People continued to move south every few weeks.

Soon the Facing Into Moon, *se'neehe*, (October) would grow. Black Kettle camped three days ride north of the river at Big Timbers. He decided to camp south of Big Timbers along Two Butte's Creek this winter. He planned one last move before the band settled into their winter camp.

In early October, when the Facing Into Moon grew, the band settled in an area east of Big Timbers for an overnight camp, intending to move on again in the morning. They camped many miles southeast of where Peacemaker Woman had led Philippe and Nigel seven moons ago.

The members of Black Kettle's camp awoke early the next morning, dismantling the camp and their vee'e, intent on a mid-day crossing of the river the whites called Arkansas, while it is low, making it an easy crossing.

The young brothers developed a routine for

loading while their mother supervised. Black Wolf straightened from his work, aware the camp had grown silent. When he glanced around, he glimpsed Pascal and Philippe on a rise west of the camp. Digging Badger's patrol waited nearby.

Philippe trotted his horse toward the camp. He led three pack mules, carrying parting gifts. One mule would carry Nigel's gear when they departed. The people in the camp returned to their loading with less noise than before.

The People have traditions about a loved one leaving. They don't linger in parting. They treated it as though the person planned to go for a morning hunt, returning in a short while. They're careful with their words so the spirits didn't think "departing" meant death and the person leaving would die soon because of careless words. They don't like to show their emotions, or embarrass one another with tears. They turned away quickly so as not to see another cry. Some whites interpreted this behavior to mean The People are cold, but in truth, they are too emotional, seeking to contain the hurt caused by a loved one leaving. Part of this tradition includes not saying aloud the name of someone who wasn't present.

And so it was as Philippe drew near. People in the camp turned away. Blossom knelt on the travois, pretending to be busy. Running Elk moved the travois harnesses between two horses, moving Black Wolf's mare from under the travois.

Black Wolf handed the rope from the *ho'ne-he ta-ne*-o'o (Pawnee) pony to Running Elk.

"The one who is my *nah-ko'e* (Mother) can ride this horse until I return."

~~~~~~

Philippe rode to Black Kettle's *vee'e*, leaving a mule loaded with trade goods. It is a custom of The People not to pay one another for favors or help, but they give gifts to another.

"These mules can't keep up. We have no place to keep these things. Is it all right to leave them here for a while? I will speak to the one who visits." Philippe reined away, riding to Nigel.

Black Kettle nodded, turning his back to speak to the women folding his *vee'e*.

~~~~~~

Black Wolf stood with his back to Running Elk and Yellow Blossom speaking aloud to no one. Tears flowed on his cheeks as he spoke to the wind.

Blossom buried her face in her buffalo robe, trying to stifle her wails.

Running Elk buried his face in his horse's mane, hugging the horse's neck.

Black Wolf spoke while he continued to separate things to carry with him.

He carried away the things he brought with him originally, his personal items. He set aside his rifle, powder horn, shot mold, and his *parfletche*, a slang French word the Cheyenne adopted to mean a "possibles-bag." He loading them along with his saddle, bridle, and blankets on Philippe's pack mule. He packed the buckskin clothes and extra moccasins Blossom had made along with other gifts given to him. The People shared many gifts with him.

Philippe unloaded trade goods from the mule onto the same travois from which Black Wolf collected his gear. Philippe knew the Way of The People and didn't make a show of giving.

"We can't carry these things. We'll leave it with you until he returns from hunting," Philippe said.

Black Wolf spoke to him in Cheyenne without facing him.

"Have you a flask of brandy and a few cigars?"

Philippe gazed at him with his head tilted and nodded. He dug in his buckskin jacket, handing over a small metal flask and a tin of cigars.

Black Wolf accepted them, staring at him for a few minutes, before saying, "*Merci.*"

The People have no word for "thank you" in their language.

When it appeared Black Wolf had no more to load on the mule, Philippe mounted, walking the animals up the rise toward where Pascal waited.

Black Wolf strode to where a young brave loaded Old Wolf's *vee'e* on a travois.

When he walked close, Old Wolf glanced, grunting a greeting.

"I hoped you had gone hunting, so we can return to roasting and eating little white babies, like the ignorant savages we are."

Black Wolf laughed aloud, touching his teeth before pointing to the old man's teeth.

"You can't fool me. Your teeth are no good. You'd choke on the little finger bones. You can't eat white babies anymore."

"I miss eating them. Too bad you grew so big."

"The Mule Man dropped his brandy and a few cigars. I'll leave them here if he comes back."

Old Wolf nodded. *"Ha-aa-he,"* he said as men did while gripping one another's arms.

As Black Wolf shifted to leave, Old Wolf whispered, "Kill many Comanche for me, young Wolf."

He noticed Philippe had reached the hill's crest when he gathered his gelding hackamore. He glanced around, lifting his lance.

I have a lance, a bow, a quiver full of arrows, a knife, a tomahawk, and a horse.

A man of The People is rich in ways the whites will never understand.

He gathered the hackamore's rope and a handful of mane. He swatted his horse to a gallop as he ran two long strides alongside, before vaulting onto the horse's back, while they ran the length of the camp to the river. Once there, he circled the animal into a full gallop, returning the way he had come.

This time, he performed all the tricks of running mounts, twirls, and dismounts he had learned. When he climbed the rise, he stood on the horse's rump holding his lance over his head and gave a long warbling war cry as he topped the rise before riding from sight.

~~~~~~

After he glanced at Pascal, Philippe shook his head in feigned regret.

"I noticed your gaze. Yes, that is a scalp on his lance. The People consider him a man."

Pascal turned his mount to follow.

Philippe reined his horse from the rise, studying the young man riding away from the Cheyenne camp.

"You sent spoiled little *Noir* away. A Black Wolf returned."

End of Part I

Look for Part II in October 2019

The Apprenticeship
Part II – North in the Spring.

Dear Reader:

I appreciate you taking your precious quiet time to read The Apprenticeship of Nigel Blackthorn. I hope the "to be continued" ending met with your approval, and you'll look for Part II "North in the Spring." In the Western tradition, one cowpuncher going along the trail talks to the next puncher, spreading word by the moccasin telegraph. If you liked our story, please tell your friends—the old moccasin telegraph, word-of-mouth, is the best advertisement. Amazon and browsing readers rate a book by the number of reviews. I'd appreciate a review if you have the time, a few lines will do. Kindle links to the Amazon review are at the end of the e-book.

Thanks
Frank

What is the line from TV ads??
BUT WAIT –There's more!

If you sign-up to receive Frank's blog, Traveling the West, from the following link, Frank will send you the novella, DEATH AT CAMP DOUGLAS, which is the prequel to California Bound.

Death at Camp Douglas is the story of Jeb and Zach's experiences in the Union POW camp outside Chicago, IL. The 23,000-word story is only available to fans joining Frank's blog. The novella serves as a transition from the fight for survival at the POW camp to Jeb and Zach's next adventure, SHERMAN'S WAR ON WOMEN, planned for release in Aug 2020. Find more information at Frank's blog http://frankkelsoauthor.com/

~~~~~~

Frank's Social Media Links

Please visit Frank Kelso's web page:
frankkelsoauthor.com

visit Facebook: facebook.com/AuthorFrankKelso

visit on Twitter: @authorfrankelso

linkedin.com/in/frank-kelso-89b077100

facebook.com/AuthorFrankKelso

authorfrankkelso.blogspot.com

frankkelsoauthor.com

TheApprenticeBook.com

facebook.com/thepossebook.1

facebook.com/CABoundBook/

facebook.com/TheApprenticeBook

Many of my author friends write westerns. If you enjoy Western Romance, please consider one of the following authors:

EE Burke – *Her Bodyguard*
amazon.com/dp/B00FIXEZUK

Lyn Horner – *Rescuing Lara*
amazon.com/dp/B00RBYFBXY

Charlene Raddon – *Divine Gamble*
amazon.com/dp/B074P686Q5

If you enjoy traditional westerns, please consider one of the following authors:

Tom Rizzo - Last Stand at Bitter Creek
amazon.com/gp/0984797793/

Chimp Robertson – *Rodeo Stories*
amazon.com/dp/B00OHWSF90

JS Stroud – *The Last Ride*
amazon.com/dp/B073X17HG9

Phil Truman – *Red Lands Outlaw*
amazon.com/dp/B06XDKSKDH

Donald L. Robertson - Forty-Four-Caliber-Justice
amazon.com/dp/B01DFSXWCQ/

Frank Kelso grew up around Kansas City, Missouri, the origin of the Santa Fe Trail. In his teen years he lived near Liberty, MO, Jessie James hometown. It's where Jesse invented Drive-Thru banking before they had drive-up windows. Writing Western themed books fit with his upbringing. A biomedical research scientist in his day job, Frank writes short stories and novels to keep the family traditions alive.

Frank won the Will Rogers Medallion Award and a Finalist for the Western Fictioneers Peacemaker Award for short stories for Tibby's Hideout. It's available on Amazon, in *The Posse*, which he gives away to his blog followers to promote a following for his coming novels. Look for California Bound with John O. Woods released August 16, 2017, the 2nd book in the Apprenticeship Series, North in the Spring released October 8 and became a best seller on Nov 11, 2019. South in the Fall set fro release in Feb 2020 and *A Message to Santa Fe*, set for release in Spring of 2020.

If you join my blog, Traveling the West, at
http://bit.ly/ThePosseWEB
You'll receive a FREE copy The Posse.

Always be kind to authors, please leave a review on Amazon.

Thanks for riding along.

Frank

Made in the USA
Columbia, SC
12 January 2020

86546649R00190